The Time Has Come

Sharron L Miller

Note

The towns, villages, street and road names mentioned in this book are indeed all real places, located in England and used purely to gain a sense of authenticity.

With a couple of exceptions, (see below) all buildings and establishments that are referred to throughout do not exist and are an entire work of fiction from the authors imagination. Any similarity is purely coincidental.

The Steam Railway is part of *The Dartmouth Steam Railway and River Boat Company* and does run from Paignton to Kingswear. A must should you visit the area.

The mention of the passenger/car ferry refers to *The Lower Ferry in Dartmouth.*

Both of the above have been used purely with the intention of gaining a sense of authenticity.

Contents

For James and Henry
xxx

No one could have known it would end like that.
Could they?
They say history repeats itself until lessons are learnt.
Well lessons were learnt.
But some things can never be forgotten.
The time had come for the truth to be told.
And she was the one to tell it.

Darkness.
Every time it ended with nothing but darkness.
And it wasn't scary.
Until...

Chapter 1

Kate

As the cool mist of the morning settled on her face, blind panic struck her subconscious, forcing her eyes wide open. She lifted her hand, bringing its icy cold fingers to touch her cheek but other than dampness, there was nothing there. The forceful pounding of her heart competed against the sharp shallow breaths that had racked her petite body with fear, rendering her near frozen to the park bench on which she sat. She knew she hadn't been dreaming. Her body told her it was too real to be even a nightmare. She had felt it. Felt it strike her cheek. But it couldn't be real either because her fingers found nothing.

"Oh God. Please God. No." A mutter escaped through twisted lips.

It had begun, again. A dark blurred image, rife with fear, somehow connected to the past and determined for her witness it. But why? That was what she couldn't understand.

She hurried to her feet, eyes flitting from side to side, checking there was no-one around as she smoothed down her clothes in attempt to take back self-control. Shoulders pushed back, the breath she exhaled was slow and controlled as she began the short walk back to work, concentrating her mind on every deliberate step. Left-right-left-right-left-right. It had worked. Her breath had slowed, her heart no longer frantic. The dampness from the mizzle had seeped through her dress suit and coated her skin, prompting an involuntary shudder. Although Spring was supposedly in the air, the remnants of Winter were still clinging on and today of all days, she wished she had brought her coat to help keep out the cold.

Kate looked down at her watch, nearly twenty minutes late. As her step quickened, so too did the grating voice in her head, chastising her for allowing it to consume her again. But she had no choice. No control over it. She really wished she had. Both now and before.

Pushing her way through the heavy revolving door, she made a left turn towards the powder room. Late or not she had to smarten herself up. After reapplying her nude lipstick and brushing the stray strands of dark hair back into place, she stared hard at the reflection looking back at her, hardly recognising the person framed in the ornate gold mirror. Physically there was not much that was different, slightly paler, a few more lines but overall, the same. But looking beyond the physical, there was something missing. The reflection that stared back at her was nothing more than a near empty shell devoid of any real emotion. The ability to really feel seemed far removed, buried deep and out of reach. Everything now fluctuated between happy and sad, black and white, all the shades of grey in between long gone.

At least that's what she believed.

When her hand reached for the office door, she was forty-five minutes late and even from behind the glass, the scowl from under the thick dark eyebrows pierced straight through her. He was not happy.

"Shit. Deep breath Kate," she told herself, "deep breath."

"Good morning Kate. Delighted you've graced us with your presence...finally." His voice acerbic as the words filled the space around them.

This man irritated her more than anything she could think of. It was typical he was in on the one day she was really late. Seconds before she spoke, her eye was drawn to his higher on the left than right receding hair line. Like a yo-yo, every time.

"I'm so sorry Mr. Collier, I just completely lost track of all time. It won't happen again." She desperately wanted to believe that last comment.

"I'm afraid it is too late Kate; this happens all too often. Your timekeeping has become appalling of late and when you are here, well...you may as well not be. Things are sliding. It is not good for the clientele or the reputation of our Hotel."

She went to speak but he raised his hand to stop her from butting in, forcing her to swallow her defence.

"You have had several warnings to get yourself

sorted out. We have paid for all sorts of help for you, not to mention the time off we've given you, but quite simply things are getting worse and we are losing business. You have left me with no option I'm afraid. I am sorry Kate. I really am."

Sorry. It was an easy word sorry. Pretty meaningless most of the time.

Unable to meet her eyes, he turned his face away from her. She had never seen him look uncomfortable before. Maybe he was sorry, she couldn't be sure. Whatever it was didn't last for long though. His cold stare landed upon her again, forcing her small hands to screw themselves up into tight balls by her sides as he continued his tirade.

"Please pack away your things Kate and leave when you've done so. All the relevant paperwork will be in order and be sent on to you."

He rose from the chair, pausing by the door frame of his own office and turned back to face her one last time, the smallest fraction of warmth in his eyes.

"Go and get some proper long-term help Kate… please." For a passing moment, he sounded almost quite sincere.

The building heat in Kate's neck crept up into her cheeks, embarrassment replacing disbelief. She let her hands relax, uncurling her fingers and began to pack away the few bits and bobs from her desk into the copier paper box Bernarde had brought over.

It had taken only five minutes for Trinity to be summoned into Mr. Collier's office and just five more for her to leave. Heavily glossed lips beamed from ear to ear as she tottered back to her seat in the impossibly high heels she insisted on wearing every day. There were no guesses as to who was taking Kate's place. Trinity was twenty-two years of age and very willing to please, in more ways than one. Since she'd been there, her rise on the promotional ladder had happened effortlessly and quickly, too quickly for it to be above board. A thought which Kate knew from the hushed gossip around the hotel had not only crossed her mind.

Gathering up the last few items of stationery, she placed them inside the box on top of the other bits that had been collected over the years, each one holding a different memory. Folding down the cardboard flaps, she took a long deep breath, letting it out as a sigh as she sealed the join with tape. Something had stirred inside of her, lodging itself in her throat. Sadness. Like an old friend she knew it well. But it was tinged with something else. Something faint that she interpreted as relief.

She was thankful that most of the desks were empty, their usual occupants were at a How to Provide a More Inclusive Service conference. The cynical voice in her knew that was the industry way of saying 'Ways to milk more money out of your clients without them realising.' She'd been around the block a bit to believe anything else.

There were only the five of them in the office, including Mr Collier. Just Kate, Bernarde, Linda and Trinity. Awkward goodbyes were exchanged with Linda, her face riddled with confusion being fairly new to the company, eleven weeks and four days to be precise. The number engraved in Kate's mind because she was due to carry out her three-month appraisal at the end of the week, her trial period coming to end. She wondered if Trinity would carry out it out? Not her problem now. Bernarde was next. She really was going to miss working with him every day, the thought prompted a slick of moisture to coat her eyes. He wrapped his arms around her and pulled her tight into one of his bear hugs. Enough time to blink away the tears. No words were needed. They were, and had been ever since the day they met, best friends who shared everything, almost, kindred spirits some would say. Kate knew she would still see him; he was not just a friend at work but outside too. Perhaps her only real friend. One she would trust with her life anyway.

Pulling away from Bernarde, her eye caught Trinity already moving stuff onto the desk she had occupied not ten minutes before, stuffing her pink fluffy pom-pom pens into the pot that had been left behind. Talk about not letting the ground go cold. Kate bit her tongue, deciding to let it pass. There would be no point in saying anything, nothing to be gained. Instead, she lifted the box of memories off the desk and made her way to the lift. Only after the doors began to close did she stop blinking, allowing the tears to escape her eyes. Tears which were swiftly followed by the voice in her head, *stop it and pull yourself together. This is your own fault. You let it happen so get a grip.* The harsh words cut clean through the tears, the thought of anyone seeing her like this unbearable. Coupled together, it had been enough to compose herself by the time the lift reached the Ground Floor, relieved there were no staff around as she walked out into the empty foyer.

Leaving her pass with security at the discreet desk they shared in the corner, she managed to avoid conversation as to the why's and wherefores of her surrendering it. She nodded a brief cheerio and stepped out of the revolving side door onto the carpeted steps of the entrance. Looking down onto the busy street below, she stood for a moment, soaking up the cool air, the sensation of prickly mounds that had formed on her skin strangely enjoyable. Leaving the last step for the pavement below, it dawned upon her that this was the end of an era.

Another one.

The streets were bustling, crowded with busy people and towering concrete surrounds. Weaving her way through, she pondered on the last few years of her life, quickly reminded of that day. That one day that had changed her life completely and each of the events before it. Ending up here in a place she had grown to hate more with the passing of each day. She came here, like many others, in hope of leaving the past behind her. To become invisible, just another head to add to an already over populated city. But she had soon learnt that the past is never far behind you.

It was how she had met Bernarde.

Kate had worked for an independent Hotel company and if she was truthful, had a love hate relationship with her job. She loved the Georgian building she worked in, decorated throughout in the Arts and Crafts style. It had a character and opulence that could, if you allowed it, transport you back to a bygone era. A magical place that would always occupy a special place in her heart, a privilege to work amongst its beauty. But beauty has an opposite, and ugliness was rife behind the scenes. Office politics, backstabbing and no respect. It was each for their own, except for a few, Bernarde being one. A world where money ruled. Its calm outer existence not at all reflective of its raging inner core. Words that resonated deeply. Her own raging inner core had become so masked by the steel veil of composure she had so carefully created for herself that there was nothing left now other than a dark abyss.

Chapter 2

Kate

She'd lost count of the times the keys had slipped from her jittery fingers as she stabbed at the keyhole, balancing the box between the wall and her body. Finally, having managed to stop her hand from shaking, she shouldered the door to the apartment open, letting it swing shut once she was inside. The small narrow hallway was dark and uninviting, its equally dark wooden flooring now home to the sorry box of belongings she'd dumped there. She reached for the light switch, keen to inject some warmth into the place as she let out a shudder, her clothes still a touch damp from the earlier drizzle. But even on a warm day the apartment always had a cool atmosphere to it. Knocking up the heating thermostat, she could hear the silent call of a hot bath beckoning.

Whilst the bath was running, she poured herself a larger than usual glass of prosecco, taking it with her through to the bathroom. Although small, the bathroom was perfectly proportioned and was her little sanctuary after a hard day on her feet. The only room that held any warmth, of any kind. She stripped off her clothes, lazily chucking them to one side, not bothered to hang or fold them like usual, she could deal with them later.

The deep roll top bath she'd begged Owen to buy was now filled to the brim with her favourite rose scented bubbles. Sinking down beneath them, she let her eyes settle on the soft glow of the spa candle she'd lit, the tightness in her forehead lessening as she watched the flame flicker to its own silent tune. The heat of the water against her skin encouraged her aching muscles to soften, as if they knew it was now safe to let go of the tension that had effortlessly built up throughout them during the day. She let her eyelids lower, grateful of the immediate peace the darkness brought with it.

But her mind, not content with being peaceful for more than just a few moments, was quick to replay the day's events. Getting fired she could deal with, well, almost. She would miss the income but certainly not the job and all the rubbish that came with it. Yes Mr. Collier, no Mr. Collier, three bags bloody full Mr. Collier was what on many occasions she had greatly wanted to burst out but had never dared. Now though, in the safety of her own home, cocooned in the warmth of the silky water, all sorts of things crossed her lips, fuelled no doubt by the alcohol, most of which were certifiably rude. Like a naughty fourteen-year-old dared by friends at school, she felt a spark of something stir within her that hadn't been experienced in years. Excitement. Just for a second.

Kate had worked hard over time to suppress her emotions. She still had them of course but had learnt how to ignore them and become numb to the feelings that accompanied them. Yet now, it was on one hand immensely therapeutic to give those feelings a voice, a route in which to escape on. But on the other hand, it scared her, because she knew she could not have feelings again. She'd come to learn that there was always too much to lose from having them.

With the how dare he drama out of her head, her mind, as keen as ever, switched back to what had landed her in this predicament in the first place. She'd only took a detour to the park to sit in the fresh air for a few minutes to try and relieve the throbbing headache she'd woken up with. But even away from the hordes of people the air had been thick and damp, oppressive. She couldn't even remember closing her eyes as she'd sat down on that park bench. Let alone what had happened next. None of it made any sense. She didn't get it, why after all this time had it started again? No matter how much she tried, she just didn't understand. Or maybe, just maybe, she didn't want to.

Finishing off the last drops in her glass, goose bumps had covered her arms and legs, the water had grown tepid, all the warmth gone. Heaving herself out of the tub, she slipped on the oversized fluffy sheep robe, a Christmas gift from Owen which had spent more time on the back of the door than on the back of her. 'A joke gift,' he'd said when he saw the disappointment behind her eyes. An excuse for still not knowing what she did and didn't like. She knotted the belt, toying with the idea of whether to get dressed or not, deciding on the latter, leaving the bathroom for the kitchen. She refilled her glass, taking the bottle and placing it down on the glass coffee table before sinking down into the cold leather settee. The bubbles tickled her mouth as she greedily swigged, sparking a temporary aliveness within it. As she took another sip and then another, light headedness slowly began to creep in. This was good, because soon it would take over and everything in her mind would be dulled, letting her escape the walls of her self-made prison, just for a while.

Her eyelids flickered, rousing her from the escape. She glanced across at the large metal wall clock, it was 8.13 pm, the day had obviously taken its toll. Still not quite awake, her palms felt around her, pressing into the sofa to push herself up. As her senses began to return, she heard before she saw Owen, shorts and t-shirt on, busy in the kitchen.

"I never heard you come in," she said, rubbing away at the heaviness that lingered in the corners of her eyes.

"I know. I didn't have the heart to wake you, so I grabbed a shower and decided to rustle up some dinner for us while you slept." A conceited smile painted his face. "What's with the box in the hall anyway? You been sacked?"

The smile from his casual joking soon faded as he realised from Kate's frown, the old saying of 'many a true word said in jest' was very apt. Conceit fast turned to unease as he quickly added, "Let's eat and you can tell me all about it baby."

Baby. It was a word she absolutely hated. It made every hair on her skin stand on end and shiver. She'd told Owen this on numerous occasions, but still he insisted on using it. As far as pet names went, there was something quite offensive about the word Baby.

As awake as she could force herself to be, she sat down at the sparsely laid glass dining table. Glass and minimal. That summed up the apartment. Looking around, everything here screamed Owen. There was nothing that would say she lived there. No cushions or trinkets, not even a candle. She'd never thought about it before but now, the reality was stark. Still after all these years this was a house, not a home. Owen's house.

"One for you, one for me," he said through a schoolboy grin, clearly chuffed as he set them down.

Pasta, great. She had begun to hate pasta. The overpowering smell of garlic sat in her nostrils, trapped there a little longer each time she swallowed a mouthful of the starchy mound. She knew she shouldn't moan but that was all that Owen ever seemed to be able to cook, or could be bothered to. She never had been sure which. Like an ungrateful child, she pushed it around the plate, filling him in on her day, being careful to edit the bits which he really did not need to know. She couldn't bear him pestering her again to see the G.P.

"So, the chunk sacked you then hey baby?"

"I just said, didn't I?" Kate snapped back, pushing herself away from the table. "Why can't you hold a proper conversation like normal people!"

"Hey, I'm just trying to lighten the mood a little baby. You hated the job anyway, or so you kept telling me. Something else will come along Kate, something more you."

"And what the hell is that supposed to mean?" Her body stiffened as it grew more and more defensive.

"For God's sake Kate nothing! Other than something you'll enjoy more, hopefully!" He threw down his knife and fork, the tinny sound as they hit the plate rang loud in her ears. The pressure building in her forehead once more.

"I don't know what's up with you lately Kate, you're either in a world of your own or snapping and sniping at people, especially me." His chair crudely scraped across the wooden floor as he pushed himself away, creating further space between them, his eyes downcast.

"Oh, screw you!" Kate shouted, snatching the bottle from the table, storming off into the bedroom. She slammed the door shut behind her, Owen's voice fading into the background. With her back against the closed door, she gulped back the rest of the wine from the bottle she had been clutching so tightly, discarding it on the floor once empty. She crawled into bed, sighing deeply as she realised her whole body was again riddled with fresh tension. Wondering how life had become like this. A vicious cycle that seemed determined to never stop. Grateful of the softness waiting to take her weight, she closed her eyes and willed sleep to come and take her back, to escape once more and shut out the day.

Chapter 3

Owen

Owen had woken early. His sleep had been restless cramped into the box room on the z-bed. He knew there was no point in just lying there, it would only feed his irritation.

He left the apartment, careful not to wake Kate and headed straight for the gym, needing to free the stiffness that saturated his body. He liked to look after himself, he always had, but it had been much easier when he was younger. The buzz he'd got from feeling the blood pumping through his veins was still there though, when he got going. As was the satisfaction of knowing that he was still in control. Admiring his sculpted frame in the mirror he was stood in front of, he smiled approvingly.

It was quiet in the gym that morning. No distractions or hanging around to use equipment meant he was finished much earlier than usual but it also meant he had nothing to stop his mind from replaying last night. He was worried about Kate; she had become more and more distant with each day that passed. Why couldn't she see it though? He couldn't put his finger on it but there was something wrong, very wrong. The fitful sleep, the vacant moments, the unpredictable moods. He had tried talking to her, but she wouldn't listen, let alone talk, urging her to see a G.P, even offering to pay for a Harley Street consultation but she'd point blank refused. He'd known all those years ago it would be tough but he owed it to her. He cared for her more than she could realise but he just didn't know what he could do to help her. Other than be there for her there wasn't much else, but even that seemed to trigger her.

It was still early as he started the ignition; he would be one of the first in the office. He watched the flicks of light appear as the dashboard came to life, sparking an idea how to cheer Kate up. He would take her out to dinner, this evening, to the oldy-worldly restaurant she had always wanted to try. Stuffy and old fashioned was his impression but this evening was about Kate, not him. He just hoped it would be enough. Waiting patiently for the screen to clear, he watched as the steam faded into nowhere, wishing the worry that sat behind his forehead would do the same.

By the time he had pulled out of the car park he'd made another decision, that this was going to be a good day, regardless. And as he allowed that thought to linger, his face had no option but to break into a smile, filling him with a different kind of buzz.

Chapter 4

Kate

Awoken briefly by the sound of what she thought was the door, her eyes had struggled to open even a tiny bit before it hit her that she had nothing to get up for. Breathing out heavily, she pulled the crisp cover of the duvet back up around her and encased herself in the warmth of the bed, rolling over on her side to bring it around her further still. Owen had slept in the box room last night, for that she was thankful. She couldn't face him this morning, hoping he would have already left for work.

'Never go to bed on an argument.' Words her aunt used to say sat at the front of her mind, as if keen not to let her repeat the same mistake again.

An ache of guilt mixed with sadness moved through her.

But it was too late. Both for last night. And before.

Outside, the rain continued to pour, thrashing

against the windows as if it were looking for a way in. It had picked up momentum throughout the morning and the howling winds were what had roused Kate from her sleep. She checked the clock; almost lunchtime. For a split second, she thought she'd overslept and was late for work. But memories of yesterday swiftly replaced that thought, but not nearly as much as the reminder of the wine that she'd mindlessly drunk. Sitting up, the throbbing in her head increased as she eased herself to the edge of the bed. She sat there for a moment, head cradled in hands, mentally preparing herself to move as soon as the spinning had stopped. With a bit of concentration, her feet began to take her full weight. The large vulgar wardrobe that dominated the bedroom provided respite for her nauseous frame; her hands pressed firmly against it to aid her balance. The steps towards the bedroom door were slow and considered, debating whether to go straight to the bathroom or hunt around the kitchen for pain relief. Opting for the second, her hands gripped the worktops as she edged her way round, reaching out only to flick the switch down on the kettle as she passed, assuming it would still have water in it from yesterday. It usually did. The same hand reached up into the cupboard above, fingers locating the paracetamol box. Guiding herself round to the sink, she filled a tumbler full of cold water, swallowed the pills and downed the rest of the water. Her mouth dry and claggy, dehydrated from last night's wine. She bent over the worktop, fingers pressed hard into her temples, circling an attempt to squeeze out some of the increasing pressure the throbbing had caused. She swilled back another glass of water and made for the bathroom. Coffee could wait.

The jet of water hit the back of her neck, trickling down around her body. Its warmth welcome, washing away the weariness felt not only by her body. Her mind, still fuzzy, found a way to dwell on the events of the previous day again and she tried, really tried to make sense of what had happened. Not with the job, for she somehow knew it was inevitable that her role there would come to end, it had to. What she didn't understand was why. Or why she had become host to this mystifying intrusion. Again. Its vice like grip growing tighter by the day. Eager to loosen its hold, she focused her energy on imagining the water that fell down around her took with it the ramblings of her mind, washing them away.

It was just one of the many techniques she had learnt over the years. She remembered well the therapist telling her on many occasions how it would help her cope. But the therapist really had no idea, how could he? It had helped a few times, but only short term. Her mind had become like a never-ending game of ping pong, back and forth, from noise to quiet and back again.

Wrapping herself up tight in the oversized bath sheet, she stepped out of the shower, wet hair dripping down her back, contemplating if things might have been any different had she told just one of them the truth. Told them what had really happened and how she felt. Maybe. Maybe not.

With the last of the moisture patted away from her skin, she sat down on the bed. The throbbing in her head had begun to subside and she gave a silent prayer of thanks for the wonder that was paracetamol. She reached over to the drawer, retrieving her notebook from its secret hiding place, away from the prying eyes of Owen and opened it up with the ribbon marker. Her own eyes rested over the open page as they tallied up how many times it had happened that month. Six. That number alarmed her. Six. Making a note of yesterdays, that made it seven.

"Jesus, this is mad," she muttered.

The words triggered the pounding in her head to return, spinning round, trapping her in the middle of a whirlwind. A hard, quick pulse formed in her throat, tightening her jaw as trepidation crept up inside of her. Invisible hands closed in, restricting her breath, the space between each one becoming shorter. In her mind, the four walls closed in on her, ready to take her. She knew she had to get out. Escape to the fresh air. She needed to think. Properly. But first she had to breathe.

Several concentrated breaths along with the need to escape those four walls aided her ability to calm herself swiftly. After hastily pulling on a tracksuit and pumps, she guided a brush through her half dry hair, teasing out the cot that had formed at the back. Lashes coated with a quick brush of mascara, she rubbed balm over her dry lips. Out in the hallway, she caught a glimpse of herself in the mirror above the console table as she bent down for her bag, reassuring herself acceptable, and not her usual pristine would suffice. With the notebook safely stuffed inside, she swung the bag onto her shoulder and picked up her keys. She was ready to go.

The rain had slowed to a light drizzle and the brightening sky ahead looked as if it might give way to some afternoon sunshine. Kate hated the rain, she always had. Even as a little girl she was always the one who wouldn't jump in the puddles, opting instead to watch from a safe distance. The rain served to darken her mood the older she'd got, leaving her distracted and tired, wanting to be alone. Over the last couple of years, she had tried all manner of things to help with her increasingly volatile moods but trying to explain to how she felt was hard. Like trying to reason with a bull, the Doctors and therapists didn't listen, hearing only what they wanted to hear. Depression and SAD were a couple of things that had been suggested but she had known it was neither of those. The pills they gave her ended up down the sink, they were the very last thing she wanted. On explaining to one that she felt so much worse whenever it was raining, she was sure he thought she was ready to be carted off. She wondered if maybe he was right, figuring after what had happened it would be understandable. Enough to send anyone mad. But in the end, she gave up on them, the endless searching for words to explain how she felt was tiresome. Nothing had helped shift the burden, lighten it even. If anything, the burden had grown heavier and heavier. Unhappiness engulfing her in its dark cloak.

She found herself in the little coffee shop that sat nestled away down a quiet side street, away from the droves of busy people. It was the kind of place only few knew about, tourists happening upon it but mainly the retired, the generation who still had time to stop and stare. She urgently needed to think, and this was the ideal place. Quiet but not totally isolated, its relaxed atmosphere was just what her head craved. She didn't need anything to add to the familiar pressure that was building between her ears.

Her favourite table was free, tucked back into the quirky wall alcove with a view out of the faux vine covered window. Undecided whether the fast spin in her tummy was from hunger or anxiety, she guessed it was probably a combination of both. Thumbing through the menu, she was pleased to see the all-day breakfast, or hangover cure as Bernarde used to joke, still sat at the top of their offering. The waitress came promptly to take her order, bringing the large cafetière of fresh coffee just a few minutes later. She looked around, appreciating just how cosy and discreet this coffee shop was. She had been on several occasions with Bernarde when they had needed to chat, moan about work or if they had just wanted to be away from the hustle and bustle for a little while. The pace was so much lighter in here and you could be forgiven for forgetting you were in the centre of a busy city. Down to earth, space to breathe. Her thoughts began to trail off, wondering how two things so close to each other could seem like worlds apart. As she gently plunged the cafetière down, the bittersweet aromas wafted up her nostrils, stirring her thoughts back to why she was sat there. There were decisions to make but where did she begin?

Retrieving the notebook she'd stuffed into her bag earlier, she opened it up on an empty page and drew a line down the middle creating two columns, heading one Problems, the other Options, and began to write.

Problem One. No Job. *Option.* Find another Job.

But doing what? She had no proper qualifications and couldn't see herself working in some funky young boutique or department store which seemed the only positions available.

Problem Two. Owen. *Option.* Shut up and put up or leave.

The theory sounded much easier than she knew the practice would be.

Problem Three. December 1996. *Option.* Tell the truth.

She couldn't. She wouldn't know where to start now after all these years so that left her with no option. She'd resigned herself to the fact some time ago there was nothing she could do now and would just have to continue to live with the shame and the guilt that had infected her. A dirty disease with no known cure.

Problem Four. Darkness. She knew of nothing else she could call it or even how to explain it without sounding crazy. *Option*. GP/Therapy.

No chance after last time. The voice in her head keen to remind that the last time had almost certainly made things worse.

Elbow perched on the table, she rested her cheek in its hand, giving a little shake of her head as she asked herself wasn't the whole point of therapy to help combat the problem and assist you to move forward? Not push you further into the depths of despair, leaving you feeling more trapped and confused than before. Her mind backtracked to the sleepless nights she had spent staring blankly at the dark space out in front of her. Only to be replaced with another type of darkness, an altogether scarier one.

From out of nowhere came a voice, silently screaming within her, finding its outlet through the pen she was holding as she scrawled – I CAN'T STAND THIS ANY LONGER!!!

All she wanted was to reach inside the depths of her soul and tear out all the memories, all the hurt, the confusion and guilt that consumed her daily. Scrub away the invisible scars that had been left behind, but she couldn't, and her head continued to pound from the constant whirlwind of chatter it had become home to. She slammed the book shut, stuffing it back inside her bag as if all the shit she was tirelessly wrestling with would somehow, miraculously go away once she was no longer looking at the words, the book out of sight.

She gulped down her coffee, praying that the caffeine hit would shock her back into now, the present. It worked. When she looked up, she caught sight of the waitress moving towards her with what she hoped was her breakfast.

Her fork picked over the plate's contents as she soon realised the idea of food had been far more appealing than the act of eating it. Pushing it to one side, she let her attention wander to the other occupied tables in the coffee shop. Two ladies sat at one, big mugs of hot chocolate and half-eaten cake, seemingly putting the world to rights if the language of their hands was anything to go by. Another occupied by an elderly gentleman, engrossed in his broadsheet, taking in the day's news from across the world no doubt. But it was the couple who sat at the table closest to her that gained her interest the most. She watched their body language as they exchanged words, one hand from each of them touching across the table. The soft smiles, full of love and adoration for each other, perfectly comfortable in one another's company. She hazarded a guess that they were perhaps in their seventies but so much younger in spirit. As the lady glanced over, her eyes met Kate's. The heat from Kate's cheeks caused them to flush and she nodded and smiled, swiftly averting her gaze in the opposite direction.

"I bet you think we're daft don't you dearie...a pair of oldies like us holding hands." The voice was light and calm.

Kate turned her head to where the couple were sat, meeting the kind smile that flowed towards her.

"Absolutely not. I was actually just thinking how lovely it is to see two people..." She couldn't finish, couldn't say it. Couldn't tell them she enjoyed watching how much in love they were with each other; they would think her loopy.

Sensing her growing embarrassment, the gentleman turned and spoke. "Let me tell you something sweet child, if a man doesn't make you feel like you are the most important thing in the world when you are with him, then my darling, he is not the one for you."

Kate's mouth dropped, stunned. It was as if they were reading her thoughts for the old lady added, "Each and every one of us has a true soul mate, the other half of us that makes us whole and complete and it is our mission, God willing, to find them. We have to be brave enough to look at what we have and if it doesn't make us feel good, then be even braver to let it go."

The resonance of those words vibrated deep inside of Kate, feeding the restlessness that grew hungrier by the day. Unsure how to answer, she strained a half smile and sighed. The type you give to someone when you're sad, because words would only send a signal to lift the floodgates. And that was exactly how she felt but it was no good, the smile hadn't worked. Her lip started to tremble before a tear skimmed her pale cheek. This was not supposed to happen. She was supposed to be regaining control, not letting go of the last shreds she had left. Frantically searching her bag for something to dab her watery eyes with, a pretty lace edged handkerchief was offered out for her to make use of.

"I'm Joan. May I?" The old lady pulled out the chair opposite Kate.

Kate nodded as Joan gracefully lowered herself down in to the empty chair, silent. After a few moments, with a good many tears shed and wiped away, Kate looked up at her and mouthed a thank you. Joan took her hand, placing it in between her own as she began to speak.

"My dear child, whatever or whoever those tears are for, listen to them. Listen to what your heart is trying to tell you for it never lies. Patrick and I spent many years apart. Far too many years apart because we let our heads rule our hearts. We did what was expected of us by our families and we were both miserable for an infinite amount of time. Only when we were both widowed did we finally listen to our hearts calling. So much time wasted that we can never get back but you my dear child, act now and do not waste this precious thing we have called life." Her voice remained as genteel and delicate as the lines that scattered her hands. "There is so much to life that you know nothing of yet, but allow yourself to be innocent in how things will best work out for you, climbing the hurdles as they appear, and you too will find your missing piece."

She let Kate's hand slide from her own, rose to her feet and held her arms out open. Following her lead, Kate stood too and allowed herself to be wrapped in the warmth of Joan's affection.

"For the light to truly come my dear, we have to first embrace the dark." The soft etheric whisper in Kate's ear sent a shiver spiralling through her.

As they parted, a tiny spark of hope took hold deep inside her.

Patrick, already on his feet, tipped his hat to bid Kate a warm farewell, clasping Joan's hand in his own as they left the cafe. Sitting back down, the spark of hope was swiftly extinguished by the knot of anxiety that had formed. Did they know? How could they know? Had they been in here when she and Bernarde had been deep in conversation and overhead their words? No, she knew that wasn't possible. They had told her they were just visiting for the day. It was nothing more than a coincidence. A nice old couple who were imparting their wisdom on someone who happened to be there. She reasoned that it wasn't too difficult for anyone to tell that she was not in a good place. Her fingers rubbed the back of her neck, wanting to ease the jagged prattle of her mind. She watched the couple from the window, strolling off down the narrow street, hand in hand before disappearing around the corner. Finishing off the dregs of her coffee which had gone disgustingly cold, a lightbulb moment came. At least in relation to one of her problems.

She didn't ask for the bill, figuring that twenty pounds would amply cover what she had ordered. She passed the note to the waitress along with a thank you on her way out, not bothering to enquire or wait for any change. Time was getting on and if she was to do this, she had to act fast.

∞∞∞

Knowing that for her, this was the only option, Kate began throwing random bits and bobs into her suitcase. She needed to get away, from here, from Owen, from everything that had gone on. A break to help spring clean her head of its accumulated clutter. Time to straighten herself out from the contorted version she had become.

A quick google of the train times told her if she made haste, she would manage the 3:13 pm train, enabling her to make it there at a reasonable hour tonight. With the phone still in her palm, she began to scroll through the list of names it held, tapping on his to reveal the contact details. The pulse in her finger prominent as it hovered over the name, but she couldn't bring herself to do it. She couldn't call him. She questioned for a moment whether just turning up on his doorstop would be a bad thing, quickly convincing herself into believing it wouldn't as she slid the phone into her pocket, pulling the zip round on the case. Heaving it off the bed, she wheeled it through into the hallway, knowing there was just one more thing she had to do before she left.

She couldn't face talking to Owen, even over a telephone. He wouldn't understand, no matter how hard she tried to explain and she was in no doubt that he would attempt to talk her out of leaving. Picking up the pen from the kitchen worktop she began to write, the nagging voice rearing up to remind her how cowardly it was to do such a thing. Folding the note over, the start of a tear began to swell in the corner of her eye, she couldn't just erase away the time they'd spent together, even if what little feelings she had for him had dried out.

Out in the hallway, she propped the note against the bowl on the console table, feeling the trickle down her cheek. Wiping away the solitary tear that had paused on her chin, she pulled on her jacket, leaving it unzipped. Without looking back, she secured her handbag on her shoulder and reached for the suitcase handle. She flicked the hall light off with her spare hand, allowing the door to her life and everything she knew to slam shut behind her.

Chapter 5

Owen

After watching one o'clock pass, then two, Owen glanced again at the digits on his monitor and saw it was coming up to three. Through the sparkling glass of his office window, the area beyond was quiet and getting in early meant he had finished his outstanding business dealings before lunchtime. Normally by this time, the office was a hive of activity which meant the afternoons flew by but today, with everyone in meetings, it seemed to drag on and on. Without much to occupy him, he sat doodling, shape upon shape, their edges as straight and sharp as the thought that appeared. Voicing his yes louder than he had realised, the word travelled through the slightly ajar door raising a couple of heads, just for a moment, from the desks nearby. Switching his computer screen over to the search page, he typed in City Breaks, assuring himself that they both needed a break for Kate to relax. As he scoured the travel page, the perfect break stared right back at him. A mini break to Barcelona. He could manage a few days off but nothing more. Even though he was not that busy today, he couldn't take more than a few days at a time, so a weekend break was ideal. Fly out Friday morning and return late Monday evening. Perfect. He could manage that.

Calling back the restaurant he had booked, he requested a bouquet of Kates favourite flowers, pink peonies and cream roses, be arranged to be delivered this evening, along with a bottle of their finest champagne. It was important for tonight to be special and he would spend what it took. Working hard over the years to build the business up along with a few wise investments had ensured that money was not a problem for Owen.

Ending the call, the text to Kate would have to wait as an email alert flagged up in the corner of his monitor. Not recognising the address of the sender and with a subject field left blank, he hesitated, laying his mobile back on the charging pad. He switched the computer screen back to his email page, his eyes fixed on the one now sat at the top of his short and tidy list. The oddness of it growing. No-one had his direct business address unless he had met them personally so why didn't he recognise the senders address? An uncomfortable niggle began to gnaw away at him, his fingers tense as they drummed the desk either side of the keypad. He was being dramatic; it was only an email and anyone of his business associates could have shared his address. So why was his gut telling him otherwise.

He eased off the drumming and clicked the email

open, not expecting the words it contained to jump out of the screen at him, lunging forward, imaginary fingers clutching at his throat. Those two words embedded themselves firmly within him, growing and twisting, draining the blood from his veins and the air from his lungs. Those two tiny words carried such weight, forcing his world to move inwards, crushing him with it.

He's out

Owen stared at the screen, at the obtrusiveness of what it held, his mind frantic in its search for something, anything that could help him understand what was happening.

But he found nothing.

And for the first time in his life, he felt like he was losing control.

Chapter 6

Kate

K ate had reached platform seven just as the train was pulling in. Catching her breath, she eyed up the other waiting passengers, thankful there weren't too many, a seat almost guaranteed.

She headed through the half empty carriages towards the quiet one, easing herself down in a forward-facing window seat. Even though the train wasn't particularly busy, she yearned for some peace and quiet and was not prepared to risk ending up near someone who spent the whole time talking away, either to her or at their phone. Settling herself for the long journey ahead, she remembered her own was still switched on, prompted by the no phones sticker on the window in front of her. Rummaging through her handbag, her fingers finally unearthed and pulled it out. She held down the button on the top to switch it off but seeing the slide to power off message appear sparked a sudden change of heart. Pressing cancel, she opted instead to flip the side button onto silent so it would not disturb other passengers seeking quietude if it happened to ring.

As the train engaged its gear, it jerked forward, advancing slowly out of the station. A quick welcome announcement was made on the tannoy, informing passengers of designated stop offs and the location of the buffet cart should they be in need of refreshments. Almost effortlessly, within seconds, the train gathered speed, whizzing past adjacent buildings, everything soon becoming a fast blur. Kate relaxed herself back into the seat, letting out a deep breath and closing her eyes simultaneously, struck by how comparable it was to her life again these last few months. Nothing but a fast blur whizzing around inside her head.

The monotonous voice announcement that they were roughly an hour away from the final destination roused her out of dreariness. She must have nodded off. Allowing her eyes to regain focus, she became aware of how the quiet carriage had emptied out of most passengers, leaving behind just herself and an elderly gentleman who she hadn't noticed up until that point. She was almost certain he wasn't in the carriage when she boarded so he'd obviously got on whilst she was snoozing. Whoever he was he appeared quite content immersed in his thick hardback book.

Knowing she had another hour or so before she

had to change trains, she decided maybe now was a good time to locate the buffet cart, she would need coffee to help keep her awake. Nearing where the elderly man was sat, she casually snook a look at what he was reading, inquisitive eyes drawn to the ornate gold embossing on the book's cover. He peered up over the pages, meeting her wandering eyes, smiling straight at her. A smile that lit up his whole face, holding her in his gaze. She was, just for a split second, mesmerised by its sheer intensity. Returning the smile, albeit slightly embarrassed at being caught being nosey, she turned her head away, hastily making for the door. Unsure of what had just happened, she found immediate relief as she stepped through into the next carriage, amazed to find that one empty too and wondered if maybe every Wednesday was as quiet as this.

After ordering coffee, the progressive gurgle in her stomach alerted her to the fact that she was hungry, her mind cast back to the café that morning and the hardly touched breakfast. The server joked with her that all they had were some day-old packet sandwiches which would be best avoided wherever possible and the biscuit or snack bars would probably be her safest choice. She opted for a flapjack and rather than going back to her seat, decided to stay and eat it there, getting the impression he was probably glad of a bit of company too as he passed her the coffee.

They made small talk about how it wasn't terribly busy, how long he'd worked on there, which was only a couple of weeks and Kate couldn't help but wonder if the bulky ankle tag that poked through his black nylon trouser leg played some part in that. Whatever it was for, he was easy to talk to and she found it was nice to communicate with someone who didn't know her or her background. He enquired if she was travelling on business or pleasure but she didn't go into any detail. Just off visiting someone that she hadn't seen in a while was the easiest thing to say, feeling just a tad awkward when he answered, 'I bet they are looking forward to seeing you?' She let out a half smile, unable to answer because she didn't know whether that would be the case or not.

Doubt soon began to creep in. Was it wrong of her to just turn up out of the blue, especially after all this time. And after last time.

No.

If she'd rung, he would have questioned her, tried to talk her out of it and she was simply not prepared to take that risk. Nudged from her thoughts by the voice asking if she was ok, she smiled again and apologized with a, "Just tired." Until the words had left her, she hadn't realised just how tired she had grown.

Interrupted by the tannoy informing all that the train would soon be arriving in Exeter, the final stop on this leg of the journey and all passengers would need to alight here, Kate pushed her empty cardboard cup towards him and said goodbye.

As she headed back to the quiet carriage to get

her things together, the announcement followed her with details of which platform was required for those continuing their journey to Paignton.

Arriving back at her seat, Kate reached across to pick up her oversized print scarf, wrapping it around her neck and then leant in for her coat. When she turned to put her arm in the other sleeve, she noticed the old man was no longer in the carriage and assumed he must already be waiting to get off. No, she would have noticed if he was and the foyer was definitely empty when she passed through it so where was he? Feeling creeped out, she grabbed her handbag from the other seat, what sat beneath it caused a sharp intake of breath.

Picking up the heavy book, she turned, looking from side to side for its owner but all her eyes found was the slip of white paper that just poked out over the top of the pages. She tentatively pulled it free, a handwritten note with the words;

For the light to truly come, we must first embrace the dark. For the journey both begins and ends with the past. Have faith dear Kate

What the hell? What the actual hell? None of this made any sense. How did he know her name and what was this all about? If she wanted to catch her connection, there was no time to stand and think though. She stuffed both the book and note inside her bag and zipped it tight before heading to the luggage hold to retrieve her case.

Those few seconds passed like hours as she willed the train to hurry up and stop, her hand hitting the door release button as soon as it was able to. She stepped out onto the platform, loosening the scarf around her neck, taking deep breaths to try to rationalise what had happened, all the time looking around her for signs of the old man. But he was nowhere to be seen. Telling herself she had to make her way to platform two, like pronto if she didn't want to be stranded there in Exeter was enough to pause the mass of confusion that had erupted in her head.

She stepped inside the connection train, having already made the decision she was going to sit herself somewhere where there were at least three or four other passengers, more preferably, just to be on the safe side. It wasn't difficult, there were only two carriages to this train and she presumed it was down to the time of day. She couldn't remember a time that she had ever been this grateful for a busy train before, looking around at the good amount and mix of people already onboard. Leaving her case in the luggage hold, she spotted a seat just down from it, which she promptly parked herself in before anyone else did.

The sigh was long and drawn out, her mind back to the old man, the book and the note. Unzipping her bag, she took out the note and stared at it, utterly bewildered. As she read the words once more, there seemed to be something vaguely familiar about them now, at least some of them. A few moments passed before the efficient filing assistant in her brain pulled out the relevant information and showed her why. Joan, the lady from the café earlier that day. She had said something more or less the same. Something about the light coming and embracing the dark. A sudden heat began to rise as a wave of nausea tumbled over her. She took off her coat and scarf, attempting to convince herself it was all coincidence. Nothing more. But there was, something more. She could appease herself with that theory for the café conversation but the man on the train, no, something wasn't right. She just couldn't shake off how he knew her name or why he had left her his book, *Passages of Time.* A book which meant nothing to her. And what was the note all about? And how had he just disappeared? None of it made any sense. But then nothing made sense anymore. Questions, always more questions but never any answers.

She shut her eyes against the uneasiness, unaware of the trickle that fell down her face.

Darkness, always darkness.
But something was different this time.
Sounds, muffled sounds.
Flashes of light then...
Darkness once more.

Chapter 7

Owen

The email had kept Owen occupied much longer than he had anticipated and when he finally left the office, darkness had gripped the sky. Knowing he hadn't enough time now to get home to shower and change then over to the restaurant, he turned around and went back inside. He always kept a toilet bag and fresh shirt in his office, just in case he should ever have to attend a last-minute business meeting and needed to freshen up. Well that was one reason.

Before changing, he pulled out his phone and dialled home. After several rings it went through to voicemail. "Hi, Kate it's me, again. Don't forget I have booked a table for eight thirty this evening at Rowlands. Get a cab and I'll meet you there, been held up at work. See you soon baby."

Fresh shirt donned and a spritz of aftershave, he sat on the bench in the washroom to give his latest designer shoes a quick once over. From nowhere, the reality of the implications of that email suddenly hit him as memories flooded back with force.

"Shit!" His clenched fist banged hard against the

side of the locker.

Kate must never find out.

Ever.

∞∞∞

Arriving at the restaurant with ten minutes to spare, he was greeted by the Maître D who confirmed the flowers had indeed arrived, relieving Owen of the envelope that he insisted must accompany them. Assuring him that everything was under control, he led him through the maze of precisely positioned tables, stopping only to pull out the scalloped back velvet chair at the table reserved for him.

Taking a long greedy gulp of the much-needed beer he had ordered, he pulled out his phone to view the message he'd heard ping through whilst being shown to his table, hoping it would be Kate.

But it was just a fifteen percent off at the local DIY store this weekend.

It struck him as strange how Kate hadn't replied in some way, but then she had told him endless times how she hated being at everyone's beck and call, and it was only just nearing eight thirty. As eight forty came, he picked up the mobile and scrolled through to call home. It rang out till it reached voicemail; she must be on her way. Placing the phone face down on the table, his fingers began a nervous tapping over it. As ten to nine came and went, he snatched the phone and dialled her mobile. Straight to voicemail. He tried again. And again. But each time it connected to her voicemail. 'Leave me a message and I'll try and get back to you.' After the fifth attempt, Owen replied to the silvery voice. "Kate it's me. Where are you? Did you get my message? I'm sat at Rowlands. I booked a table for eight thirty. Hope you're en-route. Ring me...please."

As the phone touched the table, it began to ring, prompting raised eyebrows from nearby diners.

"Kate..." Owen answered quickly.

There was no reply.

"Hello?" Owen moved the phone to look at the screen. Only it wasn't Kate. Number unknown. He cut the call, blasting the damn call centres. Agitation had slipped into his body making him restless. He picked up his beer and guzzled down the remains, holding up his empty glass to the waiter, a vulgar signal for another. But as the waiter gave a discreet nod in response, Owen had a hunch she wasn't coming. Leaving a twenty-pound note on the table, he picked up his phone and suit jacket and left the restaurant, his hasty exit fuelled by the fusion of annoyance and embarrassment.

Outside, as the rain lashed against him, his phone began to ring. Through his attempts to shield the screen from the constant spats, he could just make out it was an unknown number again.

"Hello."

Nothing.

"Hello, who is this?"

Nothing other than the click of the dialler ending the call.

This was no random call centre.

It had to be connected to that email.

And Kate.

And in that moment, he knew exactly why she had failed to show up.

Chapter 8

Kate

Kate woke abruptly to the sound of a distant voice calling out that it was time to leave the train as they'd reached Paignton, enquiring if she was okay. Disorientated, she looked around to her left and then her right, taking a few seconds for it to register where she was. She must have been sound asleep. She began fumbling about with her scarf and coat, striving to get them on quickly, aware she was holding him back as events such as this would surely not be factored into his schedule. Helping her off the train with her case, the guard checked again to make sure she was okay, suggesting it might be wise for her to get a strong coffee before leaving the station. She nodded a thank you, agreeing. But it was something far stronger than coffee that she could have done with.

She shivered against the damp air of the evening and zipped her coat up. Only a handful of passengers were at the station and her uneasiness echoed out amongst the quiet. She shrugged it off, guessing it was her body's way of settling back down from getting off the train feeling all at sixes and sevens.

After a strong word, she pacified herself that it was all down to heightened emotions, unfamiliar territory for her after all. Figuring a coffee was perhaps sensible as the last thing she wanted was to arrive at Billy's all flustered, she headed across to the small station café, taking in how dark and low the sky had become.

Kate was the only person inside the station café other than the girl behind the counter who, from the irritated expression she wore, was not particularly pleased to see she had a customer. She watched Kate walk in and park her case at the nearest table, rolling her eyes at the inconvenience. The little chalkboard sign on the table stated it was waitress service but to avoid any more of the perfect eye rolls, Kate made her way to the counter. The waitress prised herself off the countertop and making no rush to put her phone away, she finally looked up at her and uttered, "No food as we close at nine," whilst shoving the mobile in her back pocket. Really not in the mood for anything Kate fired straight back.

"Good job I only wanted coffee then...Isn't it?" Her sarcastic smile gave the girl no chance to interrupt as she added, "Large flat white, skinny with an extra shot."

Taken aback by her curtness, it was evident the inconvenienced teen was not used to being on the receiving end of such a response to her appalling attitude. Well tough Kate thought, returning to her table, it had been a long day and she was in no mood for obnoxious teenagers. With Kate's annoyance plain to see, the girl brought the coffee over, along with a strained smile, enquiring if there was anything else she could get for her.

Looking out over the station, Kate's mind rolled back over the last few hours. And to Owen. He must be home by now which meant he must have read her note. A sudden rush of guilt pulsed through her making her question if she had done the right thing. She wondered if he had called her. Text her even. Digging out her phone to look at the screen she saw several missed calls and voicemail messages. She had no idea why she was so surprised. She knew he would want to call her after a you're dumped note to try and talk her round. Owen was not the type to take things lying down. He never had been. She couldn't listen to them, or want to listen to them because she knew how weak she was and how persuasive he could be. She comforted herself with the notion of it being for the best, she'd messed up too many lives.

Knocking back the last of the coffee, she typed a quick message to Bernarde before turning off her phone, making a silent pact with herself as she stood.

Time to find herself.

The last part of the journey to Billy's was always

a pleasant one. The little steam train from Paignton to Kingswear was like jumping back in time. Its quaint cosy carriages akin to those from the Harry Potter films but the best way to travel on here was in the observation carriage. With its large glass viewing windows and deep velour swivel seats, it had a charm even more appealing than how she'd remembered it. She found herself reminiscing on the happy school holidays spent there, a rush of love coiled within as she remembered the hot summers with trips to the beach. All loaded up with buckets and spades, picnic baskets and blankets, the only way to get there was by taking the Devon Belle, feeling really special because they always sat in the first-class observation carriage, even though it had only been a few pence more. She was content to let the snapshots of happy memories flash by, feeling the most at ease with herself than she had done in ages. She closed her eyes and allowed herself to pretend she was back there, happy go lucky sweet little Katie, until something ripped through that perfect memory.

The hairs on her arms stood on end, her body tense, riddled with goose bumps. A face. Frozen. Suspended in time. A face she didn't recognize but at the same time strangely familiar. She blinked hard, but it never moved. Her chest became tighter as the invisible force of fear pushed her further back into the seat. She reminded herself to breathe, to switch her focus away from the rising anxiety that was building inside of her, threatening to take over.

She screwed her eyes tight shut; pushing her hands down hard on her thighs, she was not going to let it happen. Not after all this time. It was insane. After all it was just a face. An image. It wasn't real. It had gone.

The mantra she had not had to use in such a long time was now silently repeated, "I. Am. In. Control," over and over until it had started to work. Slowly her body responded, the tension that had stiffened her muscles slowly loosened and her erratic breathing became steadier. She opened her eyes, just a touch, relieved as they saw the station in the near distance, telling herself to hang on in there. In and Out. Inhale...Exhale. Focus.

A couple of minutes later, the heavy clunking of the brake finally halted the train. She was out on the platform before she knew it, breathing in the cool salty air of the river Dart. Without looking back, she hurried out of the station, wheeling her case down the jetty towards the passenger ferry, knowing that in another few minutes she'd be in the safe haven of Riverview cottage.

With Billy.

"Kate! What are you doing here? Come in, come in!"

"Hey Billy, thought I'd pop by and say hello." Her grin nervous, unsure of how she'd be accepted after all this time as she walked through into the large hallway.

Even though Uncle Billy had never blamed or judged her, Kate had never been truly certain what he thought about it all, deep down.

"Trisha, Trish, come look who's here!" Billy's arms opened wide as he moved closer towards Kate.

"Kate!" Trish screeched. "Oh my goodness, why didn't you let us know you were coming? It is so good to see you!"

Kate caught Trish's glance of the suitcase she'd left just inside the doorway. "Is everything okay Kate? Are you okay?"

"Yeah... course." The lump that had formed in her throat served to remind her that everything wasn't okay. Far from it. And it wasn't long before she was stood in their hallway, sobbing her eyes out in the warmth of Uncle Billy's embrace. Hoping and praying that he could make everything right this time.

Just as he had tried before, all those years ago.

Chapter 9

Owen

S lamming the door behind him, Owen dropped his dripping wet suit jacket on the floor letting out a head to toe shiver as he kicked off his shoes. The hollow darkness of the apartment struck him immediately and instinctively he knew that Kate wasn't there. After turning the light on in the kitchen, he reached for the towel that hung on the cooker door and rubbed it hard over his head and face. Rubbing away not only the water but at the cocktail of emotions that had mixed inside of him.

"Jesus Kate." His mutter thrown with the towel down onto the worktop. Reaching into the fridge for a beer, he noticed the faint light of the answer machine flashing away. He walked over to hit play, hearing not Kate's voice but his own, relaying his earlier message back to him. Taking the handset, he rang Kate's number, but it came as no surprise that it went straight to voicemail.

The gnawing frustration was met with a growing concern. Something wasn't right, he wasn't sure what but he could feel it. Deep in the pit of his stomach something had stirred, spreading out, rising up through his chest to form a spinning lump at the base of his throat. That spinning lump dissolved into a wave of dizziness and the sudden urge to vomit. Only just making it to the kitchen sink in time, his whole body wretched until there was nothing left. He reached over for the towel to wipe his mouth, his lid had been forced off, letting out years of deceit and there was no way of getting it back in. Like a caged animal that had escaped out into the wild, the lies and deceit had too escaped, out into the world and were now free to roam and wander and be exposed for exactly what they were.

For the first time in his life, Owen had no idea what to do but go and clean himself up, he was in no fit state to see Kate when she came back. From the corner of his vision, he caught sight of it, the note propped on the console. He snatched it up, unfolding the paper to reveal Kate's beautiful handwriting.

"Dear Owen, I'm so so sorry. I can't do this. I have to get away. I need to get away, sort my head out. It's just too much for me and now everything is coming back to haunt me. I don't know what else to do or say. If only you'd been a bit more open with me then maybe we could have got through this. Who knows? Please don't hate me, I just couldn't face you after everything. I can't even face myself right now. I'll be in touch K xx

His strong muscular legs buckled instantly, giving way from under him and he slumped down against the wall, his body made weak from the weight of words he held between his fingers.

He just didn't understand. Just how had Kate found out?

Chapter 10

Kate

"Morning." Kate was met by Trish's smile as she made her way into the large airy kitchen. "How did you sleep?"

"Honestly...I can't remember the last time I slept that well. What time is it?"

"Nearly eleven. I thought you'd maybe appreciate the lie in after your long journey." Kate knew what she really meant from the sympathetic look she had in eyes.

"Want some coffee?"

"I would love a cup please."

They sat at the large granite topped island in the middle of the pale grey kitchen, both silent, gazing out across the river. The view from here was a picture postcard. Billy had worked hard on the house after Pamela had died, pouring every last bit of energy he had into completing the renovation. It was a true labour of love with everything about it worthy of being in a copy of Homes and Gardens. With floor to ceiling windows that looked out across the river, no matter where you were in the house, he had ensured you could always see it. With its New England cross Coastal Chic look, its atmosphere made you feel like you were on a permanent holiday.

Trish broke the silence. "I know you said you just needed some time away Kate but what is really going on? I don't want to pry but I want you know you can tell me anything. Anything at all."

Kate hesitated before she spoke, one side of her mouth curled. "It's all a mess Trish, a real mess. I'm a mess and I have no idea what to do." Tears began to roll, gently at first, one by one, gradually building momentum until her whole body became a blubbering wreck.

She hadn't noticed Trish move to the side of her, or her arms working their way around to cradle her shaking body as her soft voice encouraged, "Let it all out Kate, you need to release it all. That's it, you take as long as you need."

After last night, Kate didn't think there were any tears left inside of her to do anymore crying but evidently, she was wrong. After the last of the tears passed her cheeks, she used the sleeve on her dressing gown to wipe her eyes and looked up at Trish.

And so, it began.

She told her everything.

Nearly.

As she poured out her heart, she felt vulnerable, bearing her soul for someone to cast judgement over. From that day that it all began, the problems with Owen and losing her job, she missed out nothing. Except that one thing, darkness. The very thing that had always been there lurking in the background. But there was no point in bringing it up. Everything Trish needed to know was out in the open. She was certain Billy would have told her the first part, he must have, he wouldn't keep secrets from her. There would be no point and judging from her unwavering calmness, Kate was right. Trish knew.

With each word spoken, she became braver, a strength to reach down into the darkest depths to years of stored memories and the emotions that accompanied them. Things she'd worked so hard to suppress. Like shedding layer upon layer of heavy clothing, the burden lightened as she gave voice to what had been concealed, yet it drained her both mentally and emotionally, resulting in her feeling heavier than ever. But it was done. She couldn't take it back. Any of it.

"It really wasn't your fault Kate, none of it. Yes, you made a wrong choice, but you must stop blaming yourself. No matter how much you rack yourself with guilt, you can't change the past. The only thing you can influence now is your future." Trish's tone was kind but edged with firmness.

"I miss them Trish, so so much. I have nobody left only Uncle Billy and you and even that doesn't feel the same anymore. But then I guess I'm not the same person anymore. How can I be? Every time I look in the mirror, I see nothing but a selfish bitch."

"Kate you have to stop this. What's done is done. It's time to move on."

"But what if I don't know how to? Let alone deserve to." Hearing herself speak those words, Kate knew how pathetic she actually sounded.

"Then it's time to let people help you. Let us help you. Nothing will bring them back Kate but you have the rest of your life in front of you to do as you please, it's time to let the grief go. Do you think your parents would want you to feel like this? Wasting your life dwelling on what you can't change?"

"But..."

Trish raised her hand. "It's not open for discussion. It's time to move forward and let a bit of light back into that life of yours." Prising herself up off the breakfast stool, she asked, "More coffee?"

"No, thank you. I think I'll go and get showered if that's okay with you?"

As she shifted off the stool, she considered herself well and truly told.

"Take as long as you need. Billy shouldn't be too late home and I thought it would be nice for us all to have a late lunch together. And put a smile on that pretty face of yours, you'll turn the weather else."

Kate flashed her a brief smile as she left the kitchen.

"Mackerel pate with breads and salad, how's that sound?"

"Yummy!" Kate shouted back, climbing the stairs with a seed of enthusiasm planted.

It had been the right thing to do and she was glad to let it all out.

All except the one thing that had really brought her here.

∞∞∞

The relaxed ambience over lunch was a tonic in itself and Kate felt part of a family once more. They chatted about all sorts and Billy had them in stitches, laughing until they were almost crying as he recoiled his funny stories and jokes. Everything felt normal. Safe. And just for a while, it was like the past had been erased as a sense of fresh hope impressed itself upon her.

They had eaten in the dining conservatory that looked out down river and it surprised Kate to see just how much had changed in the years since she had last been. The houses that stood on either side of the river had altered massively from the renovations that had took place when new owners took possession. Gone were most of the brightly coloured rendered facades, that had dotted the hills, replaced with softer pastel tones or mass upon mass of glass frontages. Everything appeared bigger, grander and more tightly packed together but the charm of this place was still the same.

As Billy and Trish filled her in on who now lived where Mr so and so used to live and Mrs such and such, her eye was drawn to her favourite of all. Glad to see it was still there, she quizzed them both about the grand cream house that still stood so prominently, nestled into the hillside on the opposite side of the river, totally unchanged, looking down over everything and everyone. King of the castle. She remembered the fascination she'd had with it as a little girl, simply because it was exactly the same as the doll's house her gran had given to her one Christmas. Ever since she had opened that present, she'd always looked upon the house with complete wonder. A sense of pride that she too had a big house like that that, all to herself. She would spend hours making stories up about the people who lived there, pretending that her little peg dollies were them. Funny how the land of make believe seemed so real and true at the time.

"Who lives there now?"

"No one." Billy answered. "Always been empty as far as we know. No one seems to know that much about it."

"Always been the talk of the town. Sandra from Equilibrium seems to think it's probably a holiday home bought with good intentions by some rich couple to add to their portfolio, never to be used." Trish added

"Well that's one of her conclusions." Billy winked at Kate.

"What do you mean?"

"Oh nothing, Sandra is full of theories that's all. Barking mad most of the time too!"

"Billy! Don't say such things, Sandra is lovely. Kate just you ignore your Uncle, he's pulling your leg that's all."

Trish stood and began to clear the table, shaking her head at Billy like a disappointed mother would at a child.

He flashed Kate another one of his winks, his humour still there. Sensing Trish was not impressed, Kate offered to help take the pots away, changing the subject by thanking her for the lunch, asking for the recipe for that delicious pate.

As the two women tidied away together, the chat continued, light and easy. Kate had made the right decision in leaving London, this was where she was meant to be.

For now.

Forever.

Chapter 11

Kate

She was completely engrossed in watching the world go by on the river below when Trish came up behind her, causing her to let out a startled jump when she heard her say, "Uncle Billy's gone back to work and I have to go down into town if you fancy a wander around?"

"Sorry Trish, I was miles away there. Yeah that would good, it has been years since I've had a mooch around, be nice to see what it's like these days. I'll just go and get my stuff together."

They ambled down through the narrow streets that led to the lower part of the town, passing many of the houses she remembered from her childhood. Memories of happier times freely popping back into her mind again, quickly fading into tarnished fragments of something altogether much darker. She was glad of the interruption caused by the jolly old man who shouted out "Good Afternoon" from across the road, pulling her from her thoughts.

"Hi Tom," Trish called back. "How's Mary doing, she feeling any better?"

As they crossed over the road, Tom leant his brush against the small gate and filled Trish in on Mary, she would be ready for visitors soon and he was sure she would love to see her.

"Anyway, enough about us, who is this fine young lady?"

"Tom, this is Kate, Kate this is Tom."

"Nice to meet you Tom." Kate said, offering out her hand over the top of the low brick wall he was stood behind.

"No, it can't be, not Pammie's Katelyn, not my little Kitty Kat!" His mouth stayed wide with shock as he shook her hand in slow motion.

"Yes, but... how..."

Trish stepped in to answer. "Tom was your Aunt Pam's gardener, don't you remember?"

"Oh my...no, not Mr Hilkins!"

"That's me love, or H as you used to call me, especially when you used to steal my tomatoes!" His jovial chortle still the same as all those years ago.

"Wow, gosh, I am so sorry, I didn't recognise you. I was just taken aback a little when I heard that... that nickname. It's been a long time since anyone used it that's all. It's so good to see you, H!" She smiled fondly, her heart melting yet aching just that tiny bit more as another reminder of what once was smacked her in the face.

"How long are you stopping for Katelyn?" Tom's

question took her by surprise.

"Oh, I'm not quite sure just yet." Her answer a lie.

"Well you must come and see me my love, you know where I am, anytime. But for now, I must get on, lots to do. Regards to Billy Trish. Cheerio both."

As they continued the walk down to the lower town, Trish relished the opportunity to fill Kate in on Tom and his wife Mary. How Tom had to retire sooner than he would've liked and how Mary was recovering after a sudden heart attack. She was only half listening though, the sing song voice in her head gluing her attention. *Kitty Kat, Kitty Kat, Sweet Little Kitty Kat.* A name she thought she would never ever hear, ever again. How could something that was so sweet and innocently given be turned into something so sordid and dirty. She shuddered, her body's attempt to shake away the memory bringing Trish's voice back into full focus with a loud "Righto."

"So, I have a few errands to run then I'm off to see Sandra in Equilibrium. So how about I meet you in there in say, an hour? I know she would love to meet you. It's on Foss Street, you can't miss it."

"Sure," Kate answered. "See you later."

Kate waited until Trish had disappeared up the street ahead before turning in the opposite direction, keen to see if her favourite shop was still up and running. Making her way through the quaint little backstreets, she was amazed at the ease in which she could remember the way, even though it had been many years since she'd walked them. She guessed it was like riding a bike, you just never forget.

Turning onto Market Street, her eyes lit up as still there, straight in front of her was Edmunds Book Emporium. She was delighted that even in this age of most things in life being carried out on a screen that there were still people, like her, who appreciated the value of holding an actual book. She smiled with the tingle of excitement as she pushed open the heavy door, still complete with the overhead bell that used to make her giggle so much as a child. Inside, it appeared to be largely unchanged. The old oak top counter with the now ancient till still stood proudly in the same place. The dusty smell of the well-thumbed pages of books scented the air around her, a smell only true book lovers could feel at home with. The only notable change was the wing backed chairs and shiny stiff leather sofas that she used to unintentionally slide off as a little girl had been replaced with a more welcoming choice of comfy chairs in varying shades of blue checked fabric. Surprised to see no one inside, she beamed out a "Hello" at the white-haired lady, who, busy at one of the shelves, half turned and told her to shout should she need any assistance.

She wandered slowly past the bookcases, the urge to run inquisitive fingers across the endless rows of books intense. She pulled one out from the brimming shelf and took it over to make use of the comfy chairs that were crying out for company. Knowing she didn't have long, she opted for the lower backed chair that faced the main windows overlooking the street. A large imposing grandfather clock stood between them so she could keep track of the time, she didn't want to be late meeting Trish.

She turned the pages of the book she'd pulled down; it wasn't anything that held any interest for her, a book about boats, but it felt right to be here. Like it was intended she was to return one day to enjoy the atmosphere once more as an adult. Closing her eyes, she'd forgotten how good it felt to just sit. No thinking, no organising or formulating plans, just sitting quietly in her own little sanctum, surrounded by the tranquillity that she'd always felt in there. Just appreciating it more so being older.

Growing conscious of the time, she reluctantly opened her eyes, standing to return the book to its home on the dusty shelf. Ten minutes, that should be plenty of time to get to Foss Street and she was looking forward to meeting Sandra, if not a little apprehensive after what Uncle Billy had said. The last thing Kate needed in her life right now was some crazy woman. Her life, after all, was crazy enough.

Sandra was certainly a character; she would give Uncle Billy that. She supposed that to those who could not understand her eccentricity she might come across as barking mad, but Kate figured she was harmless enough. Sandra was a shapely woman who she would estimate somewhere around mid-sixties in age. Incredibly vivacious with the wildest auburn hair that perfectly complemented both her personality and striking hazel eyes. There was an air about her though, an air of ease capable of making anyone feel relaxed and welcomed within a few moments of being in her company.

Kate hadn't managed to get three steps inside Equilibrium before Sandra flung her arms wide open, expressing how fabulous it was to finally meet her. Like an electric shock, her touch surged through Kates body.

As Sandra ushered her forward, her senses soared, near ready to explode. Her eyes flicked from one side of the shop to the other taking in the plethora of crystals and the like. The musky hue of the incense that burnt away on the reception swirled into her nostrils. Her ears, gently awoken by the twang of cymbal like chimes every few seconds. It was crammed with stuff yet deceptively peaceful, emitting a strange air that permeated the fibres of her being, forcing her to relax. She wondered if Billy had felt it too and that was why he thought Sandra 'barking mad.'

Before she had chance to ask where Trish was, Sandra showed her through to the back area where there were a couple of doors leading off into the treatment rooms and another into what was obviously used as a staff room. Trish was in there, quite at home sitting with a steaming mug on her lap, leafing through a magazine. Sandra proceeded to reel off a huge list of various herbal teas and fruit infusions for Kate to choose from, minus anything that resembled real tea or coffee. She could have done with some caffeine but with none on the offering, opted for a peppermint tea instead.

Settled with drinks, Sandra asked questions about Kate's journey and how long she was staying with Trish but nothing that even bordered on being personal. The conversation was easy, and she made Kate feel like they'd known each other for much longer than the half an hour that they had. Kate couldn't help but wonder what Trish had and hadn't told her though. Nothing from their earlier conversation of course, she wouldn't have had the time to, but she must know about Pam, she just wasn't sure how much. If she did know, she wasn't letting on but then the first time of meeting someone you would hardly say, "Hi, nice to meet you, and by the way, I hear you're the one who killed your Aunt." A silent laugh rattled inside in response to the utter stupidity she housed.

She re-joined the conversation which had turned to Sandra trying to convince Trish that she should do her next degree in Reiki. Kate had zero idea what that was.

"Maybe Sandra, I don't know if I'm ready for it." Trish's protests were half hearted.

"Well I think, no, I know you are ready to take it, trust me. Look, come along to the next Reiki share evening I'm holding tomorrow and have a chat with some of the others, then you can decide whether it's time or not. Bring Kate along too. How does that sound?" Sandra was clearly persuasive.

"Okay, I will, thank you. Do you fancy it Kate?"

"Well I have no clue what you two are on about but sure, I'm up for anything. Be good to meet some other people too."

"Great that's settled then." Sandra stood, conversation still flowing. "I'll see you both tomorrow then at seven thirty. Now if you'll excuse me, I have a client due in quite soon and need to go and prepare the treatment room. Can you see yourselves out?"

Kate took those last words as being more of a request than a question given as Sandra was already in the corridor with the "Lots of love" trailing off into the distance. She looked back at Trish who had already stood up, straightening down her bright floral dress, noting it as their cue to leave.

Walking back through the shop, she was drawn to the bay window and the large display of pink crystals it held. From behind the glass, between the pointed specimens, a glimpse of a face flashed before Kate. A face she vaguely recognised but at the same knew she possibly couldn't, not around here. As quickly as she caught it, she'd lost it and a faint disquiet began to spread as she stepped outside.

"Kate. Are you alright? You look like you have just seen a ghost." Concern poured from Trish as she fussed around Kate.

Shaking off the disquiet, Kate replied with the first

thing she could think of, "Yes, yes, erm...sorry. I think all that incense stuff must have got to my head and then coming out into the fresh air just made me feel a little dizzy that's all. I'm fine honest, probably just need a shot of caffeine."

Fortunately, Trish didn't question her further, accepting her answer as being completely plausible.

If only she could have accepted it herself.

Chapter 12

Kate

Arriving back at the house, Kate ran straight upstairs, in need of lie down. The events of the last few days had finally caught up with her, taking their toll on her already run-down body. Taking the phone from the bedside cabinet where it had been housed since her arrival, she held it still for a moment, a silent debate going on inside her head as to whether to turn it on or just shove it back where she'd took it from. She thought back to the note she'd left for Owen and felt the pang of guilt still sat heavy, draining her further. But she couldn't do it, couldn't turn it on. She was plainly more of a coward than she first thought but by now she'd gone beyond caring. Her head was a mess, a hundred people all shouting at her at once, the noise had become too much, too intense and she had to find a way to stop it. Retrieving the metal prodder from her make up bag to remove the sim card, she stabbed it into the tiny hole on the side of the phone. She couldn't live without a phone, but she could live without her old number. Other than Bernarde, there was no one who had it who would miss her, nor she them. Except Owen. Though she doubted if he would really miss her. Maybe he thought he would, but he would soon adjust. He would have to. Just like she'd had to in the past and will have to again. From now on in, she had to do what was right for her. As she nestled back into the bed, she allowed its softness to absorb any uncertainty she had.

Billy's cheerful tones drifted faintly in and out as he moved about downstairs. It was time for her to make amends with the past, let it go and build a more peaceful life for herself and here was just the place to do it. Of that she was positively certain.

A pinprick of light pierced the vast expanse of darkness.
Just for a fleeting moment came a glimmer of hope.
Desperate hope.
Disappeared.
Then darkness swiftly regained its place once more...

Panting heavily, her eyes jolted open, unable to move and a sticky cold sweat draped her rigid body. A nightmare, that was all. But she didn't believe the voice in her head. It was like all the other times, only somehow now, more vivid. Yet there had been no images. The debate of how something could be more vivid when there was nothing there was too loud. Every single thing she told herself was a contradiction. Maybe the therapist she so strongly resented was right. Maybe it was the aftereffects coming out of her, taunting her with shards of her broken past, making her paranoid and unable to adapt to normal behaviours. She struggled with the thought that had her question what if she had got psychotic tendencies? No. Some tiny little fibre in her being knew it was rubbish and that was why she walked away from it. No one got it. They all concluded she was suffering from post-traumatic stress syndrome.

Except Bernarde.

Bernarde was the only one who got her, didn't make her feel like a freak. She really must call him but not now. He understood why she had had to leave, assured her she was doing the right thing and only to contact him when she felt ready. He was a darling, an absolute star and if she was brutally honest with herself, the only thing that she missed from her old life. She certainly didn't miss the office politics or Trinity and her endless celebrity magazines.

Nor did she miss the sense of urgency that everyone carried as they went about their daily business, too busy to even smile. Everyday had reached the stage of sleep, work, eat, repeat, with the occasional night out thrown in for good behaviour. How could anyone in their right mind honestly miss that? But she didn't miss this either. Yet it was something she couldn't free herself from. This thing that had shackled itself firmly around her, taking control whenever it chose to with no consideration for what she wanted. The voice in her head that had lain silent for so long had been freed to converse with her mind in any way it wanted. But even that had grown tired as once more, sleep swept her up, bringing reprieve from the grating voice as it returned to where it had risen from.

Chapter 13

Kate

"**A**re you ready Kate? Trish is just getting the car out of the garage."

"On my way down now Uncle Billy." Kate yelled back appearing at the top of the stairs.

"Right, remember what I said Kate, if you need help escaping tonight, just stand outside with the incense and let off a smoke signal and I'll come and rescue you girl." Amused by his own humour, Billy couldn't contain his laughter.

"You are incorrigible!" Kate laughed back, pecking him on the cheek as she passed.

Trish was waiting in the car, engine running, having decided earlier it would be best to drive down to town for the Reiki share as heavy showers had been forecast for later in the evening. Kate was pleased they didn't have to walk as even after sleeping on and off for most of the day she was still tired.

"Just enjoy this evening Kate." Trish had started talking before Kate had had chance to pull across her seatbelt. "Take it as a chance to relax and unwind. Now, just briefly, there may be a couple of folks there who are a little way out there but they are perfectly harmless I assure you."

As Trish pulled into the rear car park of Equilibrium, she let out a long slow breath and Kate contemplated if her step aunt was more nervous at the thought of what was in store than she was. Approaching the rear entrance, a sign directing them to the front had been sellotaped to the gate. The bright orange front door was bolted shut and rapping gently on the glass, Trish pressed her face against the gap between the patchwork of leaflets and adverts so Sandra could see who it was. Flinging the door wide open, she welcomed them both with the same greeting as yesterday, happiness oozing out of her.

"Come in, come in," she almost sung in-between cheek kisses as she beckoned them through. "Grab a seat, the others shouldn't be too long."

In quick succession, the others began to arrive. Introductions were exchanged, drinks were made and the homemade cakes that one of the ladies had baked were handed round.

After half an hour, Sandra picked up a smaller version of what looked to Kate like a wooden baseball bat and struck the gong that was positioned to the side of her. Within seconds, the room fell silent and still, the sign for everyone to pause. Sandra took the floor and gave an official welcome to everyone, thanking Rose for her generous cake contribution to the evening, asking others to share the gratitude. She explained how the evening would work, asking for preference of the two options. Exchange experiences and have a question and answer session or have models for which the others could practice their Reiki on then a Q and A. The majority voted for the latter and because Kate was not a therapist or student, was volunteered to be a guinea pig.

She slipped off her shoes and shuffled on to the beauty couch that had been draped with brightly patterned thin blankets. She was asked to remove her belt, purely for her own comfort, before Joyce, a short plump, curly haired lady talked through what they were going to do. All that was required was for her to lie back, close her eyes and relax. Joyce explained that she may feel warmth coming from their hands, the universal energy they were channelling to help clear any energy blockages she may have. Not wanting to sound like she wasn't taking it seriously, Kate held back on asking on how long they had got and politely nodded her head to express her understanding.

As Sandra dimmed the lights, the room fell quiet except for the faint background music. Through squinted eyes, Kate was desperate to see what they were all doing but the low amber light made everything hazy. Deciding it best to go with the flow, the squint softened as her eyes relaxed against the soothing touch of hands on the top of her head and the soles of her feet and it wasn't long before she had drifted effortlessly into some other place or time.

She didn't know. She couldn't explain it. She was there but wasn't there.

Contradiction.

Again.

She was drifting along, not quite floating, but almost. Unsure of where she was drifting, she couldn't tell but it felt wonderful. Light. Clean and pure and whole. She didn't want it to end, this welcome wave of peace but a voice in the distance slowed that drifting down. Right down until she had stopped drifting completely and began to feel the heaviness of her body pressing against the couch underneath her.

A hand gently squeezed her shoulder and she knew that whatever it was she'd just experienced had now come to an end. What had felt like just a few minutes had in fact been forty-five. The light buzz of chatter started to make its way to her consciousness and slowly blinking, her eyes adjusted to the backdrop of the room. As her surroundings came into focus, she was greeted by a beaming bright smile, asking if she would like some water. The Ferrari red lips belonged to Marcel, as did the hand with matching red nails that had gently stopped the wave Kate had been riding on. The simple yes please took some forming. After a few moments, Sandra had brightened the room and Kate started to feel more compos mentis.

"Are you feeling alright?" Joyce asked.

"I think so, just a little lightheaded that's all." Kate sipped the water, her dreamlike state still there, just.

"That was quite intense." Marcel's smile beamed again. "Would you like to share what you experienced?"

She paused before answering, the environment where she didn't have to edit her responses for fear of reprisal new to her. She shared the sensation of drifting and the lightness of her physical body that she had experienced, not wanting either to end.

"Thank you for allowing us to work with you. It has been an honour, hasn't it Marcel?"

"It certainly has."

That was it. Kate looked at Marcel then back over to Joyce, half expecting an explanation but she got nothing, no more words, just two wide smiles. Sympathetic smiles if she listened to her cynical mind that had now decided to kick in.

A strike of the gong had the room fall silent once more, allowing Sandra's voice to fill the space. "Ladies...If you have all finished and your models are okay, would you all like to come back into the circle. We will have some light refreshments and sharing time." Sandra struck the gong again, its deep bellows echoed much further than just the space in the room, somehow throughout Kate too. Well at least that's what it felt like to her.

Swinging her legs over the side of the couch, she managed to untangle herself from the pile of blankets that had been laid over her before bending down to pick up her shoes.

Sitting back in the circle with a mug of some restorative infusion she'd been handed, Kate listened intently to another of the guinea pigs speak about her experience and the shared findings of the ladies who'd carried out her treatment. The voices fell muffled as part of her now wondered if this was why Marcel and Joyce had both been reluctant to tell her anything whilst she was on the couch, because things were shared afterwards, when everyone was together. She wasn't quite sure she liked the idea of that. She never had been one for open sharing.

She'd only lasted for three meetings at the counselling group for that very reason. If she'd wanted to share something personal, then she'd do it with someone she knew she could trust and not in a group with a bunch of strangers that could use and manipulate the information for their own gains. She could hear Bernarde's voice in her head laughing as he teased her, 'You've watched way too many psycho dramas Kate that you think everyone has some ulterior motive!' Bernarde always had a way of making her see sense, if only temporarily. He was the only reason she had attended meetings two and three. Two because he persuaded her to 'give it another go' and three because it was his last one before he flew the nest on his own and she wanted to show him her support. They had become firm friends, there were no two ways about it. There was nothing they hadn't shared and little by little she had begun to feel better about herself, knowing there was someone who understood her, understood a little of what she had gone through. Was going through. Their lives strangely mirroring each other's at the time.

The differences now though many years on were

stark. Bernarde, settled and secure. Married to a very handsome IT Programmer. General manager at Greene's. A beautiful home and knows exactly what he wants from life...and gets it. She on the other hand, had no job, no man, no security and questioned often whether sanity should be placed on that list too.

The pit pat of claps pulled Kate away from her maudling, Sandra's thanks to the ladies for sharing their 'magnificent experiences' vague. Taking another sip of the fragrant liquid, she had grown acutely aware the attention had been directed towards her as Sandra asked if she would share what she had experienced. Kate's face flushed in response. Vulnerable amongst the silence, everyone's eyes fixed onto her, patiently waiting for her to start. With both Joyce and Marcel nodding and smiling reassuringly that it was fine, her mouth opened and the words started to tumble from it.

She shared everything that had happened during her time on the couch, no holds barred, the group fully engrossed in what she had to say. When she came to a natural end, Marcel took the lead thanking her for agreeing to be a model for the evening with Joyce nodding in agreement, before remembering something she wanted to ask. Throughout the session, she'd been shown a music note and the words Summer Rain, did this mean anything to Kate?

It did.

It had been one of her long time ago favourites when she had stepped into her teenage years. Played countless time, over and over.

But why would it come up?

"Not to dwell on Kate, it may become relevant at some point in time should it be important."

That was the only answer she was getting.

General chit chat was soon resumed by the ladies in the room, their focus from Kate gone. She sat herself back in the squishy chair she'd bagged, doing her best to make sense of the last couple of hours, that song stuck, jumping when Marcel sat down beside her.

"Sorry my love I didn't mean to startle you, I just wanted to check in with you to make sure you're okay?"

"Yeah, I'm good thanks Marcel, just lost in my thoughts is all with that song on repeat."

"Listen Kate," Marcel lowered her voice as she moved in closer, "you must tell someone about the episodes you are having. Now they have restarted they will only grow in intensity and you have a responsibility to understand them."

Stumbling around for words she managed to stutter, "But, but how do you know? Did, did something happen while I was having my treatment? They are not seizures if that's what you are thinking, I have been checked over with scans and stuff. Doctors think it's probably just anxiety."

"Nothing happened, just what I picked up on that's all. I've been working with energy for a very long time now and I know when something is unfolding. It may well be a touch of anxiety now Kate but that's not the root cause. They are trying to tell you something, show you something even. I'm not a hundred percent sure because I didn't work with you for long enough to become fully connected to your energy field but I urge you to have another session, a private one. Or at the very least, talk to someone about them."

The start of the all too familiar lump wedged in her throat and she swallowed hard to keep the tears at bay, a slight tremor taking hold of her voice as she spoke. "I'm tired of speaking to the professionals Marcel, believe me I have seen a fair few and all that happens is I feel more and more confused, let alone crazy when I leave."

"There are therapists and then there are therapists Kate. Like everything in life, it's not a one size fits all. I'm guessing you just haven't found the right person yet." Marcel's brief pause thoughtful. "Look, why don't you come and see me for a cuppa and we can chat informally and go from there eh? I only live across the river, so not too far, and I'm hazarding a guess that you're sticking around for a while?" She held out a card that had her number and address on and insisted Kate call her tomorrow to arrange before bidding her good night.

She stuffed the card into the side pocket of her bag, agreeing she would call.

Seconds later, Trish appeared. It was time to go.

Chapter 14

Owen

'*K*itty Kat Kitty Kat, sweet little Kitty Kat*'. The sing song eerie voice pounded every ounce of flesh on Owen's body forcing his eyes to thrust open in horror. A thin film of stickiness covered his shaking body and for moment, he had no idea where he was. As his senses started to come to, he scrambled around for the switch on the bedside lamp, knocking the glass from the cabinet, his hands doing their own thing. The sound of the glass shattering on the wooden floor beneath rang through his ears like an explosion. Finally, his fingers locked onto the switch and as light punctured the darkness, the fear that had pinned him down so forcefully slowly began to dissolve. Pushing himself up, the enormity of the past had begun to set in.

"Fuck!" He beat his fist down in the empty space aside of him.

The torrents of thoughts that crashed inside him left him with no choice, he would have to answer that email and find out exactly what was going on. Remembering the broken glass just before his feet touched the floor, he rolled over to climb out of bed on the other side. Kate's side.

Even though she had been gone for three days, her scent was still strong on the pillow Owen had picked up, hugging onto it like a child would with their most treasured teddy bear.

Still clutching the pillow, he padded out into the hallway, through to the kitchen where his laptop sat on the breakfast bar. The tiny sleep light flashed away, usually intrusive but tonight most welcome against the darkness of the room. Flipping the lid open, the screen powered up, its bright glare lightening the room a touch more and his hand wrapped tightly around the mouse, hovering the cursor over the mail app icon. As much as he didn't want to do this, he had to, needed to. If he could just hit a rewind button and go back and change everything he would, but that was not an option and realistically, he had to stop kidding himself that he could have made a difference or stopped any of it from happening. But he could put a stop to what was happening now which spurred him to click it open and retrieve that email. Reading over those two tiny words again and again, he struggled to formulate his scrambled thoughts into words.

I read your email. Got the silent phone calls. But why now?

Pathetic but that was all he could muster.

Now all he could do was just wait.

Chapter 15

Kate

Mesmerised by the brightly coloured higgledy piggledy arrangement of the houses she passed, it took Kate longer than she had expected to locate Upper Wood Lane and Marcel's house. She stood for a moment, at the foot of the steps, admiring the quirky exterior. Far removed from the modern boathouse style of Uncle Billy's and many of the other renovations, Marcel's was one of the few that had kept its original double fronted façade. Painted in the most vivid daffodil yellow colour, it had a cottagey charm that contradicted its size. Wisteria draped effortlessly over the door and bay fronted windows, its buds beginning to swell and Kate tried to imagine what the lilac petals would look like once in flower against their domineering background.

She never heard the door open, only Marcel's soft voice inviting her in. "Lovely to see you again Kate, let me take your coat for you."

"Thanks Marcel, it really is good of you to see me at such short notice."

"Nonsense!" she declared, throwing her hands up

in the air, "I'm glad you decided to call me this morning and I just happened to be free so, here we are. Go on straight through to the kitchen while I hang your coat and then I'll put the kettle on."

Kate eyed the vast number of jars filled with different varieties of loose-leaf teas and powders that sat neatly across the back of one of the thick wooden worktops and the shelf above. She opted for an earl grey.

"Good choice. You ever had a Blue Earl Grey?" Marcel held up the jar in Kate's direction.

"No, never heard of it either but I'll give it go, thanks."

Marcel busied herself preparing the tea, scooping the dried leaves and petals into the chamber of a glass teapot, leaving Kate to take in all the little nik naks that were dotted around. Inspirational quotes were plentiful, and she spotted at least seven before Marcel picked up the vintage tea tray, nodding towards the large conservatory that adjoined the kitchen.

"I thought it would be nice and airy in here to sit today if that's fine with you Kate." She placed the tray down on the wicker coffee table, holding up the teapot. "Right, shall I be mother?"

Small talk was in plentiful supply as they sipped on the tea but Kate knew Marcel was waiting. Waiting for her to broach the reason why she was there although the right words to initiate it proved elusive.

Marcel placed her cup and saucer back on the tray

and threw out a lifeline. "Whenever you are ready Kate, in your own time, just start wherever you feel led to start from."

She was overthinking this, she knew her ability to do so only too well. Endeavouring to catalogue everything in order to try to make more sense out of it herself, afraid of what an outsider might make of it all. She had done it every single time with every therapist she'd seen but this time, it had to be different. What was the point of being here if she was to censor what was inside?

Knowing it was time, she too returned her cup and saucer back to the tray. Positioning herself halfway in the chair, she clasped her shaky hands, sandwiching them between her thighs and looked up at Marcel. "O...k...ay..." The word stretched out, prolonging the inevitable. "I guess I best ask if you know about my past and what happened to Aunt Pam?"

"I know a little Kate, but I would like you to tell me your story. Anything you want to share; I invite you to. The only way I can help you is if you are completely true to yourself. What I mean by that is that you must fully acknowledge everything that has happened and is happening because somehow, it will all be interconnected."

Marcel was unlike any other therapist she had ever spoken to before. She held no notebook, no pen and there was no formality in either herself or the surroundings Kate sat in. She exuded a kindness that stretched beyond the usual parameters exhibited by previous therapists. The nature of the job demanded a tolerance of sorts by way of kindness, but she always got a sense that it wasn't real. A part they played until their shift had finished whereas it felt different with Marcel. She couldn't explain it, let alone understand it, but there was a connection she had never experienced with any of the others.

Knowing she had to start somewhere, losing her job and how she'd ended up here to escape everything was as good as any. Not quite ready to delve into the darkest part of her past, Marcel never once tried to steer her in that direction. Instead she listened and asked simple questions with none of the interrogation she had previously felt in therapy.

"I don't really know what happens Marcel. It's like I'm perfectly fine one minute, daydreaming or just having a few moments shut eye time and the next, I have this overwhelming sense of dread and see nothing but darkness and scraps of possibilities, then open my eyes and I'm in a blind panic. It was never like this before and then I went ages after all the stuff with my family where it didn't happen at all, but just recently, these last few months or so it's started up again. Only this time I'm scared. Fearful. And sometimes there's a face. Everyone told me it was a PTSD thing, but I went through all of that, this is different. And this was happening before that night anyway."

When a natural break came in the conversation, Marcel kindly suggested that it would be a good place to end for that day and schedule a full appointment in the diary. She advised that a session of Reiki might be beneficial in order to help restore more balance in her energy field and that in turn would allow her to return to the story she clearly needed to let go of.

Agreeing, they pencilled a mutually convenient date in the diary and Kate raised the question of payment.

"Nothing Kate, honestly. But there is something you could do for me in return." She cast a look that said 'no point in trying to insist you pay.'

"Thank you, but I must pay you moving forwards. What favour can I do for you?"

"Would you be able to take these books into the town bookshop for me? Only I promised Mrs Clifford I would drop them in today, but I have an appointment later on and just won't get the time now."

"Sure, it's not like I have much else to do at the minute."

Marcel lifted the muslin bag which sat on the chair by the door, turning back to face her. "Thank you, Kate, I really appreciate it. And for coming to see me today, you did fantastic you know."

"Thanks Marcel, I really mean that."

Handing her the cloth bag, Marcel opened the front door and waved her off, lines of thought wrinkling her brow as she watched her disappear down the Lane.

On her way down to the ferry, she passed only a couple of ladies, deep in gossip about some poor soul. Once over the other side of the river, it took her just ten minutes to reach Edmunds.

The welcoming jingle of the bell above the door prompted the same white-haired lady from before to look up from her paperwork.

"Hello dearie, you must be Kate." She removed her half moon glasses, allowing them to hang down from the chain to which they were attached.

Assuming this was Mrs Clifford, Marcel must have let her know Kate was dropping the books in instead of her.

"Hi, yes I am. Marcel sent me with these for a Mrs Clifford." She held up the cloth bag as if in need of corroborating her story.

"Thank you, Kate. Bring them over here would you, my legs aren't as good as they used to be." A chuckle accompanied her reply as she tapped her thigh.

"Has this always been your shop Mrs Clifford? Only I used to come in here as a little girl when I was visiting my family during school holidays and I was so happy to see it still here now all these years later."

"It has been in my family for many generations and I took it over some years back when my father passed away but I too am getting no younger and neither my son or his children seem interested in helping out sadly." She strolled out from behind the counter, adding, "So, if you know of anyone who is looking for some part time work, send them my way. Now, are you stopping dear or do you have to get back?"

"I'll stick around for a bit if that's okay. I've not got much on at the minute and to tell you the truth, I'm quite at home here amongst all these books."

"You stay as long as you like dearie, it's nice to have some younger company around. Now don't mind me but I do have to get back to my paperwork. If you need anything, help yourself."

Oblivious to the satisfaction that had sparked inside the old lady, Kate watched her move back behind the counter, positioning the half-moon glasses back on the bridge of her nose.

Glad of the opportunity to spend some more time in there, Kate happened upon a book titled *Dartmouth Through the Ages.* Realising she didn't actually know an awful lot about this area she adored so much, she pulled it down, blowing away the thick layer of dust that had accumulated on it.

A heavy hardback book with most of the images and sketches in black and white, save a few photographs from more modern times, she slowly leafed through the pages. With most of the houses in the photographs having now been renovated beyond recognition, there was one that stuck out like a sore thumb. The grand double fronted house that sat nestled high in the Kingswear hillside on the bank of the river looked completely unchanged since it had been built. The house that had enchanted her as a child still fascinated her now. With no one knowing much about it or who lived there, it was shrouded in mystery, making it appealing to all on the outside. A forbidden fruit that kept you guessing. Expecting to turn the page and see yet more pictures of houses and buildings from times gone by, she was saddened to see that several of the subsequent pages had been shamefully torn out. It was always the risk you took if you bought a book from a second-hand book shop.

Staring blankly at the bookshelves, she considered how many books had had parts of them torn away over the years, scraps of history lost to enquiring minds, leaving the reader guessing as to what was once there. Only on the second call did she hear Mrs Clifford call she was ready to shut up shop for the day.

"Sorry, miles away there!" Kate shouted back through. "I'll just put this book back, won't be a jiffy."

Mrs Clifford was by the door, securing the belt of her long beige mac. "Righto dearie, thank you again for bringing in Marcel's books. See you again."

Not sure if it was a farewell or a question, "Yes, I'm sure you will," rolled freely off Kate's tongue.

Chapter 16

Kate

S tacking the dinner plates in front of her, Trish couldn't hold off any longer. "How did you get on with Marcel today Kate?"

"Yeah, it was erm...different. In a good way though. I'm actually going to see her again in a couple of days so she can balance my energy fields."

That was enough of an answer so as not to appear rude. After all, had it not have been for Trish introducing her to Equilibrium and taking her along to the Reiki share evening, her path with Marcel's would probably never have crossed.

"Balance your energy fields! Christ not another one sucked in by all this mumbo jumbo." The mocking from Uncle Billy prompted a sudden scolding from Trish.

"Billy! Enough! If it helps Kate, then that is all that is important."

Blowing kisses that sounded more like goldfish impersonations with the whispered "Sorry darling" triggered the three of them to chuckle. Adopting a more serious tone he added, "Trish is right though Kate, if helps you then that is fantastic. Whilst we are on the subject of help, how long do you think you'll be sticking around for?"

"Honestly, I haven't given it much thought." The lie flowed too easily. She had no intention of going back. "I mean, obviously I love being here but I don't want to outstay my welcome."

"You are welcome to stay here as long as you need Kate but the longer you stay, the harder it will be to go back."

She knew what he was getting at and what she longed to say, but the last thing she wanted was him thinking she was running away. Again. Exactly the thing she was doing but she couldn't risk hearing disappointment, not from him. Opting to stay silent, she pushed the words back, giving a simple nod of acknowledgement.

Trish was swift to interject with a story of 'You'll never guess who came into the shop today...' a knowing smile in Kate's direction as she retold the tale to Billy.

Not one to let anything go, he was quick to turn the conversation back to Kate as soon as Trish had finished. "Are things really beyond sorting out with Owen?"

The unspoken answer pulsed inside her, there was nowhere to run to now.

"I think they are Billy. We have nothing in common. All this stuff with losing my job has made me realise that I just don't love him. Coming here has made me see that even more. We got together at a time when I was looking for something normal.

A time when I was low and needed someone to divert my attention from what I'd lost. After a while, I knew I'd made a wrong decision but it was like that trustworthy pair of shoes everyone has. Comfy and serve their purpose but they just aren't you anymore, yet you can never seem to bring yourself to throw them away." She pulled her arms around herself, dropping her gaze. "I know it's not fair on Owen, he doesn't deserve this. Any of it, but I just couldn't face him because I know he would have tried to talk me out of leaving. Then I would have stayed and got more and more miserable by the day and I would have ended up hating him which I don't want. He's a good man, just not the right good man for me."

Trish leant forward, placing her hand on Kate's arm. "If that's how you feel then there is nothing to say other than you must call Owen. At the very least he deserves more than a bit of paper telling him that you have gone and he must be worried, not to mention confused."

"I know, I will call him. I promise." Kate chewed her lip, the thought already filling her with dread. "Now I don't want to seem ungrateful, but would you mind terribly if I had an early night?"

"Not at all, you go on up and we'll see you in the morning." Billy opened his arms to her, "Sweet dreams my darling girl, sleep tight"

"Night both and...thank you."

Devastation seeped out, twisting around
the thick dense atmosphere.
Devastation.
Loss of Hope.
Light fading fast.
Darkness...

Chapter 17

Owen

"You must know where she is Bernarde, just tell me please. I have to speak to her. Make her understand." Owen pleaded as he spoke and hearing the longing in his voice, Bernarde couldn't help but feel sorry for him.

"If I could Owen I would but I promised Kate that I wouldn't tell a soul. She just needs some time away to help get her head together, but she's safe."

"Please Bernarde, if you speak to her, tell her I miss her and I never meant for any of this to happen, not like this. Ask her to call me."

"I haven't heard from her but if she does get in touch again, I'll pass on your message. Try not worry."

As Bernarde hung up, Owen now knew how it felt to be powerless. He had no idea where she was or how much she knew. To make things worse, he'd had no reply to that email either, or how to reach them. He pinched the bridge of his nose and in slow motion, shook his head from side to side. His once perfect world had, bit by bit, begun to crumble away, preparing to turn into a full-blown landslide. The false exterior he'd had to gain was slipping away uncontrollably and there was nothing he could do other than wait for the carnage that would unfold. He slumped down onto the sofa, picking away at the label of the beer bottle, knowing that before long, he would be exposed for what he really was. And that absolutely terrified him.

Lying drunk and helpless, he didn't feel the empty bottle slide from his grip, joining the pile of others that were strewn over the plush rug beneath the sofa where he lay sprawled. Nor did he see the glow on the screen of his phone from the incoming call.

It would have to wait until morning now for his drunken stupor had finally taken over and sleep had won the battle.

Chapter 18

Kate

As cheerful as ever, Uncle Billy had been up since half past five that morning and was busy filling his flask when Kate joined him in the kitchen.

"Morning Kate, you're up and about early. I didn't wake you, did I?"

"No, you didn't wake me up. I was already rousing when I heard you come down so I thought I'd get up."

The lingering dregs of sleep were soon pushed away as she padded bare foot across the cool Carrara marble tiles to the sofa.

"Do you fancy a coffee with me before I get off? I have something to put to you."

"Love one please."

Silently hoping he wasn't going to bring up the subject of Owen again, she settled herself back into the enormous corner sofa, thoughtfully positioned to enjoy unobstructed views out across the river. Attempting not to spill the coffee she had taken from him, Kate brought her legs up into the seat next to her, curling her feet tight under. Just one of the many coping mechanisms she'd adopted, according to one of the counsellors.

Billy rubbed his chin, thoughtful before he spoke. "Right. I'm not sure how you would feel about this Kate and I don't want you to think Trish and I are trying to get rid of you, because you know you are welcome here for as long as you want, but, I have a proposition for you."

She brought her feet in even tighter, sliding her mug onto the table in front of her. The faint churning in her stomach fast turned to Olympic standard somersaults as she waited for him to continue.

"So, my mate down the boat yard has an apartment on the other side of the river and he is looking for someone to act as a property guardian while he's away for the next few months. He asked me yesterday if I knew of anyone, what with me in the renovation business. Anyway, when I was chewing it over with Trish, we both had the same idea and that was why I asked you last night if things with Owen were really at an end."

Confusion smeared itself across Kate's face.

"Sorry girl, I'm not making that much sense, am I?" His mouth widened, lips breaking into a gentle laugh. "The upshot of it is, both Trish and I thought if you were planning on sticking around, then you might like your own space. Like I say, we don't want you thinking it's an attempt to get rid of you."

"Billy, I really don't know what to say!" With a squeal of delight, she shifted her numb feet, turning to throw her arms around him.

"Have a think about it, there's no rush. I said I would let him know tomorrow for definite."

With excitement bubbling away, she didn't need to time think.

"I would love to Billy. I mean, I'm not really sure what a property guardian is and I do love staying here with you both but my own space is very appealing and maybe that's what I need to help me sort myself out once and for all."

Seeing his niece ooze with genuine excitement after all these years filled Billy's heart. He lifted her hands, keen to feel and share her happiness.

"If you're a hundred per cent sure that's what you want then I'll give him a call when I get down the yard today. He'll be so relieved that it's someone we know."

"Uncle Billy, just one thing." The reality of her situation made itself known, drawing her brows together in concern. "I have nowhere near enough money to pay rent so how will I afford his apartment?"

"That is exactly the reason it is perfect for you my girl." Billy smiled inward at her naivety. "A property guardian lives in a property rent free. Jack, the guy that owns the place, is prepared to foot the bills too, for the right guardian. In return they would need to keep the property ticking over and look after it as if it were their own. We'll chat more later but I must get down to the boatyard now. Do tell Trish when she gets back from her run, she'll be thrilled you are sticking around!" Standing, he bent forward, kissing the top of her head before exchanging his coffee cup for his flask. With a perky "See you later," he left her with two words that yanked away the earlier excitement. "Ring Owen."

Words that echoed throughout the whole of the room.

Even though it was a Sunday, Kate knew most of the shops in town would be open and she was determined not to waste the day moping. Assuring Trish she would be fine on her own, she slipped her arms into the borrowed rain coat and promised to call if she changed her mind about meeting for lunch.

The intention to visit Edmunds Book Emporium so soon had never crossed Kate's mind, let alone the words that followed. "Morning Mrs Clifford, sorry I know it's early but I was erm, wondering if I might have a word?"

The deep plaid skirt suit from yesterday had been replaced with a lighter weight brown skirt and cream woollen sweater, complete with a string of pearls that sat neatly around her long swan like neck. Kate appreciated the style of this elegant old lady, even if it was terribly dated.

"Don't sound so apologetic dearie. It is never too early to see a beautiful face. I knew you would be back. Now, let me guess, you would like to come and help me out in the shop, wouldn't you?"

Kate stood open mouthed, wondering how on earth this woman knew why she was there when it had only just become apparent to herself.

"Close your mouth dearie else the flies will get in. Now come along and sit yourself down over there. I'll be over in a minute." A graceful bow of her head to the chairs saw Kate do as she was instructed, followed seconds later by Mrs Clifford, complete with clipboard and pen.

"Right Kate, it was Kate wasn't it? Let us start your interview, shall we?" The mischievous glint that twinkled behind the half-moon glasses was lost on Kate.

Interview? For a part time job in a bookshop? It hadn't taken long for her mind to chip in, after all it had an opinion on everything these days. Or at least seemed to.

"Only jesting with you dearie, I don't go in for all that nonsense. I know the right person for a job when I see them and yesterday you were very much at home in here. Now relax." Using both hands to lower the glasses, she chuckled away, lost for a moment in her own merriment.

She was a funny character was Mrs Clifford, first impressions were definitely not always what they seemed, particularly in her case, serving a quiet reminder to not to be so judgemental. As she spoke, Kate studied her with great care, watching the harshness of the woman's angular features softened by an inner glow.

Agreeing to two days a week, Friday and Sunday,

with the prospect of more should the need arise, the two women shook hands. The pay was minimal but Kate didn't care. It was a chance to do something she enjoyed and earn a bit of money for it along the way.

"Righto' then dearie, that is sorted. If that is all, I will see you this Friday, nine thirty sharp." With effort, she pushed herself out of the chair, condemning it as a modern-day bad back creator.

Kate took the outstretched hand once more, its bony fingers wrapping tighter than she would have liked around her own, holding her in their grip. The wink that accompanied the words, "Now don't you let me down dearie," sent a strange tingle down Kates spine that didn't leave her until she was back outside, in the fresh spring air.

Walking past the quaint timber framed shop buildings that lined Duke Street, Kate couldn't quite believe her luck. A potential new place to stay, rent free, and a part time job in a book shop of all places. She remembered another of her Aunt Pam's sayings, 'Luck happens in three's'. She deliberated on what the third thing might be, knowing as she waited to cross over from The Quay what she more than anything hoped it would be.

Finding an empty bench that overlooked the cast iron bandstand, Kate took a seat. The Royal Avenue Gardens were already alive with visitors and she prayed the hungry gulls would keep their attention on the child that offered out handfuls of bread and leave her alone.

Glancing at her watch, the time had come. She knew that at eleven twenty on a Sunday morning the chances of Owen being at home were incredibly slim. But she'd promised both Billy and Trish she would make the call and as much as it pained her, knew they were right. Having changed the sim card so he couldn't contact her, she had also been careful to turn off show caller id in her settings. The last thing she wanted was for him to gain her new number.

Dialling the number to what was once her home, she held her breath as the line connected and began to ring out. She prayed so hard that she was right about Owen being at the gym but on the fifth ring, one before she knew the answerphone would take over, she hit the red button on the screen as fast as she could, unable do it. The thought of his voice stimulated a pang of conscience she just couldn't bury. But adrenaline began to fuel her, it was now or never and she owed it to him, she'd said it herself. With redial pressed, she poised herself as she waited for the ring tone. And this time she let it ring until the virtual voice of the answerphone answered her call. The message she left was short and to the point.

"Owen it's me, Kate. I just wanted to say sorry and to let you know I'm safe. I think its best if you try and move on. I'll be in touch when I've figured out what to do but that could be a while. I'm Sorry."

Bitch. After everything he has done for you. All these years and that's all you give him. Don't you think he de-

serves more?

Of course she knew the harsh, critical voice to be correct for once but short of going back to him, what else could she do. No, she'd done what she'd promised and called him and that was that.

It was time to let him go.

Chapter 19

Owen

Playing back the voicemail for the umpteenth time, Owen was distraught he had missed that call. He sat hunched up on the floor, his finger hovering over the play voicemail button of his mobile so as not to let a single moment pass between the end and the start. The intensity of each and every word sunk deep within him, surging his veins like a bolt of electricity.

There was always something about her voice that made every inch of his body come alive. But that was then and the aliveness now was overshadowed by the throbbing gloom that had collapsed upon him. He ran his thick fingers through his unwashed hair, second guessing how things had managed to change so quickly. Dropping from the clutches of his fingers, his head fell forward, resting on his knees as he allowed himself to be consumed by the downward spiral his of his thoughts. As he rocked gently backwards and forwards, the truth of how tiring his life had become descended upon him and finally, Owen set free the stifled cry, allowing it to escape until it filled the room around him.

Chapter 20

Owen

The rays of the morning sun shot spears of light through the flat window, breaking his restless sleep. Owen rubbed hard at his eyes, willing them to open properly. He looked down at himself, lying fully clothed on the sofa with no recollection of why, until he caught sight of the empty beer bottles scattered on the floor around him.

Swinging his legs awkwardly to the floor, he sat hunched, his limbs not quite yet his own. Forcing his arms above him, he stretched out as far as possible, wincing at the tightness that had set in from a night spent on the stiff leather sofa, his back and shoulders sore.

He closed his eyes against the memories of a distant past that flooded back. Dark memories intermingled with her voicemail message, and then Kate's. All spinning round together fast and furious. Lines blurred between what was right and what was wrong. Knowing if he screamed, things would only get worse. It was time to pull the break and get off this ride from hell. If he was to salvage anything from this mess, he had to pull himself together and that couldn't be done by wallowing in self-pity. Self-pity led to alcohol fuelled binges which led to rendering him useless.

He'd taken his eye off the ball and he needed to get it back on. Firmly.

The time had come to pay the past a proper visit.

Chapter 21

Kate

The sharp increasing downpour had walked with Kate all the way to Marcel's leaving her shivering on the slabbed doorstep.

Bringing her in from the dreariness, Marcel joked, asking what she'd done with the sunshine while relieving her of the jacket that dotted drips into random spots about her. Thankful for the towel, Kate frantically rubbed away the wet from her hair, unaware of the frizz she had caused.

The familiar scent of lavender and citrus hung in the air, becoming stronger as Marcel led her down the black and white tiled hallway, opening the last door on the left. The room beyond was beautiful. Painted in the warmest of lilacs, its rectangular shape was dressed with two dark purple wingback chairs at one end of the room, separated by a gnarled oak coffee table. The therapy couch was positioned just off centre, draped with an intricate patterned throw. The small sash window was concealed with a slatted oak blind, its sill home to various crystals and ornaments, some she recognised as similar to those she'd seen in Equilibrium. With two shelves stacked neat with books and another home to a colourful collection of glass bottles, the room was light and inviting, the incense that had taken over the lavender unfamiliar but quietly soothing.

Marcel spoke softly as she helped Kate onto the couch, explaining that it would, in essence, be very similar to the session she had received at the Reiki share. Placing a cushion under her knees, Marcel covered her with another lightweight throw, giving just one instruction. To breathe in deeply and close her eyes as she exhaled.

Within moments, the familiar drifting she'd previously experienced was ready to welcome her once more.

Trees.

Endless rows of trees all around.

*Their leaves bouncing back the light the sunshine
had coated them in.*

Slowly fading.

Evaporating light.

Dampness pushing through.

Then darkness, weighted down with fear.

The force with which Kate's eyes opened startled her. She could see Marcel holding her feet, too engrossed in her work to notice the wide eyes staring down at her. As her gaze flitted, she took slow deliberate breaths, relieved that they had helped loosen her tight chest by the time Marcel removed her hands. Remaining silent, Marcel turned to reach over to the shelf, taking down a blue glass bottle that sat amongst the collection. Using what appeared to be an eagle feather, she wafted the spritzed contents of the bottle at some height above Kate.

Entranced by her actions, Kate wondered if she should speak but instead, she lay there, waiting to be guided.

Marcel placed the lid back on the bottle, returning it to its home on the shelf along with the feather. Returning herself to the foot of the couch, she brought her hands together and bowed, muttering words that were inaudible to Kate. Once finished, she excused herself and left the room, re-entering moments later with a tray.

"Just allow yourself a moment Kate and I will pour us both some water."

Pushing herself up into a seated position Kate yawned, stretching out her arms.

"How was that?" Marcel passed over a tumbler full of water.

Kate answered simply, "It was interesting."

Tilting her head, Marcel smiled, "Let's go over and get settled in the chairs and you can tell me why."

Kate fidgeted from side to side, too nervous to sit back and let the chair take her full weight. What she wanted was to pull her knees up tight, take her safety position, but instead, she perched halfway back, both feet flat on the ground. She tightened her grip around the crystal tumbler she was holding, the indents of its pattern pressing into her fingers.

"Whenever you're ready Kate. Just start and the words will flow."

The ball had been placed firmly in Kate's court now. She'd been in this position before; she knew it was time.

"The session itself was good. Interesting. It was kind of like the last time, at the Reiki share evening but different." She was well aware how contradictory that sounded.

"Different, in what way?" Marcel leant back in her chair.

"Well, I had that wonderful floating sensation again. It was so peaceful. Then I could see trees. All around me. It was odd because one minute I felt safe, happy. The sun was shining and I remember noticing how bright it was as it fell on the leaves. In a strange way I had a sense of feeling complete. Does that make sense?"

"It does," Marcel said.

"That feeling was wonderful. It really was. I could have stayed there forever. But then the light disappeared, and, and I couldn't see anything." Kate picked at her thumbs, lowering her head a fraction to the floor. "It just went pitch black but I had this overwhelming sense of fear, like I was trapped. That's when I must have panicked because my eyes sprung open and I saw you standing at my feet. And well, that was it."

"Well done Kate. I know how difficult it must have been because this isn't the first time this has happened is it?"

Kate shook her head, lifting it slightly.

"How long have you been experiencing these happenings?"

"Years."

There. Done it. She had finally admitted the thing that had plagued her for so long and the rest was now begging to follow, leaving her no choice but to dig deep.

"The first time was when I was around five years old. I would often have dreams of floating and everywhere around me was dark. But they were different back then. I was never afraid. Until..." She couldn't say it. She knew if she did then she would have to admit the real reason her family were dead.

"Until what Kate? You can tell me you know. Remember there is no judgement here. Just a safe space to let go." Marcel's words paled into the background, drowned out by the sobs that had pushed their way out of Kate.

"It is not up to me to force you Kate but know this, If you chose to bury again this thing that is bothering you so, there may never be another opportunity to let it go."

Marcel was straight, honest and direct. Things Kate admired.

The clenching in her stomach made her shift uncomfortably in the chair.

"I have never told anyone Marcel. Not a single soul. If I tell you this then I have to tell you everything. Completely unedited and that scares the hell out of me."

"Take your time. There is no rush."

Kate pressed her palms together, resting her lifted chin on outstretched thumbs, lips squashed against the sides of her index fingers. A few seconds passed and she lessened the pressure, readying herself to talk.

"So, these dream type things, they changed when I was a teenager. I guess as a kid I just accepted them as being there, everyone around me teased me for daydreaming. 'Off in her little world' they would all say. 'Away with the fairies.' But when I got older, I didn't understand them. Didn't understand what was happening to me." Sighing, she looked at Marcel. "I got scared and wanted them to go away. I needed to understand why but there were no answers. I was tested for the usual epilepsy as the school thought I was having absences but nothing abnormal showed up. They couldn't find any explanation for what was happening to me. They wanted me to see a psychiatrist but thank god my parents refused. They just put it down to rampant hormones that my body was adjusting to."

Reaching forward, she took the tumbler, its contents soothing against the simmering fire in her throat. Pushing the empty glass back, she tucked her knees into chest, locking her arms around them, self-preservation.

"I was miserable. Not all the time but most of it. People thought I was crazy and if I'm honest, I started to believe them and nothing I did seemed to help.

"When I hit sixteen, I got involved with a crowd of people that were into a bit more than the usual bottle of white lightening down the park. At first, I declined. But as the weeks went by, I gave in and tried a bit of weed. The occasional joint every now and then helped me forget what was happening to me. I felt happy. And normal." Back in the memory, her face softened. "None of the crowd were bothered whether anyone was weird or crazy. Each and every one of us had some sort of crap going on in our lives. Then I ended up getting involved with someone. A guy who was a bit older than me." Her voice faltered, anguish pushing away the softness.

Pulling her arms tighter around her knees, she clasped her hands against her calves, the sharpness of her nails digging in through her trousers, caused them to sting. But she didn't mind the pain. Daring to go back to him, even to think of him, there would always be pain. Ever so gently, she rocked back and forth, eyes wide, holding a silent plead to Marcel to give her the strength to continue. As their eyes met, there were no spoken words of encouragement, no coaxing to continue. The powerful intensity of this woman held Kate captivated, building a fearless courage as a whisper flashed into her consciousness.

'You must first embrace the dark.'

"His name was Mark. He was nineteen and I was sixteen. We were friends for quite a while before it naturally developed into something more. Our friends used to call us cheese and onion because we complemented each other perfectly. We were so good together." A half smile that held so much pain crept out as she was back there. Sixteen and in love.

"That's cute."

"Hmmm, it was. Mark was my rock. And I was his." All the good times they'd shared in the near three short years together were fondly remembered, momentarily brightening her eyes. "Or at least I thought I was."

Marcel was keen not to let her dwell for too long. "What happened Kate?"

"For nearly three years we were happy. Really happy. My dream things had lessened, only happening every now and then. Mark was in a steady job and had got himself a flat. The plan was for me to move in with him once I'd finished my college course. We had what I thought was a normal lifestyle for people of our age. Went to parties every now and then. Held a few ourselves. Drinks down the pub. The occasional meal out. All that sort of stuff. But Mark got distant. Every now and then he would snap at me over nothing.

"I didn't see him as much when I went on placement but when I came back, he was awkward around me. He wasn't sleeping well, and we didn't talk as much. Then there were days when it was like it always had been, happy. So, I would ask if everything was okay. Broach the subject of my concern. He reassured me he was just stressed with work and his degree. He would stroke my face, plant a kiss on my forehead and tease about how stress was part and parcel of being a grown up. Even though I was a grown up too I never took offence. I knew what he meant by it. Rent, bills and responsibility.

"I had no reason to be worried. It all made sense. We were on the whole happy. And I wasn't stupid, I knew every relationship had its ups and downs." Her grip had loosened from her knees, the need to defend herself in Marcel's presence had gone.

Kate admired her patience, curious if she ever got bored of hearing people's stories drag on before they finally got to the point. Whether she did or not, Kate had to tell her everything. It was important she didn't miss anything out. Her shoulders softened, dropping a little further as she welcomed the effect that Marcels unwavering serenity had on her.

"It was a couple of days before my nineteenth birthday and I was so excited. Mark was taking me away for our first proper holiday together. I went over to his flat to surprise him as I'd bought him a new pair of sunglasses. He'd wanted them so much, but he never bought things for himself. So, I decided I would treat him. I loved him so much and he deserved to be spoilt."

Something had re-stirred inside of her. Something she was unable to label. Taking the crystal jug that sat proudly on the table, she refilled her glass. Even though it had turned lukewarm, the sips were soothing against the knots in her belly. Setting the glass back in line with the jug, she sat back, inhaling sharply.

"I called out to him, but there was no answer so I assumed he wasn't back from work. I decided I'd have a tidy round so that when he came home, there was nothing to do except chill. That's when I saw it. When I went into the bedroom. The end of my happy world." She lowered her head again, staring hard at the floor below, needing to take a breath. The deep ache returned, bringing tears to her eyes.

Giving Kate time to compose herself, Marcel left to replenish the jug with fresh cool water. On her return, she refilled both glasses, setting the jug back down, covering the top with a beaded lace doily.

"You are doing amazing Kate. Do you feel able to continue?"

Discarding the wet tissue in the small bin underneath the table, she straightened in the chair, "I think so."

Fuelled once more by Marcel's calmness, Kate was determined to carry on and let it all out. Determined that the past would loosen the tight grip it had held onto her with. She pushed her fingers between the backs of her thighs and the chair beneath them, inhaling deeply. She was ready to continue.

"Nothing could've ever prepared me for what I saw when I went into the bedroom Marcel. Nothing. I stood there longing to scream but even the scream itself was that shocked that it couldn't find its way out. I just froze to the spot like I'd been cast in stone. I remember every little detail of what I saw in that moment. I can still smell the pungent smell of disgust and deceit that filled the air. I remember how I felt in that moment. Betrayed. Bereft. And then numb. *I'm sorry sweet kitty kat.*" She bit down hard on her lip. "That's when everything became hazy because the next thing I remembered was waking up in a hospital bed and not knowing how or why. Hooked up to machines. The constant beeping. Wrists bandaged. Confused."

She edged her fingers out slightly from under her thighs, using her thumbs to subtly pull down the sleeves of her jumper a little more, just in case Marcel happened to cast a sympathetic eye upon her wrists. All the others had. But her eyes never moved.

"When the nurse came in, all she would tell me was that my parents were in with the doctor and they'd be allowed in to see me soon. Although drowsy, I could sense their disappointment from the deafening silence in the room. In the end I gave in and opened my eyes, waiting for one of them to ask why. But it never came. They never asked. I think somehow that made it worse because I wanted to tell them why. I wanted to share why I felt so betrayed and numb. I needed to feel like I wasn't alone.

"I guess now I was just naïve. They would have known why I felt like I did. After all they were my parents. I know they were probably trying to protect me, save me further pain but in the confused state I was in, I needed them to show me that in some way I wasn't alone.

"That night in hospital was one of the longest in my life. I longed to see Mark. Longed for him to explain. But of course, he never came. And I was all alone and scared. Again. And I never did find the answer to my question – why?"

Stepping inside her meandering mind, she allowed the shadows of the past to reflect there, questioning if she would be sat in that room, with Marcel, if they were still together. The answer never to be known.

"The days and weeks that followed went by in a blur because Mark leaving me left a huge void in my life. But then, well that void was quickly filled with these strange happenings. They'd been dormant while I was with Mark. While I was happy. But they reared their head again once that distraction was removed, becoming more and more frequent. Leaving me feeling out of control and out of my depth.

"I'd made several visits to shrinks at the doctor's insistence, and by then, my parents too, but every time I tried to explain to them about the absences, they politely told me I was suffering from PTSD and they were the minds way of blocking out traumatic events.

It didn't matter to them that I had experienced them before. It was like they weren't listening. They just assumed it was my mind playing tricks on me, convincing me it was a covert resistance tactic which stopped me looking at what had really happened.

"In the end I just agreed they were right, just so they would discharge me." Her eyes shifted around the room, settling on the shelf of glass bottles, taking in the different shades of blues and greens before turning back to Marcel. "Am I taking too long? I just feel it's important I tell you everything now."

"Absolutely not. I am honoured that you feel able to share your story with me. But know that you don't have to tell me anything that you don't want to. We can stop at any point you know." Turning slightly in her chair, Marcel shifted position, uncrossing her legs to reveal the deep creases in the linen of her trousers. Time was clearly not an issue.

"Thank you." Kate eyed the large amethyst pendant that hung from Marcels neck, a real statement piece. "I'm actually finding it quite a cathartic experience to talk about this...openly...without having questions fired at me."

Marcel moved her weight forward, resting her hand on Kate's knee. "I'm glad you feel comfortable here Kate. Such bravery deserves a safe, peaceful space."

The warmth of her touch flooded throughout Kate. Even after she'd moved her hand and settled back into her seat, resuming another crossed leg position, the tingle from her touch was still with her. Whatever had happened was more than she could comprehend. Unaware she had mirrored Marcel, Kate too sat back and crossed her legs, ready to go on.

"After I was cleared on the grounds of being stable, I tried to get on with my life. Tried to be normal. But these moments started to take over me. I would find myself losing track of where I was or what I was doing. The next thing I was gripped with fear. And on occasion I would see a face. But I knew somehow these feelings I felt didn't belong to me.

"Sounds crazy, doesn't it? I even started to believe I was crazy and didn't know who I could turn to or talk to. I felt completely isolated. I needed Mark but that wasn't an option. In the back of my tiny mind came this idea."

Sat there, with Marcel, the idea she'd had that would allow her to experience the connection her and Mark had once shared was now clearly so vulgar, stupid.

"Anyway, I tracked down the local weed seller and started smoking joints again and for a while, things were okay. I never smoked it at home. I couldn't risk anyone finding out. After a while though it stopped taking the edge off.

"Whatever these happenings, absences, blackouts, call them what you will were, well they'd found a way to let me know there were still there. Still in control. Because they returned stronger. And foolishly I moved onto something stronger to keep them at bay. The guy with the hood, I never knew his name, suggested I try one of his specials. I never questioned him. I just handed over my money and slipped the wrap into my pocket along with desperate hope and want.

"Later that night, when I knew my Mum and Dad were asleep, I sat on my bed and swallowed what I thought would be the answer to my prayers. It wasn't very long before my body responded and I started to loosen up. I felt chilled. Calm. In control and not alone anymore. I finally felt connected again, to Mark. I even heard his voice telling me how sorry he was. In that moment I could forgive him and pretend the last few months had never happened. That they were the dream and now I had woken up. I was in his arms, his hand caressing my hair. Laughing and kissing like we always had. Making plans. Just in that moment it was all so real. Or should I say that it felt so real, just in that moment.

"I was hallucinating though, off my face big time and had no sense of what was real and what wasn't. If I had of done, then Mum and Dad would still be here. And Aunt Pam. My own selfishness wiped out my family."

She started to fidget, growing uncomfortable from the strength it had taken to fight back the rising emotions. She inhaled deeply against the unwanted heat, exhaling equally as deep, determined to carry on. She had to say it. Needed to say it.

"You see Marcel, it was me who started that fire. Not on purpose. But it was definitely my fault. I could remember dancing around the flames in my room. For Mark. My naked body putting on a show for him. A replay of a night in the woods we had once shared long ago. Teasing and tantalising him so I could feel him inside of me again, just like that summer's night. But I never did feel him again. The next time I opened my eyes, I was lying in a hospital bed. Again."

Unaware of the tremor that had been steadily building, her body began to shake. The sheer force of muddled emotions that had been silenced far too long had at last found their outlet and tears came at speed, stinging her cheeks as they fell. She pressed the heels of her palms hard into closed eyes, letting her fingers tap away at her head, hoping the motion would tap away the pain. Using sleeves which were still half pulled down over her hands, she rubbed at her snivelling nose and tear stained eyes, apologising to Marcel for getting into such a state.

"Let it all go." The response was short and all that was needed to give Kate the final push to continue.

"My parents weren't there, at the hospital. Nor Aunt Pam. By this time, I really was all alone. The nurse who had told me my family never made it was kind. Really kind. She put me in touch with various bereavement organisations and because of my past, I was also assigned a case worker. The nurse knew of course that I'd been off my face, toxicity levels would have shown up in the blood tests. The police came in to talk to me. Going through the motions of explaining the state of the house. Asking if I had somewhere I could go to. Apologising for my loss. I wanted to scream losses at them but there was no point. It wasn't their fault I had killed my family. I waited for them to question me about the fire, but they never did. To this day, you are the only person except Bernarde I have ever told that it was me who was responsible for that fire. Can you understand now why I feel so dirty and selfish."

As grief and shame swung before her, she couldn't look at Marcel, not wanting or deserving her sympathy. She twisted her head to the side, her stiff neck relieved of the change in position. With the bookshelf now in her line of vision, her eyes flitted over the titles of the neatly lined books when one stuck out like a sore thumb. She was sure it was the same book that had mysteriously made its way into her bag. She would remember that gold embossed title anywhere. But in the grand scheme of things, it was irrelevant. Just a mere coincidence.

She plucked up the courage to turn back to Marcel's question. "You don't have to answer this Kate, but how do you know it was you who started it?"

"I'd lit a few candles in my room earlier that evening before I took that pill. Something I did often, me and Mark always had lots on the go. One of the candles must have got knocked off and instead of panicking or trying to put it out like someone of sane mind would do, I didn't. I remember how I relished in those rising flames. I was tripping out by this point, someplace else. My bedroom long since gone. Cavorting around them without a care in the world, my sole aim to feel close to Mark. I don't know how I ended up in the back yard. The doctors assumed I'd tried to escape the fire and collapsed out there as I was unconscious when they found me. Dad had tried to get to my room to rescue me and Mum had gone to get Aunt Pam. She'd had a knee op just a few weeks before and was staying with us so Mum could look after her. It was Uncle Billy's suggestion as it was far too hilly around here for her to get around easily.

"Anyway, none of them made it. Nearly my whole family wiped out in one sitting. If I could go back to that day, I would never have taken that pill. Not if I'd have known the devastation that would follow. All I wanted was Mark, and to block out these happenings Marcel.

"Uncle Billy came to visit me, begging me to go and stay with him but after a few months, I couldn't bear him being so kind to me. I tried to tell him it was my fault but he wouldn't listen, insisting that it was just an accident. I'd made my mind up that if I was ever going to sort my life out then I had to try and do it by myself." With too much effort to keep it upright, her head hung again under the weight of the confession.

It had taken everything Kate had to be this frank with her words. She knew she'd relayed most of it in a matter of fact way, but it was the only way she could cope with opening herself up. An 'adopted coping mechanism' was the phrase the last shrink had used to describe her manner. Whatever it was, her story had now been told and she knew there was no going back.

With no text-book answers or clichés, Marcel was wise with her words. There was always a delay before she spoke, not one of hesitance, rather more like she was waiting for the right words to appear to her. If Kate hadn't, on more than one occasion, felt the warmth and kindness this woman emitted, she might have been slightly unnerved by it all. She surmised anyone coming for alternative therapy such as this should not expect normal. But then she'd long given up thinking what was normal, another question whose answer proved elusive.

"I can't begin to imagine how awful things must have been for you Kate." Marcel's hands came together into a prayer position, her chin resting lightly on the tips of her long slender fingers, suspended in thought. "But these happenings, as you have named them...I feel they are trying to tell you something. Show you something even. Naturally, you have pushed them away because you are fearful of them. But in life, the more we resist something, the more forceful it becomes. In order to allow our energy to flow, we must learn to feel our feelings...without getting lost in them. Does this make sense?"

"Yeah...kind of...I think. So, are you saying that I have to actually feel this fear that these things leave with me?"

"I am Kate. A willingness to experience a whole array of feelings. But one cannot do that while they are caught up in their thoughts over it. Befriend your feelings. All of them. Let your heart listen to what they have to tell you." Her hands fell down into her lap, her signature bright red lips widening into a knowing smile.

Kate couldn't ignore the sensation that rattled against the silence. What was Marcel holding back? She groaned inwardly; hadn't she just been told to listen to her feelings more? But then who was listening, the judgemental voice that lived rent free in her head or the wise one in her heart?

"You see Kate, sometimes we play a pivotal role in something much bigger than we can ever begin to imagine and..." Her words trailed off, a reluctance to continue, confirming she was definitely holding something back.

"Hmm like what? I'm sorry but I don't understand. Listening to my feelings is one thing but this..." she shrugged, shaking out a sigh as her head moved side to side, "this...what you just said, it'll just take some getting my head around that's all." She chose her words carefully, not wanting to offend.

"I know it must sound odd Kate but sometimes... well...things in our lives are orchestrated in such ways to help us reach our destiny. Sometimes we can deviate from the path we chose to walk, particularly during difficult times. What matters most is getting back on it." Marcel held out her hands, palms facing out towards in defence as she watched Kate's face crease with confusion. "Like I said, I know it sounds odd. And I know that you're probably thinking but what if I don't know what path. That's why it's important to learn to listen...from the heart."

She was spot on because that was exactly what Kate had been thinking.

"What should I do then? Because right now I am seriously confused."

"First all of you have to let go of the past." She shifted to the edge of her chair, resting her arms across her legs. "Carrying guilt and blame around constantly is not healthy. As much as you loved Mark, it was not your fault he betrayed you. If it was you that caused that fire, well...you didn't intentionally set out to burn down your house, nor for your family to die. What's done is done Kate. Now, I think there is something I should share with you..."

Kate's eyes followed her to the bookshelf, watching as Marcel removed a heavy leather-bound book, catching a glimpse of the gold embossing on the spine as she turned back to face her. Kate reached for the water, her mouth suddenly dry, sipping nervously, not daring to think about what would happen next. Returning to the chair, Marcel rested the book on her lap, heavy black leather against soft white linen. Her hands lowered down on top of it, holding it like it was the most precious thing in the world.

"A long while ago Kate, I was in a dark place and wasn't sure which way to turn. One evening I had taken myself down to the beach...casting pebbles into the water...imagining what it must feel like to be taken by the water. It was late summer and there was nothing more than a slight breeze in the air, then from nowhere came a sudden gust of wind, taking my cardigan with it, pulling it across the sand. I got up, naturally, to chase after it and when I returned to where I had been sat, went to put it in my bag. I couldn't believe what I saw. When I opened my bag, there was a book in there. This book, *Passages of Time*." Marcel looked down at the book that was lying on her lap, her hand moving back and forth in a gentle stroking motion. "It was strange you see...because it appeared from nowhere. There wasn't anyone around that evening. It was just me sat on the beach. But that wasn't all that was left." She stopped the stroking and opened the book, retrieving a piece of paper that had been carefully concealed between the pages.

Kate was now transfixed on the contents of her hands.

"I think you might already be familiar with what is written on this..." Marcel began to read. "*For the light to truly come, we must first experience the dark, for the journey both begins and ends with the past. Have faith dear Marcel.*"

Kate's mouth fell open, her hand covering the pounding in her chest. "I...I...don't understand. That is exactly the same as the note that was left for me. In the same book. On the train when I came down here. There was a man. Disappeared. Gone." Her scrambled thoughts struggled to form any sort of coherent order before leaving as stumbled words. "I...what does...the note...why?"

"I read the note over and over Kate, putting it away, taking it out again, but it was months before I had any inclination to read the book. Call it a hunch or a sixth sense if you like, but I knew you had received one too. You were drawn here for a specific reason and to me to help you. It is all symbolic in some way but that is what you are yet to discover."

Kate could do no more than strain a tight-lipped smile in response, fearing that the next thing to leave her mouth would not be words, but vomit, as a heavy mass of entangled thoughts churned round in her stomach.

Chapter 22

Kate

She skipped dinner, unable to face conversation or eating. There was plenty to digest already without adding more to her overloaded system. Trish and Billy were as understanding as ever, allowing her space, no questions asked.

Lying on the bed, she stared blankly at the shadows on the ceiling, the scene too familiar. She attempted to make some sort of sense out of the day, out of yesterday and the days before that too. Going over and over all she'd encountered in her life, questioning what it was all for. Its purpose.

Thoughts of that book pushed their way to the front, along with the note. What bothered her more than anything was that he had known her name. Like he had Marcel's. But how? It didn't make sense to her logical mind. The only conclusion she could draw was that he was obviously some weirdo that got his kicks out of scaring women. Vulnerable women. Easy to spot, easy prey.

But he looked so kind, and normal.

His face came into her consciousness, blurred and out of focus, but if she closed her eyes, she could see easily his soulful eyes and broad smile which illuminated not only his face, but his whole being. The luminosity he had radiated was much more than charm, it had to be. But she no idea what.

Unwilling to think about it any longer, it was doing her no good. She frowned, what if running away had just made things ten times worse? It was always the same, more questions and never any answers. Clicking off the bedside lamp, she rolled over to her side, pushing an arm under the pillow her head was lay on, bringing the other to hug it tightly. She was exhausted, not just physically but emotionally too. She didn't know who she was anymore or what she was supposed to be doing. She was fading away from herself, adding to the dread that was already present.

The Noise.
Unbearable.
Then muffled noises.
Falling.
Fast.
A face...evaporating with the light.
Floating.
Light and Free.
Pitch black darkness.

Chapter 23

Kate

"Morning Kate, sorry I have to dash, meeting in town then late lunch date. Make sure you eat some breakfast please!" Trish was busy stuffing folders into a cloth tote bag moving at a speed far greater than Kate who, still half asleep came down the stairs.

"Oh, and don't forget we're off to see Jack later about the apartment. Have a good day!" She was out the door before Kate could reply.

Leaving the last stair, she eyed the oversized roman numerals on the hall wall as she passed, she'd overslept again. She made a mental note to set an alarm for Friday, her first shift at Edmunds. She did not want to be late.

Opening the fridge door, she smiled inwardly at the colourful range of food inside, a perfect extension of Trish's personality and energy. She pulled out a tub of organic yoghurt and the bowl of prepared berries that sat at the front, Trish's way of knowing that she would eat.

∞∞∞∞

"Right Kate, you ready?" Billy swiped his keys from the kitchen worktop.

"Ready as I'll ever be." The army of butterflies in her stomach showed no signs of letting up anytime soon.

She'd spent ages getting ready that afternoon, changing her outfit several times, eager to make a good impression. She had no idea what to expect when they got there, let alone was expected of her. There was one thing she did know though and that was how much she could do with something to settle her nerves.

Keen to avoid conversation, Kate remained two steps behind Billy and Trish as they strode into town to board the lower ferry. It struck her that having not questioned Billy about the property she would be potentially looking after, she knew nothing other than it was an apartment on the other side of the river in Kingswear. Already loaded with cars and a couple of bicycles, they'd arrived at the right time and walked straight on the ferry, the only foot passengers for this crossing.

Returning the permit back into his wallet, Billy wrapped his arm around Kate, rubbing her shoulder. "Don't look so nervous."

A couple of minutes later, they had reached Kingswear and waited as the ferryman swung the gates of the pontoon wide open.

Turning right after leaving the slip way, they climbed the steep narrow lane, coming to a stand-still outside the drive of the old rectory.

"Here? Are you serious?" Kate's stomach now home to a game of ping pong between nerves and excitement.

She wasn't sure what she imagined but it wasn't this. As a child, she remembered the old derelict rectory standing dark and lonely, its true beauty concealed by swathes of dark green ivy, tendrils snaking up and around, clinging to anything it passed. Now, its exterior had been carefully reno-vated to its former Georgian glory, injected with a new lease of modern life.

"Yep, well half of it."

As they walked across the sweeping drive, Billy gave Kate a quick overview of the renovation, ex-plaining it had been restored and converted into two apartments with a communal lobby.

Apartments or not, it was big, elegant and grand and Kate brimmed at the prospect of actually living here. Good luck really did come in threes.

"I've always wondered what these look like in-side," Trish whispered to Kate through a curious grin as they entered the lobby.

"Lift or stairs?" Billy asked once all three of them were inside.

"Lift for me." Kate straightened her back, pushing back her shoulders, "I don't want to be out of breath when we get up there. Wouldn't be a good first impression would it!"

Stepping out of the lift, the face that greeted them was far more than a pleasant surprise to Kate.

"Billy, great to see you, and you too Trish!" Jack embraced each, then turned. "And you must be Kate?"

As she met his look, their eyes locked, holding the welcome longer than either of them realised, the spark of an untold bond ignited.

"Yes I am. Really good to meet you Jack." The effort to keep her voice calm huge.

"Right then come on in, let's go in and get a drink."

Following behind them, what the inside held was not at all what Kate had expected from the outside. Beautifully decorated and styled but not in an overdone way at all. Its modern twist on the Art Deco style was incredibly tasteful. The mink and beige colour scheme accented with flashes of black in the geometric patterns of the cushions sat perfectly against the dark wood of the parquet flooring. The mix of rosewood furniture and mirror topped coffee tables gleamed as the light from the stepped glass chandeliers bounced upon them. Everything oozed with sophisticated class.

She was in her element, a beautiful apartment decorated in the style of her favourite period that she could potentially be living in next week, rent free. Yet the drips of doubt came swift. She studied the toned outline of this handsome stranger, appeasing herself that the reality of the opportunity hadn't sunk in yet, but in the depths of her being, she knew it wasn't that. Shaking off the feeling, she welcomed the glass that was offered to her. She sipped the contents slowly, the fizzy liquid cold as it passed her lips, lightening her legs as it slipped down to her stomach.

Stood outside on the wraparound balcony, a peace descended on Kate as she watched the hypnotic motion of boats sail up and down the river, reflecting on how strange it was that something can feel both so familiar yet so new at the same time. Brought out of her daydreaming by the offer of a refill and a tour around the apartment, she accepted both, following on behind Jack as he led her back inside to see the rest of the rooms.

The two bedrooms were huge, both complete with spacious en-suite bathrooms. A separate guest bathroom, a study and a gym. The living space, split into three sections, was all open plan with a utility room branching off the kitchen. A white gloss kitchen which appeared more accustomed to champagne and eating out if the gleaming black quartz worktops were anything to go by.

Ready to sit and join Billy and Trish, Jack's mobile rang. Glancing down to the coffee table at the flashing screen, he mouthed an apology as he picked it up to answer, leaving the room.

"Well, what do you think Kate? Can you see yourself living here?" Kate's roving eyes brought back to Billy and Trish.

"Who couldn't see themselves living here? It's just beautiful, stunning. Way beyond anything I could have ever imagined." Kate span round, arms wide open as she took it all in, stopping dead and feeling rather foolish as Jack returned. Throwing her a boyish grin, their eyes locked together once more and for a split second, everything faded into the background.

Jack tapped his phone against his palm, "I'm so sorry but something has come up that I have to go and sort out. But listen, Kate, let me take you for lunch tomorrow and we can discuss the arrangement then if that's okay?" Not giving her any time to object, he added, "I'll meet you at The Bistro at 1pm."

"Yes, thank you." The reply came from a voice that Kate was sure did not sound like hers.

"Everything alright Jack?" Somehow Billy figured that everything was the opposite of his question.

"Will be Billy." Jack eyed each of them turn. "Thanks for coming and I really am sorry to have to cut short like this. Pitfalls of running your own company and all that." He shrugged, unaware of Kate's rising heartbeat as his own muscles tensed.

Once outside, after a brief exchange of bye for now's, they parted company, leaving Jack to deal with business.

Back on the ferry, Trish wasted no time in delighting at the interiors of Jack's place. Kate half listened, nodding and agreeing with a smile and a "I know!" in the right places but the other half of her mind was elsewhere as she stared back at the balcony she'd been stood on not an hour before.

Watching it shrink as they floated further away from it.

The last thing she remembered of that day was everything around her moving in directions that didn't make sense, everything slowly fading away.

Alone…
Everything has gone.
Taken.
Coldness clasping tight.
Light fading fast.
Silence.
Wrapped in darkness.

Chapter 24

Kate

Her aching limbs lay dense and heavy on the bed, eyes firmly fixed on the ceiling again, wondering what was happening to her.

The doctor who had been called was not overly concerned but wanted her to get some blood tests ran, just to be on the safe side. His diagnosis, likely caused by low blood pressure. She hadn't cared to tell him it had sort of happened before, reassuring herself that this time it was different. Different because it was a full-on black out. All the other times she'd just lost track of time, usually always when she'd been sitting down, resting her eyes. Except for the one time in the bath when Owen had come in to bring her a drink to find her under the water, semi-conscious. Scared them both but luckily it never happened again.

Not prepared to lie there battling with her thoughts any longer, the days of self-pity needed to end. Thousands of people pass out every day for no reason, nothing to make a fuss about.

Unsure of the time, she heaved herself out from the warmth of the bed, sliding her feet, right first, then left into the slippers that sat at the side of it. Hearing Billy and Trish moving around downstairs, she pulled the belt of the cotton dressing gown tight around herself, tying it into a knot as she stood at the top of the stairs, mentally preparing herself for the tirade of questions she anticipated were waiting for her at the bottom.

"Here she is. Go and take a seat and you can join us for breakfast."

Answering Billy with a forced smile, she sat at the table, watching both buzz around in the kitchen like a couple of bees. She shuffled the chair round so she could look out over the river, her mind drawn to the apartment that she would soon be living in, prompting a reminder of the lunch engagement she had at one o'clock.

"Right here we go." Appearing from the kitchen with a laden wooden tray, Billy's voice was overly cheery. Forced. "Mixed berries, granola, yoghurt, oven baked croissants and fresh coffee, all prepared by yours truly!"

Trish followed closely behind, holding a cut glass jug of fresh juice, giving Kate a wink as she smiled affectionately at him. "Help yourself Kate," she said, sitting herself down opposite.

Kate needn't have bothered to mentally prepare herself as the conversation didn't once veer to how she was feeling or what had happened the day before, leaving her at one point questioning whether she had imagined the whole thing.

After breakfast had been eaten, she offered to clear

away, not listening to the protests of Trish and Billy as she loaded up the tray with the used crockery, carrying it through to the kitchen. About to unload it, the hushed voices took her attention. Edging over ever so slightly, she could easily make out what they were saying without being seen.

"Do you think she is okay Billy?" Concern wrapped around Trish's words.

"Maybe she is just exhausted and needs a good rest. I mean she has been through a lot on her own. Living in London and breaking up with Owen, it's bound to take its toll isn't it?"

"I know, I hear what you're saying but I can't help thinking there's something else going on. Something we don't understand. Did you see the exchange between her and Jack yesterday?" She rubbed at her arms, "It made my hairs stand on end."

"I didn't see anything but what's that got to do with anything?"

"Oh, I don't know Bill, there's just something making me think all isn't as it seems. Call it gut instinct if you like and I hope that I'm wrong but..." Her words tapered off as Kate returned to the dining table.

"All okay?" Kate pretended she had heard nothing.

"Yes, my girl, all is okay." Billy reassured her; totally unaware she'd heard their whispers just a few moments ago.

"Right, well I'm off to get ready, meeting Jack at one remember?"

"How could we forget eh? Go and have a nice

lunch, enjoy yourself and we'll catch up with you later."

She caught the brief glance of worry pass from Trish to Billy before she spoke. "I will!"

On leaving the room, Kate could hear once more the hushed tones as they continued to share their concerns.

The Bistro was a trendy new addition to the water's edge that served nothing but fresh seafood. Arriving a good fifteen minutes early, Kate made straight for the ladies. Taking out her foldaway hairbrush, she smoothed her short bob back into place, the breeze having blown it every which way on the ferry over there. She wanted to ensure she looked her best when she met Jack today, her early arrival intentional for that very reason. She hadn't imagined that spark yesterday and even if she had, decided it wouldn't hurt to be a little self-indulgent for once. She'd chosen her clothes carefully, not wanting to show the effort she'd gone to to get it right. Opting to wear her v neck, pale pink cashmere sweater over a plain white shirt, she'd teamed it up with her favourite dark skinny jeans and heels. She neatened up the cuffs of the shirt which sat over the sleeves of her sweater, concealing the vulgar scars that lay beneath. Turning from side to side, she took one last look in the mirror, acknowledging how good she felt. Pushing her shoulders back with a quick breath in and out, she held her head high and left the ladies, catching sight of Jack being shown to a table by the window.

She hung back by the pillar, watching, allowing herself time to take him in. She watched him remove the jacket of the navy-blue suit he was wearing, revealing the crisp white slim fitting shirt that highlighted the definition of his upper body. She saw him settle in his seat and roll up the cuffs of his shirt, the sunlight bathing his lightly tanned skin. He was handsome, there was no doubt about it and immaculately dressed.

As nerves kicked in, Kate jumped at the voice that appeared beside her, asking if she had a reservation. Nodding over towards where Jack was sat, she followed behind the waiter.

"Kate, hi!" Jack stood as soon as he saw her approaching, greeting her with a friendly kiss on the cheek, taking her a little by surprise.

"Hi Jack, I hope you've not been waiting too long?" A gentle heat warmed her cheeks, the answer already known.

"Not at all, just got here myself. Please, sit down."

The waiter pulled out her chair, laying the napkin over her knee, a polite nod at Jack as he backed away from the table.

"You look great by the way." His eyes took in every inch of her.

It was there again, that spark, only this time stronger. And deeper, much deeper.

"Glass of bubbles?" Jack held up the bottle that had quickly arrived at the table after she had.

"Thank you."

"Cheers! And here's to…"

Stopping mid flow as they chinked glasses, their gaze again locked momentarily before his eyes narrowed. A flash of discomfort dulled the brightness of the blue, just for a second before they softened and he finished his sentence, "new beginnings."

By the time the food arrived, whatever had passed within him had long gone.

They shared a vibrant fresh seafood platter, accompanied by several glasses of chilled Chablis and conversation. Jack was easy company and Kate had lapped it up, forgetting they were in a restaurant until the waiter came to remove their plates.

Thanking him, Jack straightened in his chair, his smooth, neatly manicured hands laid on the table. "Right…how about we go back to mine, grab a coffee and talk over the arrangement hey? Otherwise I'll be leaving tomorrow without anything in place!"

"Yeah, sure." Excitement and nerves jostled for her attention against the sarcastic voice inside her. *'Get a grip Kate, he's only asking you for a coffee, this is a business arrangement that's all.'*

The voice was right, of course it was, but she couldn't deny the sensations that tingled deep. She reached underneath the table for her bag, trying to shake off what her body felt.

"Ready?"

"But…we haven't paid yet." Kate rummaged in her bag for her purse, not looking up.

The scent of musky aftershave caught her nostrils as Jack moved behind her, taking the back of her chair. Leaning in over her shoulder, his breath warmed her ear as he spoke. "Please, no need."

She allowed him to pull out her chair and open the door for her as they left, offering his arm for her to take. It had been a long time since she had been in the presence of a gentleman and business arrangement or not, she was going to make the most of it.

On the short walk back to Jack's apartment, neither spoke, both comfortable with the quietness around them. Although the sun was shining, the breeze the river carried was cool and Kate unknowingly pressed herself in closer to his side.

"Make yourself at home Kate, I'll just put some coffee on."

She moved out on the balcony, taking the same spot as the previous day, lost in her own thoughts when her ear was warmed by Jack's breath once again.

"Beautiful isn't it?" His voice soft, meaningful.

"It's enchanting. The whole river is but especially this view of it. I could lose hours just gazing out…"

Her daydream ready to take over.

"One could say even more enchanting having you

in the picture." His breath was there again, warming not just her ear but the side of her neck to.

Her pulse quickened raising the fine hairs on her neck, unsure how to answer. He slipped his arms around her waist and she could feel not only his breath now but the fullness of his soft lips as they caressed her neck. He turned her round to face him, his arms around her waist, pulling her into him, hers finding his. His face inched closer, her eyes drawn to the tiny scar above his right eyebrow. Their hungry lips touched, sheer excitement cursed her veins as she savoured each and every delicate and gentle kiss. She wanted him so much but a thread from the past tugged at her, gnawing away at her desire. Broadening the gap between them, she pushed herself back against the strong arms that gripped her waist, her eyes unable to meet his as she muttered, "I'm sorry."

"Hey, sweetheart, what's wrong?" His tenderness full and genuine. With a thumb and finger, he held her chin, lifting it up.

She could sense the desperation within his eyes, needing her to look at him. To explain. To reassure that it wasn't his fault.

"I'm scared Jack. I'm a mess. I came here to try and get my head straight, to try and make sense out of my totally screwed up life, but all I seem to be doing is going around in circles. I'm so sorry... I shouldn't drag you into all of this." Her words muffled by the tears that stung her cheeks.

Turmoil dug its claws into her as she rubbed away

at the tears, desperate to stem their flow, pressing the heel of her palms into the stinging balls that had taken over her eyes. As Jack took hold of her wrists; she flinched, not wanting him to see the ugliness they bore, his grip was firm yet gentle as he prised them away from her face.

"Kate, sweetheart, look at me, it's fine. You have nothing to apologise for. I shouldn't have presumed you felt the same." There was no annoyance in his voice as he spoke, just a softness to his words encouraging her to look up at him. He smoothed away the stray hairs that sat across her face, tucking them behind her ear, shooting a tingle off inside her. "It's me who should be sorry Kate, please don't think badly of me."

Think badly of him, how could she? She lowered her face again, swallowing hard against her tightening throat. Jack was everything she could wish for in a man. Kind, attractive, funny, charming, handsome. The list was endless and he was attracted to her. And she was single and equally attracted to him. Yet something she found impossible to label churned away inside of her, adding to the guilt she carried. Everything had happened at such whirlwind speed. Images of Owen, Aunt Pam, her parents and Mark, all swirled together in her mind as she forged an attempt at an explanation.

"I don't think badly of you Jack, it's myself that I think that of. I got carried away in the heat of the moment, forgetting who I was...and..." Her voice had become brittle because despite what anyone said, she would never believe that she deserved to happy. Even if that happiness was temporary. How could she enjoy life fully, knowing that her actions had prevented those she had loved from doing the same?

But underneath that guilt lay something else. Something that stretched far beyond a physical attraction, something she was not yet ready to understand. A subtle fear, deep in her subconscious made itself known and whatever it was, was dangerous yet necessary at the same time.

She dug deep for the courage to face Jack, but the face that looked back at her was not kind with enticing eyes and soft smiles. It was the face of someone else altogether.

She froze.

Aghast.

She had to get out of there, break this madness but she couldn't make herself move. It was the face from the window, from the train.

A face that was both familiar and unfamiliar simultaneously.

The evaporating face of her dream now looked straight at her.

Confusion.
Unable to think.
What is happening?
Why is he here?
All hope gone.
The darkness is waiting.

Chapter 25

Owen

Having called his PA to say he wouldn't be in, Owen slumped at the dining table in the cold, empty apartment that only a few days before had been so full of life and warmth. He missed Kate. Her warmth, her smile, her smell, her energy. He missed absolutely every single thing about her.

He flipped open the lid of his laptop, if he wanted her back, a chance to explain, he had to do this. Swallow his pride, no matter how painful and sort this mess out. Staring at the flashing cursor in the search box, his breath quickened. Part of him wanted to slam the lid shut and leave everything in the box where it had been safely tucked away for the last twenty odd years. Buried away so deep in the recesses of his mind that he recalled it only as something that he vaguely remembered, disassociated from being his own memory. Kate's memory. But now it was no longer cloistered away. It had unearthed itself, waking him from a long blissful dream into a living nightmare.

With hesitant fingers, he began to type. The pulse of his index finger throbbed as it hovered over the return button, secretly knowing what would be revealed on the screen before him upon pressing it.

In big bold letters, the headline of the Herald Express lunged from the screen.

A slide of the past staring right back at him.

SUICIDE MURDERER HITS EARLY RELEASE

Chapter 26

Kate

"Kate, wait, what's wrong?"

She ran through into the hallway, every inch of her screaming to get out of there. It was the wine, had to be. She'd let herself get carried away, tried to imagine that she was just a normal average person. That's all she really wanted, more than anything in the world was to just be normal. She couldn't fool herself though, no normal person sees a face staring back at them in place of another's like she just had.

But why? She didn't understand why?

With every passing second, the band around her forehead became tighter and tighter.

"Kate, slow down, whatever it is, talk to me sweetheart. I can't let you leave like this." The urgency in Jack's voice desperate to know what he'd done to make her leave in such hysteria. To know why her face had contorted itself, twisted with fear.

His urgency added to her own, forcing her trembling hands to shake uncontrollably as she attempted to get her boots on. Trying to balance on one leg, she tugged frantically at the zip on the inside, needing to pull it up to her knee so she could escape this nightmare. As the zip pull slipped out of her grip, she wobbled, losing her balance.

"Kate. Talk to me...Please."

Jack's words tore at her, squeezing the air from her lungs, her breath became more and more ragged. Her throat stung from the bile she'd forced herself to swallow, in turn making her eyes water. Her balance grew un-steadier by the second unable to stay upright any longer.

The image of that face falling with her.

Strong arms had broken her fall and she dared not look up at the face from which the soft reassuring voice came. With eyes shut tight, she sat there, in the safety of Jack's embrace, no desire to confront the madness of what had just taken place. As bizarre as this moment was, she didn't want it to end.

A sense of belonging had replaced the irrationality of those last few minutes. In the arms of this kind, gentle man who had carefully lowered himself onto to the floor whilst holding her tight, determined not to let her fall. Nestled into him as he tenderly stroked her hair, whispering that everything was okay. How could this man that she had only met just yesterday strike such a fire within her, leaving her feeling like she had known him forever?

The answer jumped at her.

Jack was as gentle and kind as Mark had been all those years ago. And that that was what her heart was craving. So, she allowed herself to absorb his kindness, allowing it to seep freely into her. Drinking it up because her reserves had run to empty over the years.

∞∞∞

The high pitch of the intercom speared through the peace that cosseted them. The grittiness in her eyes as she tried to open them, evidence she had drifted off. She pushed away from the warmth of Jack's body, levering herself to sit up, massaging her forehead whilst trying to decide her next move. It was no good, she had to face this head on for this time, once again there was nowhere to run.

"Hadn't you better get that?" Her hands still covered her face, searching for a distraction.

"No, it's fine. I wasn't expecting anyone so it can't be important. How are you feeling now? Want to tell me what happened?"

The heat from Jack's hands was felt before he wrapped them around her wrists, gently prising her hands away from her face, again. As patches of the afternoon flooded back, her cheeks blushed, it was not fear that stopped her from looking at him this time. She had to look though, try and explain. She owed it to him.

Her behaviour always owing someone something.

"I'm sorry Jack. I truly am. I should never have come back with you." She kept her eyes downcast, not yet ready to face him. She held the long deliberate breath in as she thought. Getting the balance between explaining but not oversharing was tricky. "I came here for a break but, if the truth be told, I've got to sort my train wreck of a life out. Like I said earlier, I'm a complete mess. I've dragged down everyone I know, even lost my job over it." She scoffed, lifting her head.

With his back propped against the hall wall, Jack listened, his features soft, free from impatience. The coldness of the porcelain tiles had begun to seep upwards into her stiff limbs, she hadn't the faintest idea how long they had been sat there. Nor if Jack was uncomfortable either, if he was, he hadn't made any gesture towards being so. She shifted her weight round, leaving the comfort of his body to prop her back up against the wall, aching legs outstretched in front of them as they sat side by side. Jack never said a word.

"I'm not sure if you know of Marcel...she lives on this side of the river. Anyway, she's some sort of healer and I've been to see her recently, try and sort out myself out. You'll probably think me completely weird, but I owe you an explanation. I've seen this face sometimes. A face that isn't really there. And it's odd because although it freaks me out, I know that in itself is nothing to be scared of. But I'm scared of what I don't know. It's like it's trying to show me, or tell me something. Anyway, earlier this afternoon, when we were close..." Her cheeks turned crimson as she remembered their awkward embrace. "I saw it Jack. The face, in you. That's why I freaked out. I'm so sorry. It's like in the moment that it happens, something completely takes over me. And the more scared I get, the more I try and shut it out, but then the more intense it becomes the next time."

She turned to face him, longing for forgiveness, half expecting to see the face staring back at her, but it wasn't. It was Jack's, wearing an expression that was hard for her to read. The seconds that passed as they sat in silence were long and drawn out, feeling more like minutes. She looked away, the intensity of whatever sat behind his eyes too much.

"It's okay. I get it." Jack reached out his hand, resting it on her leg. "I don't think you are weird, not in the slightest. But then if you are then I must be too." He gave her leg a gentle squeeze, letting out a quiet snort. "We all have a past Kate. Some worse than others. There comes a point that certain things just aren't content to stay there, in the past where we think they belong. They rear their ugly heads, we confront them head on, learn our lessons, put the past to bed and move on."

"I get that but I don't see the significance of the face?" Her hopes were pinned on him being able to give her the answers she needed. To put an image to the pictureless jigsaw that had continued to form in her head over the last few weeks.

Jack lifted his hand from her leg, turning his body ninety degrees to face her. "Would it help if I told you I see them too sometimes. Faces that is." His smile grew wider as the long sigh was let out. " When I am sleeping. When I am paying for my groceries. On the phone, looking out over the river. My boat. In the bath. Even in the trees sometimes. And over lunch, in you. Just for a fleeting moment before it went."

"But...I don't get it Jack. Why? What does it mean? Who is this man? Does it not send you crazy?"

That was the connection they shared; she knew there was something, they were cut from the same cloth.

"Well...it's a little perturbing at times, I must admit. Especially when you roll over in the morning and there's a face where there should be an empty pillow." Jack let out a dry laugh. "But it's not a man's face, it's a woman's."

He rose to his feet, stretching his arms behind his back, shaking of the stiffness that was slowly setting in.

"Come on," he said, "we need a drink."

Kate's reluctance at the idea as she readied herself to move fell on deaf ears. Jack offered out his hands, insisting that the drink was a good idea, that they both needed one.

She swallowed her objections knowing he was right and followed him down the hallway, her eyes drawn to the definition of his broad shoulders still visible through his crumpled shirt. Teasing herself to wonder what they would look like without it.

"Tea, coffee, or something stronger?" The smoothness to Jack's voice as smooth and curved as the kitchen it travelled from, jolted her away from fantasising.

"Coffee please," she shouted back.

She'd made herself comfortable on the dark mink sofa, engrossed in the rhythmic motion of stroking the soft velvet fabric back and forth, forming of a pattern then making it disappear over and over. "Sorry, I was miles away there." Jumping as Jack sat down opposite her.

He held up the small black and gold milk jug, "Milk?"

She nodded, pausing to pluck up the courage to ask her question.

"Have you ever asked for help Jack? For the faces that you are seeing?" She pulled down the sleeves of her jumper, holding the edges firmly between her fingertips and palms, stuffing scrunched-up hands between her knees.

He poured the milk into the matching cups.

"It's called Pareidolia. Quite common apparently."

He looked up at her, soft and reassuring as he explained how he'd been diagnosed with it in his early twenties. She didn't probe, deeming it too intrusive and she knew only too well how that felt. Everyone has a past and some things are best left well alone.

"It's a sign of a well wired brain Kate, nothing to be worried about and you are definitely not going mad." His little laugh lit up his eyes. "Now, this coffee should be ready to plunge."

Her brain was busy trying to assimilate this welcome news to speak. Too busy processing the fact that there was nothing wrong with her. Nothing to be scared of. The needling voice in her mind quick to remind her that if only she'd told one of the Doctors about them, then she wouldn't have put herself through the anguish she had. She would have been told the term for what her brain was able to do but the worry stopped her. The worry about what they would think of her

"Do you feel better now you know you're not going crazy?" Jack's voice silenced her own voice of judgement.

"Absolutely. All this time...yes, absolutely, thank you."

Her smile was awkward but it needn't have been. The tiny hint of sadness she was sure had sat behind his eyes earlier had now dissolved, returning them to the pools of piercing blue that had first captivated her.

They carried the afternoon into the evening, drinking coffee, discussing what her duties would be as his property guardian whilst he was away. The atmosphere as light and easy as the conversation, laughing and joking like they had known each other for ever. The last time she had laughed like that was with Bernarde, reminding her that she really must call him. His fruity voice popped into her head, pretending to be shocked, *'Oh you saucy little minx!'* as she imagined telling him what she'd nearly done this afternoon with Jack, sparking her lips to curl.

As comfortable as the time that had passed between them was, a persistent pull in the direction of something not quite right still lingered in the hidden pits of her. No matter how plausible the Pareidolia thing was, there was one big difference between them.

He saw faces, in things.

She saw a face.

And except for seeing it him this afternoon, she usually saw it in nothing.

Chapter 27

Kate

"Right, got everything?" Billy's hand poised to close the rear door of his pick up truck.

"I think so."

The thumping in her chest couldn't believe this was actually happening, especially after yesterday. But Jack had seemed somewhat relieved that she would still do it. The relief mutual that he still wanted her to.

"Ring us if you need anything won't you? We'll miss having you around." Trish's lip quivered as her eyes welled up.

"For goodness sake Trisha, she's only going across the river!" Billy having clearly mastered the art of the eye roll and head shake combination flashed Kate a grin.

"I know, I know." Trish dabbed at her wet cheeks.

"Thank you, Trish, for everything. And don't worry, you'll not be rid of me that easy!"

Kate's last statement lightened the mood, lifting Trish's frown till laughter burst through the tears.

Climbing up into the high seat of Billy's pick-up, Kate could hear Trish telling him to remind her not to forget to eat some breakfast. She smiled to herself, it had been nice having someone there to mother her a bit. It had been a long time since she had and Trish was the closest thing she was ever going to get to having a mum again. And she enjoyed the warm fuzz that had begun to tingle.

∞∞∞

"Here we go then. You ready?" Billy clicked open his seatbelt.

"I think I am." Her tight-lipped smile strained.

"Come on then, sitting in here won't get you inside." Billy pushed open his door, cocking his head upwards to the sky, "And by the look of that cloud over there, if we leave it much longer it'll be pouring and I for one don't fancy getting drenched before I get to work."

Climbing out of the truck, Kate looked up at the drab blanket of cloud that had covered the sky, watching it grow darker and thicker with each passing second.

"Kate. Come on." Billy, now laden with the bags of groceries that Trish had insisted on buying, stepped from foot to foot.

His brightness burnt through the grey doom above and she found herself smiling fondly at the only true family member she had left in her life. The earlier rush of warmth returned leaving her in no doubt that this was love, for him, for Trish. She brought her hand to her chest, the sensation alien to her, the numbness to real emotion wearing off.

He was already waiting at the door as she took her handbag from the footwell. Pulling up the handle on her case, she made haste to join him.

Scrolling down to the fictional telephone number she had stored in her phone's contact list; she punched the six numbers of the key code into the pad on the outside door. As the door buzzed open, Kate took a step in, biting her lip as she turned to face her Uncle. Tipping her a wink, she continued into the spacious entrance lobby.

It struck her how odd it was letting herself into someone else's home, especially with that someone being Jack. A man she hardly knew yet one that that had shown her nothing but kindness and compassion, expecting nothing in return. She contemplated if he would feel the same if he knew about her past. But by his own admission, he had said everyone has a past, some more than others.

Given the heaviness of the bags they were carrying, they decided against the stairs. Within seconds, they'd reached the upper level and the lifts doors slid apart. As the space opened up before her, a shadow flitted across the small landing. But there was no one there. Her shoulders twitched, it must have been a trick of the light from the doors opening, or maybe a bird outside. The floor to ceiling glass panel at the end of the landing was sure to cast an array of shadows across the walls. Wasn't it?

She fed the key in to the lock, twisting it open.

As she wrapped her fingers around the rectangular bar that sat central on the polished oak door, she paused, an unknown force holding her back.

"Come on then girl, my arms are about ready to drop off here!" Billy threw her a broad smile and another wink.

She'd come to learn it was his way of saying everything will be fine.

With the bags delivered safely to kitchen, he stayed for a few minutes only, apologising he must shoot off to work.

"I love you Uncle Billy and I will always be grateful to you, for everything you have done for me. You do know that don't you." She proffered her arms for a goodbye hug.

Not one for open displays of affection, she was clueless as to what came over her, her razor-sharp edges beginning to blunt.

"And I love you too my girl. As does Trish." Billy pecked her cheek, the dryness of his lips lightly grazing her skin as he pulled away. "Now, don't forget where we are, else I'll never hear the end of it from Trish."

"I won't," she promised, her smile matching his as she closed the door behind him.

She turned, pressing her back against the door that separated her from the outside world, looking down at the spot on the floor where not even twenty-four hours ago she'd been sat with Jack, huddled together, strengthening the strange invisible bond they shared.

It felt like a lifetime ago.

Certain she was not going to dwell, her first job was to unpack the groceries that Trish had bought. Emptying the hessian bags, she couldn't help but chuckle, amused by the yellow post it notes Trish had sellotaped to certain items with instructions on how to cook and use them. She opened the cupboard doors in the kitchen one by one, keen to look inside each to discover its contents. Everything was ordered and immaculate. Inside the large pull out larder unit, a modern salt and pepper mill along with a vinegar bottle sat lonely, side by side. She got the impression Jack was not a cook. Carefully loading the wire racks with cans, packets and bottles, she moved on to fill the fridge. A huge black gloss American style one complete with ice dispenser and as she tugged it open, it was not only the fridge that lit up.

A bottle of pink Lanson had been left in the shelf inside the door and a large, ribbon tied box sat on the middle shelf. She picked up the folded note card that had been carefully positioned next to them.

For you. I thought you might like to toast your new home this evening so took the liberty of buying your favourite. Have one for me and enjoy...Jack xxx

Three kisses.

Three!

She read it over and over again. Her eyes unable to leave the three kisses that stood so solid next to his name, quickening her pulse, stirring something down below. She folded it back over, standing it on the worktop, reaching over for what needed to be put in the fridge, keen to shake of this flush of lust she so shamelessly felt. She stood the milk next to the champagne, it was such a thoughtful gesture. She couldn't recall telling him it was her favourite but she must have, how else would he have known?

She spent the next couple of hours exploring her new living space, appreciating again the effort that had gone in to designing the place. The neutral contemporary colour palette enhanced with bold geometric patterns against plush velvet fabrics had been carried effortlessly throughout the whole apartment with no expense spared. It was a perfect modern interpretation of the Art Deco period and she loved it.

She snuggled herself down into one of the recliners that had been perfectly positioned for grey dank days like today. Unable to sit outside but still able to take in the stunning landscape, shielded from the elements safely behind glass. She pulled out her phone that had been stuffed into the back pocket of her jeans earlier and scrolled through the few contacts that she had kept stored.

"Hey B, it's me, Kate. You free for a chat?"

"Kate...sweetie! How fabulous it is to hear your voice!"

Kate tilted the phone, putting distance between the high-pitched screech and her ear.

"Of course I'm free for a chat! Anytime for you sweetie and as it happens, you've caught me on a day off. Now, let me get settled and you can tell me what's been going on."

She waited as Bernarde quietened the classical music that was playing at full pelt in the background, happy that he was at home. It really was good to hear his voice again.

"Right sweetie, all yours."

She didn't know where to begin. Even though Bernarde was her best friend, opening up was not something she was good at and the last few days had been a whirlwind.

"Are you well Kate? I know you're with Billy but I've been so worried about you, you know. We both have." Bernarde's juvenile liveliness had been replaced with a grown-up concern.

"I don't know the answer to that B..." she twisted a chunk of hair around her finger, "one minute I think I am then the next, it's like someone snatches away the glimmer of hope I have, leaving me back where I was." Her body sank further into recliner, her knees close to her chest as her legs left the matching footstool. "So much had happened B, like you'd never believe but... I think things will be okay." The reassurance was more for her than Bernarde. "I start a new job tomorrow."

Over the next hour, she filled Bernarde in on everything that had happened. The complete uncensored version of events since she had left him behind in the office. It had been hard this last week not speaking to him, there had never been more than two days pass without speaking in all the time she had known him, but that's how it had had to be.

"Owen called me sweetie. Said he needed to speak with you, he was pretty desperate."

"You didn't tell him where I was did you B?" Kate drew her knees in closer still. "Please tell me you didn't."

She held her breath, waiting for his answer, her muscles tightening from the lack of oxygen they had.

"Of course I didn't. I told him you were safe and that I would pass on his message to you should I speak with you."

She let the held breath out slowly, relief seeping through her as the air passed through pursed lips.

"Is it really all over between the two of you?"

"Coming here made me see that I had just kind of fallen in with him, after everything that happened, I needed someone safe. Someone who would look after me and not care about my past. Owen happened to be that someone and at the time, security ranked far more important than happiness. I guess on reflection it was a way I could punish myself too you know. But we don't fit B. We never really have. The differences are stark when you dare look at them. He's better off without me, I can't love him in the way he deserves. It's time to set him free. He knows that." Her shoulders dropped as she gave Bernarde the explanation he deserved; the weight of the world lifted from her.

"Oh sweetie, I totally understand."

In her mind she could see Bernarde wrinkling up his nose as he spoke.

"So...does your bff get to see this fabulous pad you're living in at some point?" The usual fruity playfulness had returned to his voice now. "And if I can't meet this man in person, I need to see a picture of the fabulously buff Jack...and not just his face!"

Rambunctious laughter filled the space between them. The uncontrollable sounds that came with force from within left her belly sore, eyes full and cheeks smeared with happy tears. They say laughter is good for the soul and the way that everything had paled into the background, she understood how.

Exchanging goodbyes with Bernarde, or farewells as he liked to call them, *'goodbye is too final'* she used to hear him say to hotel guests, she promised to keep in touch with him if he promised not to tell Owen where she was or give him her new number to which he had declared *'scouts honour!'* To her knowledge, he'd never been a scout, prompting further giggles.

She placed the phone down on the mirrored top coffee table, reaching for the throw that she'd laid near gold ringed legs tucked between the recliners. Shaking it open, she wrapped the soft fabric around herself, gazing out of the folding glass doors at the shades of grey that still blotted the sky, hoping that the sun would find a way to burn its way through.

The heavy rain from earlier had driven most people indoors and the river was not the usual hive of activity it was known for. She fixed her attention on the fishing guys that were unloading their catch.

On the rigid frame of the woman with the clip-board, striking ticks on her white sheet of paper, unable to tell if she was impressed or not with what they had caught. She became so engrossed in their comings and goings that she hadn't noticed the face that was staring up at her.

The face that watched her every move.

Chapter 28

Owen

The ten minutes that Owen had spent staring at the screen before him, seemed like an eternity. His chewed fingertips tapped a nervous tune on the tabletop as he read the details of Paul's early release. He always knew this day would come. That he would never completely get away with what he had done. The hurt, the lies, the deceit. From that point forward, he had carefully designed a new life, shaped and moulded to enable him to have complete control of everything and everyone in it.

Almost.

All boxed and tied up, nice and neatly like a department store gift at Christmas. Perfect and appealing. Except now, the tightly tied ribbon had been yanked, causing the bow to unravel, beginning to reveal the hollow darkness inside. The past could never be changed but he had no regrets. He would never wish a life away but what was the use of having them, they were nothing but wasted energy. If he was to salvage anything of the life he had carefully created for himself, time was of the essence.

He switched from the glaring screen of the newspaper article to his email, retrieving the message that had yanked at the ribbon. Scanning the few words it contained, he found what he needed and pressed the digits of the telephone number into his phone. As it connected, he began to pace the floor, up and down, back and forth, waiting for the voice to answer.

"Hello." The voice was quiet, small.

"It's me. Owen."

"I did wonder how long it'd take you before calling me." The voice was no longer quiet. Or small. It was direct. Cold. Stabbing at the hairs on the back of his neck.

"So, he's out. What do you want me to do? What am I supposed to do? I told you before, I'm sorry. But it was years ago Sarah. We were years ago." He kicked the leg of the chair, sending it sideways as it fell. "For fuck's sake we were not much more than kids!"

A burning rage balled in his stomach, spreading through his body as rapid as bush fire. His free hand clenched, ready to strike out.

"Yes Owen, years ago. Years that Paul has lost. All because of you." Her voice remained cold, flat and direct. "Yes, he is out. And while I would be glad never to see you or your lousy face ever again, he wants to see you. He wants answers. Did you think for one minute that he wouldn't?"

"Sarah, please, what good can come of this?" Beads of sweat formed on his forehead. "Is it not better left in the past where it belongs?"

"While what happened is in the past Owen, what happens next has to be dealt with."

"How can you be so cold Sarah, after everything we shared. Did it not mean anything to you? I mean did Paul even know you were shagging me? We were at it day and night. Even in the same room as him on occasion. I'm sure he'd be interested to hear what we got up to." Owen was clutching at straws now; this wasn't something he couldn't win easily so had resorted to playing dirty.

Sarah's snort was as cold as her voice.

"Tut-tut-tut...Is that really the best you can come up with? Empty words Owen. We were off our faces, all of us. If Paul had of woken up, I'm sure he would've joined in given half the chance. Of course he knew about us. He was glad of the rest. Never could handle my insatiable appetite for sex." Her cackled laugh chilled Owen to the bone.

He was losing.

Fast.

"Meet us tomorrow. In Paignton at the Beach Cafe. One O'clock. Or sweet little kitty kat might have to find out the whole truth about her darling Owen."

The line went dead. She'd hung up, denying him the opportunity to answer. The only thing audible to him now was the thump thump thump of his heart against his chest. He threw the phone across the floor, an outlet for his despair.

He had to get to Kate and find out what she already knew.

Sooner rather than later.

Chapter 29

Kate

S he stirred; the corner of her half-opened eye fixed on the digits that glowered from the fancy gadget alarm clock radio. Five twenty-five was ridiculously early for her but if she got up now, she'd have plenty of time before her first day at Edmunds.

Rolling out the comfiest bed she was certain she'd ever slept in, she groaned, not wanting to leave it behind. Jack certainly had good taste, and expensive. The eight hundred thread count Egyptian cotton bedding with a hand stitched, slate grey silk border was just one of many testaments to that. Stretching out, she slid her feet into the open toe slippers she'd left by the bed.

Motion sensor floor lights softly illuminated her way as she shuffled through to the lounge, finding the remote to open the automated blinds that clothed the expansive full width glass doors. As they began to part, the sky was still pitch dark, not even a glimpse of the moon was visible, and it wouldn't begin to get light for at least another half an hour or so. The town across the river quiet and still, wrapped in the heavy cloak of the night. Without realising, she was now staring at the cream house that sat back up the hill. Her little girls' dolls house. A house that never displayed any sign of life. Ever.

Except now.

There was a light on.

She moved closer to the window, the faint orange hue flickering. But then it was gone. She scrunched her eyes shut, counting to three before looking again. The house stood drenched in darkness. No sign of any light, just the string of bulbs that festooned the fuel jetty, catching the water and reflecting out. She'd learnt as a child how water has a funny way of casting shadows and reflections, fooling you into seeing something that wasn't there. Another reason she disliked the rain. She backed away from the glass, the house becoming smaller.

She had seen a light.

Figuring out how to operate the shower hadn't been straight forward and by the time she'd prepared herself some breakfast, her tummy had grown impatient. She had just one more thing to do as she positioned it creatively on the breakfast bar, turning on her phone. She needed to take a photo and send it to Trish. Just to put her mind at rest that she was eating. As she sent it through, she laughed, remembering how she swore to all those that knew her that she would never be one of those people who photographed their food for social media. But this was different, she had no intention of showing the world.

Seconds later, a message pinged up on the screen.

'Good luck today sweetie! Don't forget your cedarwood! Love you Lots xxxxx'

She laughed again, appreciating Bernarde's sentiment and humour, startled by the buzz of the intercom.

"Hello?"

She could just about see the guy stood at the entrance door, most of him concealed by the ginormous flower bouquet he was holding.

"Delivery for a Kate Downes." Staccato words travelled through the speaker.

She checked the clock, twelve minutes past seven, surprised flowers could get delivered so early.

"Er, thank you. I'll just come down. Could you leave them in the entrance lobby for me please?"

"No problem Miss, someone is a very lucky lady."

As she walked down the stairs, several questions stirred about who they could be from. Who would be sending her flowers at this time in the morning? And more to the point, who knew she was here. It was either Uncle Billy and Trish, Bernarde or Jack. They were the only ones.

On sight of the bouquet, her heart skipped. It was even more ginormous than it had appeared on the small screen of the intercom. It really was exquisite. Laden with roses and ferns, peonies and hypericum berries, shades of delicate pinks against creams and green. Its weight surprising her as she bent down to pick it up. She opened the card that had been delicately positioned in between blooms so as not to damage them, baffled by what it held. There was no name, just a quote.

A quote she vaguely remembered. *Love. An ever-fixed mark that looks on tempests and is never shaken.*

She turned the card over, checking for a name. There was nothing. She repeated the cycle of reading the beautifully scribed words then flipping it over to the back, hoping to find some trace of the sender. She pushed the card into her trouser pocket, still no clearer as to who had sent them but they were beautiful, their scent perfumed the air around her as she climbed the stairs, a spring in every step.

Placing them in the centre of the kitchen island so they would be visible from most directions, she stood back, admiring the creativity of the florist who'd lovingly picked and tied them. Taking the card from her pocket, she read the words once more.

Shakespeare.

It was a line from one of Shakespeare's sonnets.

How could she have forgotten. The card fell from between her fingers, dancing in the air before hitting the porcelain floor tiles. The coolness freezing her bare feet to the spot. She didn't understand. Couldn't understand. But she would recognise it anywhere.

She managed to free her feet, the walk to the bedroom, heavy and laborious. Another motion sensor light lit up as she stepped inside the walk-in wardrobe, reaching up to the half empty shelf that housed the carrier bag. Pulling it down, she delved inside for the book. Her fingers trembled as she opened it up, searching for the loose piece of paper that it held tight between its pages. Casting the book to the side, she returned to the kitchen, her pace much quicker, leaning forward to pick up the discarded flower card. She lay them side by side, the only noticeable difference between them, other than the content was the background on which they were written. They had definitely been written by the same person. Each and every letter penned in the same unbroken curves. But how? Her mind raced, the question stuck like a fly trapped helplessly inside a spider's web. Her eyes, full of disbelief darted away from the writing, over to the flowers, wanting to pick them up and throw them out, cast them aside, but they were too beautiful. She held back, unable to do it.

There was no time to sort this out. Not now. She had to finish getting ready.

Her phone pinged, another text. This time from Trish. *'Good Luck today Kate and thank you. Enjoy!'*

Breakfast, shit. She'd forgotten about that. Her desire to eat had gone anyway, appetite replaced by nausea. She'd text her back later, let her know how her first day went.

But there was one person she did need to text before she did anything else and that was Marcel.

The bell above the shop rang loudly as she stepped into her first day of work.

"Good Morning my dear. Why the woeful face?"

Kate wasn't aware she had a woeful look on her face. She'd tried to put her concern from earlier to one side, not let it affect her first day, but clearly it hadn't worked. Her painted smile had not concealed anything and Mrs Clifford was sharp, able to see straight through it.

"There is nothing to worry yourself about now you go and put your things in the back." Her faced creased a little more as her mouth stretched into a smile. Although lined, it was still bright, a youthful energy shining from beneath it. "And dearie, put the kettle on, always the most important bit of the day. Milk and two sugars for me please. Oh, and use the teapot, I can't stand tea made in the cup." The glint in her eye told Kate they were going to get along just fine.

The morning passed by quickly as Mrs. Clifford took Kate through what she wanted doing, which in all honesty wasn't that much. Her main duties would be of course be assisting customers as and when required, cleaning and restoring a bit of order to the neglected shelves and last but not least, the most important task, tea. As the day went on, Kate got the feeling it was just as much company Mrs Clifford was in need of alongside an extra pair of hands. Although she hadn't made that much conversation, having someone around was sure to lessen the loneliness for her.

Arming herself with a couple of dusters, a can of beeswax polish and a soft paintbrush, Kate decided to make a start in the local history section. Not quite trusting yet of the ancient rolling library ladder, she positioned the slightly more modern stepladders at an angle to the shelves, allowing her to take down the books one by one and lay them on the oval table with minimal exertion. From the look of the dust trails, she was certain this was the first time the shelves had seen light in a very long time. She cleared the top two shelves in no time at all, wiping out the dust before giving them a good spritz with the polish, and a final wipe over. She turned her attention next to the books themselves, undecided as to the best way to rearrange them into some sort of order. She carefully wiped each book over, using the paintbrush when necessary on the older more fragile volumes. Settling on alphabetical order of the author, she arranged the cleaned books into makeshift piles, repeating the same process on the remaining four shelves.

With the books back in situ, she stood back, admiring her mornings work. The bookshelves now held a new lease of life, crying out for customers to reawaken their contents. The dark oak gleamed from its drink of beeswax; its grain highlighted as the light settled on them. Proud of her work, she enjoyed the sense of achievement and the contentment it brought. She thought of Owen, of him knowing what she was doing now, his sense of disappointment. To others she imagined it would be just a load of old books. To her they were living things. Nature repurposed and impressed with the words of another, whether fact of fiction. Something that could touch hearts, change lives and live on for many years. She didn't have to worry about what Owen would think anymore, the days of his quiet disapproval were gone.

Folding the step ladders, she turned ready to take them back to the kitchen come storeroom, clocking a book she'd left on the table. Propping the ladders up against the door frame, she picked it up, frowning. She'd checked the table twice and there were definitely no books left behind so where did this thick leather-bound one come from? She shook her head, it must her mind playing tricks again, just as it had that morning with the light in the house that she was sure had been on. She studied the cover of the book she held, an issue of The History of Dartmouth, the same book she pulled out when she came in the other day, just a different edition. She opened it, so lost in confusion that her shriek startled her just as much as the hand that squoze her shoulder.

"I'm so sorry dear, I didn't mean to make you jump. I called you a couple of times but couldn't get you to hear. I thought you might like some lunch as it's nearly one o'clock."

"Whoa, sorry I was miles away there. My Dad always said I was of a nervy disposition." She tried to make light of it. "Is it really that time already? I'd love some lunch. Silly me though forgot to bring some. I'll have to pop out if you don't mind. Would that be okay?"

She was rambling. A habit that reared when she didn't know the best thing to say. She put the book down on the table, aware of Mrs Clifford's eyes following her movements.

"No need to worry yourself dear, I have plenty enough for the both of us. Now be a dear and pop the sign round to closed."

Doing as she was told, she muttered coincidence to herself over and over again, keen to file it along with the rest of them.

"Righto then dear, come and sit yourself down." Mrs Clifford gestured to the chair opposite her at the small square dining table. It was a pretty impressive spread for lunch, not your usual cheese or ham sandwich. On the surface, she was a kind, elderly woman but Kate was twitchy, something wasn't quite right. But then what in her life was right. Or come to think of it really ever had been? Her Aunt had always told her to take people as you find them, something which she'd always found tricky living in her head, listening to the voice that had gained squatters rights there.

"Lost in your thoughts again dearie..." Mrs Clifford interrupted. "You know, try not to figure things out. Let them unfold as they shall, and the answers will become clear."

How did this woman know what she thinking?

"Don't worry yourself, I'm not reading your mind. I can just see the confusion nestled between your eyes."

She is most definitely reading your mind. The voice in her mind flooded her with uneasiness. Uneasiness which Kate hoped didn't show in her smile because silence was all she could offer.

"Righto, what are you tempted by then? I don't know about you but I for one am ravenous!"

Mrs Clifford selected several bits from the china plates and bowls, all neatly laid out on the crisp white tablecloth that covered the kitchen table. She handed Kate a sandwich plate.

"This is so kind of you Mrs Clifford. It all looks beautiful. I'm not sure where to start." Kate said, having managed to regain her voice and her manners.

"It is my pleasure dear. I do enjoy food but it becomes so very tiresome when you lay it out only for your own eyes to feast upon it." Her smile began to fade.

"You eat like this every day?" Kate's eyes widened; her jaw slightly ajar.

Mrs Clifford gave a little chuckle, the smile returning.

"I most certainly do. And so shall you if you wish to join me when you are here. Today's society have become very lazy when it comes to dining etiquette. Apparently," she clasped her hands together, resting them on the edge of the table, "it is because they are too busy to stop. Sandwiches on the go. Drinking from bottles. Beakers for coffee. It will be an evening meal out of cardboard next!" She shook her head, holding up her hands.

Kate couldn't help but giggle. If only she knew. She was of course right because Kate was one of those people. Stuffing something in quick and easy because she was so busy. But Kate had no intention of taking the conversation on this subject further or telling her you could indeed get your dinner served in a cardboard box.

"Well this is a real treat and I am very grateful." Kate took two of the finger sandwiches and a mini tartlet. "Thank you."

She was not exaggerating when she said it was a real treat, it was so relaxing. They had made a deal that in the future, Mrs Clifford would lay out and Kate would tidy away. Her offer of contributing towards the food was point blank refused with no more to be said on the matter.

She liked Mrs Clifford's directness, her no nonsense manner. You always knew where you stood with people like that. If there was something to say, it would be said and then things move on. Kate bore witness to this as she went back into the shop.

Mrs Clifford resumed her position behind the counter; palms laid flat over the escaped book. "I want you to take this book home with you dearie, it might hold some answers for you. There is no such thing as a coincidence you know. I'll leave it here for you so you don't forget to take it at the end of the day." She lifted the glasses that hung down from the gold chain, positioning them in the middle of her nose. "Now, off you go, those shelves wont sort themselves out."

Although devoid of customers, the afternoon came and went in the blink of an eye and closing time soon came around. The book on the counter was now in Kate's bag but she had no idea what answers it would give her, let alone the questions in the first place. So, not wanting to appear ungrateful, she did as she was told.

Leaving the shop and Mrs Clifford behind for the day, memories of the last few months began to fade, becoming insignificant. She'd had a rare opportunity handed to her, stirring up a pot of excitement peppered with nerves. For the first time ever, she was heading home to an empty flat, on her own, in circumstances which were fully in her control.

But she wouldn't be alone for long.

Chapter 30

Owen

The drive to Paignton had taken much longer than Owen had either expected or accounted for. The stop start of the traffic fuelled the apoplexy that had been borne from yesterday's phone call to Sarah. He checked the time, ten past twelve. With five miles left to go, he questioned whether he'd make it in time.

The car continued to crawl at a snail's pace through the queues of traffic. He'd planned to call Bernarde when he reached Paignton but now, he wouldn't have the time. He turned the music down, asking the car to "Call Bernarde."

One ring. Two. Three.

"Pick up Bernade...come on."

Impatience tapped away inside him, the gear stick on the receiving end as he willed him to answer.

Voicemail. He hung up and tried again. Finally, on the fifth ring, Bernarde answered.

"Owen...hi."

"Bernarde listen. I haven't got long but I really need you to tell me where Kate is."

"No Owen, I promised her. She doesn't want to see

you. Now please don't ask me to break her confidence. She needs time that's all. I've already told you, she's safe." Bernarde kept his tone neutral.

"For God's sake just tell me!" Owen slammed his hand down on the steering wheel, his aggression pushing Bernarde further away.

"Stop. Just stop. Accept that she doesn't want to see you and accept that I am not going to tell you."

"I have to find her before..." Owen broke off. Unable to finish. Anguish tearing him in two. If he had said what he wanted, *before...they do*, another can of worms would have been opened and he would have had to tell Bernarde who *they* were. The less people that knew the better. No, there had to be another way of finding her.

He heard Bernarde's voice. "Before what?"

"It doesn't matter. Just promise me that you will look out for her. She doesn't have anyone else. For God's sakes just do as I ask for once."

Bernarde had eventually promised he would do as Owen had asked. After all, he was Kate's best friend and whatever was going on, he didn't want to see her hurting any more than she already had.

He finally pulled into the car park just after half past twelve. Turning off the ignition, he unclipped his seat belt and sank back into the chair, letting the weight of his eyelids fall down, shutting out the business around him. He wasn't prepared for this. Wasn't prepared for the past to stand before him. To confront him. Thoughts of what he should say and how to deal with it scrambled around in his head, all weaving around the image of Kate. No matter what had happened and what she felt about him now, he couldn't let her be dragged into all this. She was fragile enough. If she found out about all of this, it would break her, shatter her beyond repair and he didn't want that, for either of them. After all these years, the sense of duty he once felt had turned into something more. Something he had never bargained for.

Love.

He loved her with all his heart and he would always be there for her, no matter what.

His phone chimed. A text. From Sarah. He knew he had to open it. He checked the time. He wasn't late. It was still only twelve forty-one.

Change of plan, meetings off. I'll be in touch. BTW Kates looking class!

"Bastards!!" He grabbed the steering wheel with both hands, his knuckles white from the intensity of his grip. His rigid body moved backwards and forwards, in slow motion, trying to pacify the venomous snake spiralling within him, to contain it. The anger he felt showed him one thing though. And that was that he would do whatever he had to do to protect Kate.

Protect her from ever knowing.

From ever finding out who he really was.

And from knowing what really happened to Mark.

Chapter 31

Kate

"Hi, come on in." Kate held the door open wide, allowing Marcel to enter the hallway.

"Hi, so this is the new pad eh?" Marcel was already unravelling the heavy fringed scarf that she'd stylishly wrapped around her neck.

"It is," Kate said, closing the door behind her, "I still can't believe it if I'm honest. Go on straight through."

"Wow Kate, this is magnificent!" Marcel turned full circle, almost bouncing on her feet as she entered the living space.

Leaving her to marvel in its opulence a few moments longer, Kate fetched a cold bottle of chardonnay and two glasses, taking them over to the coffee table between her favourite seats. Feeding the scarf into her oversized handbag, Marcel joined her, making full use of the footstool.

"So then, what's this all about?" Marcel took the wine glass Kate held out. "Your text sounded pretty urgent this morning."

Kate took a large swig of the wine, hoping it would

help her start.

"Did you see the flowers?"

"One could not miss them darling!" Marcel did a fantastic mock posh voice. "They are simply fabulous!"

"Fabulous they may be Marcel but I have no idea who sent them. And what's more, let me show you the card that came with them." Kate marched off to the bedroom, bringing back with her both the flower card and the note.

"There, look at that," she said, handing over the card.

"Love. An ever-fixed mark that looks on tempests and is never shaken. That's Shakespeare isn't it?"

"It is." Kate finished the dregs of her glass, swiftly refilling. "But do you not notice anything familiar with it?"

Marcel stared from the card to Kate then back to the card. She knew. Her face dripped with understanding. She clicked her pointed red nail against the glass, taking her feet from the footstool.

"What is going on Marcel? I mean...how?"

"Show me the note Kate." Marcel held out her palm.

Kate passed it over to her, her eyes not moving as Marcel held them side by side.

"Does this actual quote mean anything to you?"

"Yes. I guess in a way it does." Kate looked down into her glass. "Remember I told you about Mark? Well he loved the works of Shakespeare. He wanted to teach it. That quote was on a fridge magnet I had bought for him one Christmas. Why do you ask?"

It had never once crossed Kate's mind that there could be any connection to Mark but now Marcel had asked, her mind thrust into overdrive.

Marcel had sandwiched both the card and note between her flat hands. Her furrowed forehead indicative that her closed eyes were searching for something. She let out a deep breath, her voice not quite her own.

"Firstly, when you look closer, they are not of the same hand, although you could be forgiven for thinking they were. But something is telling me Kate that the past is not as it seems. There are secrets. Deeply buried secrets that are wanting to be told. And they want you to tell them. It is time to put things right. Hmm." She opened her eyes, her familiar voice returned. "I need you to tell me if anything else out of the ordinary happens, okay?"

"Is that it?" Kate couldn't help but be so blunt. After all she'd come down here to get away, leave the past behind. How then could she have a fresh start if she was supposed to be sharing secrets?

Marcel sat forward, placing both the card and note on the coffee table. "Kate, listen. I have no idea why you but I am here with you. Come what may. You're not on your own with this."

A taciturn nod was all Marcel was getting.

The silence that filled the air was thick but untroubled as they both sat gazing out across the river. Both retreating back into their own inner worlds.

Marcel was the first to leave.

"Kate, do you know that person down there? On the embankment near the bench. They've been looking up here for a little while now."

"Nope. Never seen before. Probably looking up in envy, I know I would." She'd only briefly looked at the figure, her mind already full with more important things to question. Certain that many people would sit on that bench and look up in wonder.

"Hmmm probably." Her hesitant smile unnoticed by Kate who was still looking down on the embankment, watching as the person moved on, their silhouette outlined from the overhead lights.

"I don't think you should be here alone Kate."

"Oh come on Marcel! Why ever not?"

"Call it whatever you like. I can't explain it but something is niggling away at me that you shouldn't be here alone."

There was a seriousness to her tone which Kate hadn't heard before, a gentle warning that her gut knew to believe but her mind was reluctant to. It had to be the wine talking. There was no plausible reason why she shouldn't be there alone.

Marcel swung her legs round, resting her glass down on the table, clutching her hands together under her chin. "Listen. I know it might all sound a bit odd ok, and not what you want to hear, but... I have to tell you what I feel. What I pick up on." Her eyes were almost apologetic, waiting for Kate to accept.

Following suit and resting her glass down too, Kate swung her legs round, mirroring Marcel before she answered. "A *bit* odd? I'd say more than a bit. Do you *always* listen to these feelings?"

Marcel nodded slowly, eyebrow raised, the accompanying smile hard to read. Part apologetic, part sympathetic, glued together with something unknown to Kate. Unsure of what to say or what to do, she struggled to maintain eye contact, it had become too uncomfortable. The spark inside her flickering, corroborating Marcel's words.

"I think it's perhaps time I was heading home Kate." Marcel began wrapping the fringed scarf around her neck. "Thank you for the wine and I am sorry if I have upset you." She held open her arms.

Her embrace was warm. Comforting. Needed.

"Confused me maybe but definitely not upset me." Kate grinned, wanting to reassure her.

"Right, you know where I am if you need me. Anytime." She leant forward, planting a farewell kiss on Kate's cheek.

Kate promised she would, thanking her for the company as she showed her to the door. Just about to step out into softly lit corridor, Marcel turned on her heels.

"And Kate...think about what I said...please."

Rolling.
Rolling, tumbling, rolling.
Panic.
A whirlwind of flashing light.
Distorted noises.
Panic.

Chapter 32

Kate

Despite Marcel's concern hanging heavy as she went to bed, Kate had slept well after her brief dream, waking refreshed and ready to take on the day. As she wasn't needed at Edmunds today, she'd allowed herself a slow start to the morning.

Nothing to do, nowhere to be and no one to interrupt her, heaven.

It was a pretty miserable day outside again, the sky low with its thick sullied blanket of cloud, dulling the colour of everything in sight. It was hard to believe that the sun was behind there somewhere. Thankful she had no need to go out in it, she turned on the small table lamps that were strategically dotted around the apartments grand open plan living space, the book that Mrs Clifford had suggested she take home sat on top of the sideboard next to the last one.

The book she knew she had not missed.

Her mind remembering the old lady's words. '*I want you to take this book home with you dearie, it might hold some answers for you. There is no such thing as a coincidence.*'

She picked up the book, *The History of Dartmouth,* figuring there was nothing to lose by looking through it. Snuggling down with the faux fur throw on the sofa, she tucked it under her feet that were drawn up to the side of her. Tracing her fingers over the patterned front of the hardback, she gently levered open the front cover, skirting over its table of contents. Nothing jumped out at her.

She looked again, slower this time. There were sections on Dartmouth and Kingswear during various wars. Details of the first recorded Regatta, the opening of the Floating Bridge and Queen Victoria's visit with her family in royal yachts. All the usual topics that one would expect to be covered in a history book.

Readying her fingers to start randomly flicking through the pages, a title caught her eye, holding her fingers back. The Llewellyn Family. The name sounded familiar but she couldn't recall why. She turned to page two hundred and forty-five - The Llewellyn Family. She read through the introduction, how the Llewellyns had been a prominent family in Dartmouth and Kingswear with the first records of the name dating back to 1752. The last records show that Mr and Mrs Llewellyn had been resident here until 1933 when a tragic end had befallen them both. Mr Llewellyn had been found to have taken his own life when the ancillary staff had attended him for breakfast on the morning of the 25th July. Just eight weeks after his wife had died.

This might not have been her usual read but she

was enthralled. Tragic yet intriguing like a novel you can't put can't down. Only this was real life. Or had been. She turned the page, desperate to read more. But the pages were full of pictures, not words, snapshots of history brought to life. An annual staff photograph from the turn of the century, all looking neat and smart in their smocks. Mr Llewellyn as a young boy, stood proudly presumably by his father at the grand opening of the Britannia Naval College in 1905. There was one of Mrs Llewellyn at a luncheon taken in 1931. High society ladies all dressed in their finery, tiny petite things. She pulled the book closer to look at the image, drawn to the woman taking centre stage, the grace and beauty she exuded was palpable, even through paper. Her eyes flitted over to the next page, keen to see what awaited them. It was the house on hill. The house that had filled her with such wonderment as a little girl. Her castle on the hill. Now here it sat. An image captured, locked in time and connected to The Llewellyn family. The caption beneath it simply read, 'Moundhill House, empty, 1934.'

She looked away from the page, throwing her gaze up to see the real image of what she now knew was called Moundhill House. There it stood, lonely and isolated. It was all beginning to make sense now. That's why she, or no one she knew had never seen any life there. That's why its presence drew you in. The intrigue of a lonely, empty house.

She moved the heavy book from her lap, stretching out her legs before moving to the window to get a closer look at Moundhill House. She wondered why no one had ever called it by its name, instead always referring to it as the house on the hill. A beautiful house nestled amongst trees, cradling its secrets tight. A house she imagined had once been awash with love and laughter, parties and social functions. A house that had met a tragic end. Vacant of life. Inhabited now only with memories of a distant past. Even from this distance, the sadness that emanated from its rendered facade was palpable, calling to her, closing in around her. Her sigh was loud, drawn out, in hope that the sadness would leave with her breath. But the invisible pull would not allow her to forget, wanting her to look, wanting her to feel.

Coffee.

She would go and make a coffee.

That would take her eyes and her attention away and place them both on something else.

In the kitchen she made purposeful movements back and forth, talking to herself as she made each one. For a cup, then a spoon, coffee and then the milk. Back again to the cupboard where she had stashed her biscuits. The weight was lifting. By the time she had made her coffee and taken out far more biscuits than she needed, the welcome sound of a text alert had distracted her further still. Taking both back through to the lounge, she kept her eyes low, careful not to even glimpse in that direction, not wanting to step back inside its sad story.

With the book tucked away on the sideboard, she

took her phone, eager to see who the message was from.

Bernarde.

Trust him to have impeccable timing.

'Hey sweetie, listen, I need to speak to you. Can you give me a call when you get this? Lots of Love XXX'

The involuntary smile took over her face as she read the message again. Bernarde could light up a room even when he wasn't in it. She'd call him back now.

The best place to get a signal that would hold was by the balcony. Still intent on not looking up the river, she shifted position to face the opposite direction.

It wasn't long before he picked up. "Hey sweetie, thanks for calling back"

"No problem B, what's up?"

"Now, I don't want you worrying but I have had Owen on the phone again. He was kind of strange if I'm honest."

"Strange? How? What did he say?" Kate's hand covered the hollow of her neck.

"He was asking again for me to tell him where you were. I insisted that you didn't want to see him and he needed to move on but he was almost begging me by then and... well then he said something odd. *'I really need to speak to her before...'* but he never finished. I asked him before what but he wouldn't tell me. He just made me promise that I would look after you." The seriousness of Bernarde's tone began to soften. "I didn't know whether to tell you or not sweetie but I couldn't sleep a wink last night and I can't afford any wrinkles to be setting in on this beautiful canvas now, can I?"

Their laughter was equal.

Some people never understood his dry sense of humour but Kate loved his unique knack of always making her smile, regardless.

Her hand dropped to her hip. "It's Owen just being melodramatic B. He's not used to not getting his own way and doesn't like being told no. He never has."

"That's what I thought at first but...well now I'm not so sure. I mean why would he ask me to look after you? Hang on, you are okay...aren't you?" An air of panic skimmed down the line.

An air that brought Marcel's words from last night straight to the front of Kate's mind.

"Kate...are you still there?"

"Sorry, just thinking that's all. Listen, you know you said you wanted to come down and see me. When do you next have some time off?"

"Well sweetie as it happens, I am currently off. You remember Peter and I were supposed to be taking a long holiday together, well his mother is back in hospital and this time it's looking like she won't make it. So, I'm yours anytime you want me."

"But won't Peter need you there with him? I mean...what if his mother does...you know?"

"The word you're looking for is die and it's just a formality. You know they hadn't spoken to one another for years. No, Peter's fine, honestly." Bernarde assured her that everything was okay and if Peter did mind, he would tell her, otherwise she would see him on Monday.

She held the phone against her chest long after Bernarde had hung up, staring out into the distance. A flash of light had managed to puncture the dense grey blanket, lightening it by just a shade. It caught the still water and she followed the reflection across to where it ended on the embankment. To the bench. To the person who was sat there, looking up, straight at her. Her body stiffened. Although she couldn't clearly see a face, this had to be the same person from yesterday. The one Marcel had asked if she knew.

There's no such thing as coincidence.

She took a couple of steps back so she was no longer in full view, concealing herself against the wall. But she could still see them. Concealed by a baggy dark tracksuit, it was hard to determine whether it was a male or female. Whoever it was just sat there. Not imagined. Real. Looking up at her. Edging away from the window completely, she pressed back hard against the wall, aware her breath had become shallower.

Last night she had brushed it off, an envious on-looker. But they were looking up at her, even from that distance she could tell. But she had no idea who it was or why they had taken an interest her.

She tapped the phone against her chest, unsure what to do. She forced herself to leave the wall, she had to get to the bedroom, away from prying eyes. Moving swiftly, she glanced sideways to the window as she passed, half wanting to know if they were still looking up. But whoever it was had gone.

In the bedroom, she sat, pushing her palms down hard onto the bed, keen to stop the trembling. It was her just her crazy mind going into overdrive again.

Then she heard it.

The pounding.

The heavy pounding that was coming from the door.

But it was impossible.

No-one could get through the main door without using the intercom. Without being buzzed in. So how was someone outside, banging on the apartment door. She felt as trapped as the breath that sat in her, desperate to escape but nowhere other than this room to escape to. A torrent of thoughts crashed around in her mind. How? Why? What? Had she traded in one crazy life for another?

The loud repetitive bangs bounced off the walls as the knocking continued.

Bang. Bang. Bang.

Whoever it was knew she was there. There were not going to go away. And that left her with no choice. She had to answer the door.

Each step she made was heavy and cumbersome, slow like man on the moon. Her phone was at the ready, Uncle Billy's number ready to dial in just one press.

Just in case.

Sliding the spyhole cover to one side as quietly as she could, she held her breath, not wanting to alert whoever it was that she was now on the other side of the door. She leaned forward, her eye meeting the glass.

Deep furrows set across her forehead, her eye searched left to right then back again.

But all she could see was an empty hallway.

Because there was no-one there.

And the rain began.
Gathering momentum with each passing second.
They ran.
Danced.
Laughed.
Sheltered.
Under the canopy.
Out of sight.
Clothes sodden, soaked through to the skin.
But it didn't matter.
They were alive.
They were in love.
A shared love warmer than the summer
rain that poured down around them.

Chapter 33

Kate

Confusion had been with her all night, sharing her bed, encroaching on her space and showed no sign of lessening as she left the apartment for work.

The sharp cool air was a welcome hit as she stepped outside. She had only slept briefly, fighting her troubled mind throughout the rest of the night and as a consequence, she was lethargic. She'd tossed and turned against flashes of what's and why's that intruded the silence space. But when sleep did come, it wasn't restful for it was occupied with a dream. A peculiar dream that she could remember from start to finish. Made even more peculiar because she had not dreamt properly since she'd been a little girl. Whatever was happening was not going to take over her and she knew keeping her nerves in check would be hard work.

She just didn't comprehend how hard.

By the time she had reached Edmunds, the lethargy had begun to ease and she welcomed the refuge that waited within its walls.

Mrs Clifford was her usual upbeat self and Kate was

allayed that she had not been subjected to any questioning or wise words on her arrival, nor when she brought out the tea. As well-meaning as she was, today Kate could do without it. And do without it she would as Mrs Clifford informed her that she would be out until lunchtime.

The morning passed by uneventful and she had managed to dust and reorder the cookery section in next to no time, immersing her attention on the job in hand. As the last few books were put back in their new place, the shop bell jingled its tune.

"Just a minute," Kate shouted, keen to let the customer know there was someone in the shop.

Backing down the steps, she brushed down her trousers and straightened her blouse, ensuring she was free from dust before presenting herself.

"Hi Kate!"

Jack was the very last person she expected to be stood in front of her.

"Jack! Hi!" A blush crept up her neck. "I don't understand. I thought you were away for three months?"

"Long story I'm afraid. I popped round last night but you couldn't have been in."

The temperature of the blush increased, rising rapidly to colour her cheeks now. What a fool! She couldn't tell him the truth. Instead she made up a story about being in the bath. Unsure whether she was convincing enough or not she changed the subject.

"So, what brings you here?"

What a stupid question. He was back and wanted his apartment back, that was what had brought him here. Inwardly cringing at her own naivety, she forced out a smile.

"Well..." The short pause seemed to last an age. "I wondered... if you might like to go out, to dinner, with me?"

"Yes!" The word exploded without any hesitation.

She could've kicked herself for blurting out like that, for sounding too keen. Too late now. Her belly was far too busy doing flips to worry about that.

"Great. How about this evening? That's if...you're not busy already?"

"No, no, this evening's good."

"Shall I pick you up around seven thirty?"

"I'll look forward to it."

"Me too. Until tonight then."

Her insides ached long after he had left the shop and she was still sat in the chair, miles away in her own world when Mrs Clifford came back.

"Penny for them dearie."

"Hmm? Sorry, what was that?" Kate had registered the voice but not the words.

"I said penny for them. Your thoughts."

"Oh, nothing. Just a restless night catching up with me that's all." Kate hated lying to her but she reasoned that it was, in part the truth.

Eager to change the direction of topic and aware it was nearing lunchtime, Kate headed for the kitchen, "I'll pop the kettle on, shall I?"

∞∞∞

The afternoon had stretched out and Kate had
seen every minute of it pass by. At least that's what
it felt like. Mrs Clifford had not probed any further,
her usual sharpness masked by a shroud of preoccu-
pation, spilling out and straining the atmosphere.
Kate had seen her only once throughout the afternoon and again at closing, not knowing her well
enough to ask if everything really was 'just fine'.

Her terse expression and the earlier than usual
closure of the shop was enough to show Kate it
wasn't though.

Only after Mrs Clifford had removed the key from
the heavy mortice lock and placed it firmly in her
handbag, did Kate leave her. As they parted company, it was impossible not to notice that the
usual twinkle in her eyes was absent, replaced by a
heavy brow that fell down to meet the sudden grey
shadows of her undereye.

In the time had taken Kate to reach the apartment,
she had appeased herself that Mrs Clifford was most
likely feeling under the weather or a little tired.
Everyone was entitled to an off day and she mustn't
forget her age. If she was still not quite herself to-

morrow, she decided she would make it her business to check everything was okay and if there was anything she could do to help if it wasn't. For today though, there was nothing else she could do.

Her attention deftly swung on to the evening. And Jack. The bubbling excitement that she had managed to keep contained throughout the afternoon now oscillated up and down, side to side. She was as giddy as a goat and when whatever it was that continued to build inside of her reached the full line, it found its outlet through the short bursts of spontaneous laughter she found herself having. She couldn't believe her luck. Jack was most girls dream. Full of old-fashioned charm and chivalry, he epitomised movie star perfection. And he was interested in her.

She had pinched herself several times to ensure that she wasn't dreaming as she patiently waited for seven thirty to come, but no, it was real enough.

When the soft rapping came, she hung back for a few seconds, not wanting to appear like she'd been waiting by the door. Exactly what she had been doing ever since just gone seven, sat on the edge of the sofa nearest the hallway, but he didn't need to know that. Reaching out to unlock the door, the flutters in her fingers brought an understanding of what a school girl crush must feel like.

And she was going to relish every single bit of it.

Chapter 34

Frances

A rush of both warmth and light flooded out into the drab evening as Frances Clifford opened the door, highlighting the worry that was etched across the fragile skin of her face.

"Marcel my dear, please, come in."

In the sitting room, the old lady took the decanter from the sideboard along with two cut glass crystal sherry glasses. "For my nerves," she insisted, pouring out the pale straw-coloured liquid.

Marcel had known Frances for the latter part of thirty years and it was she, that was in part the reason why she had gone on to nurture her gifts into a way of life. A career. Inheriting her Aunt's estate when she had passed away unexpectedly had brought Marcel down to Dartmouth at the age of just nineteen. With the last surviving relative gone, she had found herself in a place she could never have anticipated. The relationship with her Aunt had been somewhat unusual. An eccentric lady who Marcel had seen only three times in her nineteen years, one of which was her christening so that really didn't count. With no interest in visits or telephone calls, the only contact they had was through a yearly letter to each other, usually at some point during the festive season. The news of her death had come as a surprise for there had never been any mention that she was in poor health.

The death certificate had simply stated heart failure.

Where some would have been overjoyed at being the sole beneficiary of such a vast amount, to Marcel, it was the complete opposite. A heavy ball and chain of responsibility wrapped tightly around her young ankle. For she discovered that a covenant had been placed in the deeds that stated the house could never be sold while there was a blood relative living, and to complicate things further, a stipulation of the will was that Marcel could not gain access to the money unless she moved into the house. At the time there was no way round it, she had had to move to Dartmouth and start a new life.

As the months had passed by, she had grown more and more depressed. Dreams of forging a career in fashion faded fast as she'd had to give up on her degree. The increasing pressure of being away from the life she had wanted to make coupled with sorting out both the will and the estate took its toll on her. Encased with anguish, she was convinced her Aunt's house was haunted, terrified to stay there alone. Plagued by what was happening, there was nowhere to turn and she had no one to confide in. Finally, the isolation and torment that dominated her every moment became too much.

She had taken herself off to the beach one evening, resigned that the only way forward to was let the waves consume her. But something stopped her. An unseen force that had interrupted the mental preparations leaving a tangible offering in its place.

It was leaving the beach that evening when she and Frances Clifford met.

What followed was months, if not years of nurturing as Frances took Marcel under her wing. A strong woman who dismissed nothing and believed anything was possible. Someone who showed her there was no such thing as coincidence. Over time, Marcel began to embrace that she was a natural empath, a lightworker of sorts and that everything that she had ever experienced were small cogs in the wheel of preparation for things to come. The two of them became close and over time, an unbreakable bond forged and Frances Clifford mentored Marcel in everything she knew on the subject of metaphysics.

From thereon in, Marcel began to flourish.

"You look troubled Frances."

The shadows beneath Frances Clifford's eyes an indicator that foreboding had superseded sleep.

"Marcel my dear, I am deeply concerned. I knew this day would come but I fear it is all happening at too quick a pace."

Mrs Clifford, or Frances as she was known to only a

few, sipped on her sherry slowly. "She is such a beautiful soul but I fear she is not yet ready to experience what is to befall her."

"But what can we do Frances? We both know we cannot control time or the rate in which these things play out." Marcel fiddled with the tassel of her scarf.

"I fear there is nothing neither you nor I can do Marcel, other than to be freely available to her when…"Frances swallowed the last of the golden liquid from her glass, unable to find the words to finish. She rose, needing a refill, holding out the decanter towards Marcel, a silent offering of more.

As she positioned her thin frame back down on the chesterfield suite, it was the first time Marcel had ever seen Frances look her age. Now, against the rich emerald green of the sofa's fabric, her once rosy complexion looked whitewashed, inner worry sucked away to leave behind a drawn, dehydrated face. Her usual impeccable posture had given in to slouched rounded shoulders, the burden too heavy to hold.

She took another swallow and looked up. "We need to keep a close eye on her, a very close eye. Impress on her that she can share anything at all with us, night or day."

Marcel nodded, suspended in her own thought as Frances continued.

"Because if what I am being led to believe is correct, she is going to need all the help she can muster to get through this. And we are the only ones who can give it to her."

The two of them sat in silence, both knowing the enormity of what was to come, their biggest challenge yet. The last thread to add to the weave.

Only Marcel had no idea.

"There is one more thing Frances," Marcel said. "I heard news today that Paul has been released."

Chapter 35

Kate

Their evening had been delightful.

Good food, good drink and good company. The conversation flowed and Kate was completely at ease being with him. The perfect gentleman, text-book definition and more beyond. There was undeniably something between them. But it was a fission of something that extended far beyond the initial physical attraction two people felt when first meeting, something that was simply indescribable.

An unspoken feeling, a knowing, they both shared.

As the door to the outside world had closed, he leant in, stealing a kiss from her ready lips. The kisses as soft as his lips as he pressed them against hers, his tongue teased as he pulled them away, his stare hungry, matching her own primal desire that pulsed inside her. It had been so long since she had been touched, even held in this way. Unable to control the throb, she leant in too, pressing her lips against his. His hands grabbed her waist, effortlessly lifting her, her legs wrapped tightly around him as he carried her with ease through to the bedroom.

He was confident, considerate.

Neither of them spoke, knowing without words that this time, this was what they both wanted.

Each move he made blended effortlessly into the next and it wasn't long before they were naked. He drove her back into the bed, his tongue tracing the outline of her nipple, a sound of pleasure escaped her lips. His soft fingers snaked her body, the tiny hairs standing on end as they passed. Her own aching body melted into his, a perfect fit, locked in time as they became one.

She had never experienced anything like it. Her whole body was alive, wired. He had awoken something in her that she never knew existed. This was more than just lust; it went far beyond anything remotely comprehensible. There was no him and no her but a flawless unison of energy, bonded together so that they were one.

They both lay on their backs, the rise and fall of their chests gentle and synchronised as they looked out into the expanse of black that coated the night sky, hiding the stars beyond. The only light came from the moon and the faint twinkle of boat lights moored up along the jetty, the water bouncing them back up into the dark where tangled thoughts of happiness and regret hung.

From the moment she had set eyes on Jack, a part of her had come alive. A part which she thought she had buried with Mark all those years ago. But tonight, it had been restored and she was high on the drug of happiness, not wanting it to end.

But all good things came to an end, didn't they?

The happiness that engulfed her though was marred with regret. Regret because she had vowed never to allow herself to be so open to hurt again. To have her whole world ripped from under her. All the years spent with Owen had been her insurance policy against this. Being with him was easy, safe. He would always be there for her but she was anything but content. She had never loved him. Just needed the security that being with him had offered. But a floodlight had been shone down, exposing it for what it was and she had cashed in that policy, leaving her vulnerable to her own emotions.

She rolled onto her side, oblivious that Jack was already on his, propped up on one elbow studying her.

"Okay?" It was no more than a whisper as he smoothed the hairs away from her cheek.

She smiled, too scared to answer.

He brought his face closer, the warmth of his lips against her forehead dissolving the regret, re-igniting her earlier happiness. He rolled onto his back, held out his arm and pulled her in close to him, bare skin next to bare skin once more. The steady rhythm of his heart comforted her. Happiness seemed too fickle a word to describe how she felt in that moment, it was more than that.

Much more.

And it wouldn't be long before she found out why.

Chapter 36

Kate

T he empty space that she lay next to stabbed at her heart. It was too good to be true. She knew last night but she also knew how desperate she was to feel connection at that level again. And desperation had won that battle. Her eyes scoured the bedside cabinets for a note but there was nothing. He had just upped and left. Now, in the cold hard face of reality, she had to see it for what it was. A one night stand.

Sex.

Stupidity smacked her in the face, reminding her that he could have the pick of any female he should choose. Why did she think she was anything special? The thought of having to face him at some point gave way to a creeping shame. She had no idea what the hell she would she say to him. He might be used to one-night stands but she certainly wasn't. There was no point in trying to figure it out, she would have to deal with it when the time came.

Throwing back the duvet, she tried to push the regrets to the back of her mind, its resident voice reminding her that she could have chosen not to be so easily charmed. Could've chosen not to hand herself on a plate.

Maybe he had text her. But her phone was in her bag, in the hallway where she had dropped it last night. Images raced around as she wrapped the dressing gown around her, suddenly ashamed of her nakedness.

But if he hadn't text then what next?

She had absolutely no idea.

Opening the bedroom door, shame was soon replaced by surprise as voices travelled down the hallway from the lounge.

Familiar voices.

"Hey sweetie!" Bernarde stood up, arms wide open as Kate ambled through. "What time do you call this?"

"Oh my God...Bernarde!"

She flung herself into his arms, speechless, unable to form coherent thoughts let alone words.

"When did you...How... how did you get in here?"

"I let him in."

She hadn't seen Jack in the kitchen.

"We thought we'd let you sleep in and I wanted to hear all about you from Bernarde."

"Don't worry sweetie, I have only told him the good bits, and...I have kept my hands to myself!" Even the sound of Bernarde's cheeky giggle couldn't pierce through the bubble she'd found herself in.

"Come and sit down Kate, you've gone very pale." Slipping his arm around her waist, Jack guided her over to the sofa.

"It's the shock of me!" Bernarde's hands flailed around him. "I have that effect on many people."

Kate rubbed her hands hard over her face and wondered if she was in fact still asleep. But no, she was definitely awake. Awake and surprised. And with each sip of the coffee that Jack had made for her, she began to feel more awake.

Bernarde, perceptive as ever, asked if he could use the bathroom to freshen himself up. Jack offered to show him to the room where he would be staying, complete with its own large en-suite and told him to make himself at home, no rush. Giving Kate a cheeky wink as he passed, Bernarde tootled on behind him.

With Bernarde settled, Jack re-joined Kate on the sofa.

"Morning beautiful." He planted a welcome kiss on her forehead

He was genuine, honest, smiling with the whole of his body and a pang of guilt tore at her for thinking he was anything other.

"Morning." Her feeble smile didn't go unnoticed.

"You thought..." he teased her; his lips pressed hers in between his words, "I'd done... a runner... didn't... you!"

He knew. Was she that easy to read? She couldn't lie to him; he didn't deserve it.

"Just for a moment, when I woke up. I hold my hands up...Yes, I did. I'm sorry Jack."

His hand moved under her chin, tipping it up slowly so that she had to look at him. She'd been here before.

"Kate look at me and listen. Never say you are sorry. Not to me, ever. I can't explain it but, you do things to me. I feel things no one has ever even come close to making me feel before. When I am with you, something happens, and if I'm honest with you..." he leant in closer, "it scares the absolute hell out of me."

He waited, wanting some sort of response.

Did she tell him she felt the same? Fully surrender that insurance policy? If she could pause that moment and run to Bernarde, she'd ask him what she should do. But she had no magic button and she had seconds to choose.

"I...I...get it..." her words stuttered at first. "I feel the same and I don't understand it either. I know this will sound cheesy but it's like I feel complete when I am with you. Like..." her words trailed off; afraid he might laugh.

"Like what Kate? Tell me."

There is no such thing as coincidence.

"Like...we were meant to meet. Are to meant to be. I know it sounds crazy but I can't help it." She shrugged, her insurance policy well and truly gone. "That's how I feel."

"I think you have put my thoughts into perfect words."

He couldn't resist the fullness of her lips, pressing his own against them. The kiss was slow, intentional as their lips lingered together.

He pulled away. "Does this mean we are..." His

words broke off leaving the question unfinished.

She knew what he was asking, her heart ready to burst through her ribs with utter joy.

"Ooooh...let me think..." Unable to help herself, she teased, wanting to hold on to that moment for as long as she could.

He leant forward, the weight of his body driving her backwards, down on the sofa as their kisses mixed with giggles, light and carefree.

"You Kate Downes, have made me...one extraordinarily happy man!" He nuzzled into her neck, each kiss adding to their pleasure.

Bernarde's eccentric tones filled the gap between their laughter. "Get a room you two...For goodness sake!"

Jack pushed himself up, his toned arms outstretched to pull Kate up too. "I think we already did."

∞∞∞

Morning soon folded to afternoon as Kate showered and dressed. Jack had gone out, business to attend to, leaving her plenty of time to catch up with Bernarde before they all met for dinner, Uncle Billy and Trish included.

In the whirlwind of last night, it had completely slipped her mind that the following day was Monday, the day Bernarde was arriving. Something which proved to be of great amusement to both

Jack and Bernarde. Although in her defence, never would she have said to arrive before eleven am.

Bernarde had caught an early train, unwilling to sit with the hoi polloi that would undoubtedly occupy the rush hour trains. He despised public transport, the close proximity of complete strangers a trigger of his past, but living in central London, he, like many, had no need for a car.

It was just like old times, his company a much needed tonic for Kate. After chatting about Peter and his mum, the hotel and how Kate was greatly missed owing to Trinity being found wholly unsuitable for the job, Bernarde veered to the subject of Owen. Kate didn't want to talk about him, she wanted to talk about Jack. Her and Owen were finished, there was nothing more to add to what she had already said. Taking the hint, Bernarde finally gave up, throwing his hands up in the air in defeat, shaking his head as he laughed. Even though it had happened at lightning speed, he thought Jack was perfect for her, just what she needed and deserved, a feeling in his water that he was a good one. A keeper.

And for once, Kate finally started to believe that everything was moving in the right direction.

The choice to move away from London and Owen warranted.

That it was okay to be happy.

Secrets meetings, stolen moments.
Every second relished.
The flame now fully ignited.
Desiring more and more.
One day they would become more.
How she wished.
One day...

Chapter 37

Owen

Owen stared down at the photo on his phone in disbelief. The anger that had been simmering away in him since last week was now on fast boil, rising upwards, his breath becoming heavier. The more he looked, the stronger the urge to punch something became. He couldn't take his eyes away from the picture, nudging the screen each time it faded, forcing the brightness back to stoke the fire inside him. A strange notion passed through him that maybe if he looked long enough, he would see something other than what he thought he saw. That somehow, the arm that was fixed firmly around her shoulders wouldn't be there. Or the person it belonged to would morph into someone different.

Bitch.

He couldn't understand why she wanted to rub his face in it.

Absolute bitch.

It hadn't taken her long. But at least he knew now.

He let the screen fall into auto lock mode, watching as the picture it held faded in brightness before going completely blank. He tapped the phone back and forth against his palm, considering what his next move should be. The tapping helped ease the anger by just a notch as his thoughts became more constructive. He held down his finger to unlock the phone, the photo forced back in front of his eyes momentarily before he brought up his contacts list, closing down the social media app and the deceit it held. As he tapped her name open, the anger fell from him. A smirk as dark as the thought that stopped him from hitting call crept across his lips. He'd had enough. He was sick to death of trying to keep a lid on everything. If playing dirty was how it should be then let the games commence.

He was ready.

For each and every one of them.

Chapter 38

Kate

"Jack listen. I was thinking that when Bernarde goes back, maybe it would be best if I move back in with Uncle Billy." Kate twiddled strands of hair between her fingers, her eyes fixed on the cars lining up on the ferry that was just in sight, her mind elsewhere.

"Really? How come?"

"I don't know." She drew her knees in, her attention still split. "I just don't want to spoil a good thing that's all. I mean we barely know each other."

The last thing she wanted was to move back in with Uncle Billy but it seemed the sensible thing to do.

"Then stay here and let's get to know each other properly." Jack moved behind her, his hands either side the recliner as he bent to kiss the top of her head.

"But what if it doesn't work?" Swivelling to the side, Kate looked up at him. It was a genuine question and one that terrified the hell out of her.

He raised his eyebrows, "But what if it does work?"

He was right. What if it did. She wanted it to

but was hesitant, naturally. She was scared. Not of it not working but of how it would make her feel. After all, who would move in with someone that quickly. She didn't know of anybody. She pressed her fingers into her temples, this wasn't supposed to happen. Not like this. Jack was supposed to have been away for three months and in those three months she had banked on getting herself sorted. But it had happened and there was no denying the things she felt when she was with him. Everything had happened way too fast and although she was well aware of where the brake was and how to use it, she wasn't sure she wanted to pull it.

"Right then my lovelies, I have fresh croissants, smoked salmon bagels and cinnamon buns," Bernarde announced, setting down his boxes from the bakery on the kitchen worktop.

Neither Jack nor Kate had heard him return.

"You can stay more often." Jack turned, his voice light as he joined Bernarde in the kitchen, offering to get the coffee on.

Kate watched them both, chatting easily, her heart warmed that they got on. It meant a lot that Bernarde liked Jack and vice versa. She thought back to all the times over the years that Bernarde had tolerated Owen, just for her sake. Owen being completely oblivious that Bernarde really did dislike him. So wrapped up in his world that he never even caught a glimpse of the eye rolls between Bernarde and Peter or the near silent sighs of frustration that came usually when he was talking about himself. She had seen them of course, but had chosen to ignore them, not wanting to rock the boat.

"So, madam, fresh pastries and coffee are served if you'd care to join us." Jack had one hand on the chair he'd pulled out for her, his other gesturing towards it. A smile of approval from Bernarde standing the other side of the table.

Kate sat, letting Jack push her chair under, glad she'd held off that brake. Bernarde offered out the plate of pastries he brought.

If she had to paint contentment, this would be it.

Jack plunged the coffee, pouring out Kate's, Bernarde's and then his own. Reaching over for the milk, Kate's eye caught part of the newspaper headline that sat just behind the jug. Milk poured, she swopped the jug for the paper, unfolding it to reveal the whole of its front page.

The words meaning nothing until she saw it.

There.

In black and white before her.

The paper fell from her fingers, her head swamped with confusion.

"Kate, Kate." Feeling the hand that had taken hers, Jack disturbed the fog that had descended over her.

"Sweetie, what's wrong?" Bernarde's voice came into focus, then Jack's.

"Kate, darling, what is it?"

She spoke but remained motionless, the air around her oppressive, freezing her in time.

"The paper. His name. I don't...don't understand."

Bernarde picked up the newspaper, eager to see what had caused that much shock. Five seconds being plenty to see, two words enough for Kate to know he had seen it too.

"Bl...oo...dy hell!" The words left in slow motion, Bernarde's mouth unable to close.

"What?" Jack had no idea what had caused the shock they had both had as he looked from one to the other. He held out his hand, his fingers beckoning, "Pass me the paper Bernarde."

He read the article, still confused. "I don't understand. Do you know this guy?" He looked to Kate; his question unanswered. He scanned the headline once more, his tone more demanding, "Will one of you tell me what's wrong...please?"

Kate lifted her head, expressionless.

"Bernarde...he...he will tell you..." Her voice faltered, the shock accompanied by a desire to go and hide, be left alone to try and make some sense of it all. She pushed herself away from the table, her movements robotic as she stood to turn and walk away, down the corridor, into the bedroom, locking the door behind her. Without so much as a backwards glance at either of them.

Bernarde himself had never expected this, who could have? But Jack needed an explanation and he was the one who'd been left to give it.

"Right Jack, I'm not sure how much of Kate's past you know about but many years ago, in fact she was just a kid really, she was with this guy called Mark." The discomfort at sharing Kate's past had him shift uncomfortably in his chair. "He was the first love of her life and I think she was his. They were inseparable by all accounts. Anyway, she came home to the flat they shared, all excited as they were due to go on holiday and...well...I'm sorry Jack, could you just give me a minute?" Bernarde's voice broke, his hands wrapped around the cup that held the dark brown liquid he was staring into. "So," Bernarde cleared his throat, a new composure to his voice, "Kate came home, went into the bedroom and found him. Dead. He had slit his wrists. It destroyed her Jack. It was the start of a downward spiral that resulted in the death of her parents and her Aunt."

Jack lifted the newspaper, his eyes scanned over the article again searching for answers. "But what has that got to do with this guy?"

"Because up until a few minutes ago Jack, Kate had always believed Mark had committed suicide and had no reason to think otherwise. Read the name in the paper Jack." Bernarde took the paper from him, pointing to the name on the first line of the story underneath the headline, "Mark Blackwood. That was the name of Kate's Mark. Imagine finding out after all these years that he hadn't committed suicide but had been murdered. I didn't know him, or Kate at that time, but it sure as hell has shocked me. To the core." Moving from the table to the window, Bernarde was unsure what came next, knowing had he been at home he would have reached straight for the brandy to settle his nerves, regardless of the time.

"I'm still confused Bernarde, how the hell did she never find out?" Jack scratched his head, joining Bernarde at the windows. "Surely the police would have told her? Her parents? Court?"

"Whose side are you on Jack? Does that really matter? Surely right now Kate is the most important thing. At least she is to me." Bernarde was not used to being so stern with his words.

"You're right Jack, how? I don't understand it either." The meek voice had them both turn round.

"Darling, I'm so sorry." The red rings under her eyes hadn't gone unnoticed. "Come here." Jack opened out his arms, taking a step closer, wanting to take away whatever pain invaded her.

She raised her arms up, palms flat, not wanting what he was offering. "I have to get out. I need air." She backed away, turning.

Jack took her arm, not wanting her to leave or be on her own like this.

"Please Jack, let go." She shook his hand free, unable to cope with talking, explaining.

As she neared the door, the intensity of his thoughts, wants, needs, bore through her back, the heat rising as Bernarde reassured him she'd be fine, let her have some space. Shutting the door on both of their voices left the one in her head to have free reign.

How long she had walked for was of no concern. The more she concentrated on her feet pounding the ground under them, the clearer her next step became. She had to go and see Uncle Billy.

The damp concrete of the quayside discharged its cold as she sat waiting for the small boat ferry to come. She preferred this to the car and passenger ferry, free from fumes, free from noise, slower. He would row over as soon as he caught sight of her by the red waiting pole and she prayed that wouldn't be long.

As much as she tried, she couldn't shift that article out of her mind. Although it was a shock, it had turned to relief after a while. A selfish relief that he hadn't chosen to leave her. That he hadn't given up on them. All those years she had felt so angry at him, couldn't even go to his funeral or speak to what little family he had. Blaming him for everything. Torn between love and hatred for him. Whatever had happened on that god-awful night, she had to find out. Needed to find out. It was now her responsibility to them both, the very least she could do. She was so mad with herself now, if only she...

"You getting on love?" It was an unfamiliar voice that broke her trail of thought. She hadn't seen this guy before and she was expecting, hoping that it would be Frank.

"Where's Frank today?"

"Dentist love, you getting on or not?" He was impatient and Kate didn't care for it. It wasn't like it was busy.

"I've got a bit of a problem," she started, "you see I need to get to over to the other side but I haven't got any money on me. I came out in a rush and forgot to pick up my purse. Can I owe it to you? Please?"

"Sorry love, don't know you from Adam and times are hard. No fare, no ferry. You'll have to walk round." The shake of his head long and exaggerated, his smile sarcastic.

Tight arse. One pound ten pence, that was all. Walk round, she'd like to see him walk round. Frank would've subbed her; knew she would have paid him back. But this guy was not backing down.

"Please!" Begging wasn't her thing but she had to get to see Billy.

"Take for us both please." The woman's voice came from the side of her, similar in age, maybe a bit older.

Not usually one for accepting charity but beggars couldn't be choosers.

"Thank you," Kate said, steading herself as they sat on the wooden slats of the boat seat.

"No problem. Glad I could help." She offered out her hand. "It's Sarah by the way."

Kate took her hand, shaking it in return. "Thank you, Sarah, it really is kind of you. I'm Kate."

The crossing took no more than a couple of minutes but Kate was relieved to be on dry land once more. Ready to thank Sarah again before saying goodbye, she got in there first.

"Where you headed?"

"My uncle's." Considering they'd only just met,

Kate thought it quite a nosey question.

"I'll walk with you, shall I?" There was something behind the woman's smile that didn't sit well with Kate.

"Ah no need. Plus, you don't know which direction I'm going in and it'll probably be out of your way."

"No, it's cool, I'll walk with you. I'm going up town, the same way as you." Sarah's cheeks lifted unnaturally high for the smile to be genuine.

How could she know Uncle Billy lived up town? She hadn't told her. Shrugging it off, she was low on Kate's list of things to be bothered about.

"You're not from round here are you Kate? What brings you here?"

No chance to answer before Sarah struck up again.

"Let me guess hon, relationship troubles. Definitely boyfriend, not a girlfriend. Break up. Am I right?"

Whatever game she was playing, she appeared to enjoy it immensely.

"Bang on." Kate was annoyed. But she wasn't letting her have the upper hand. Just who the hell did she think she was prying into her life. She picked up her pace, hoping, praying she would get the message. It wouldn't be long before she was at Billy's and could be shot of her. All that for one pound and ten pence.

"Ooh, just call me mystic meg eh hon?" She was relentless. On and on.

Kate managed to ignore her, mostly, she enjoyed

the sound of her own voice too much to notice. They turned the corner, the path to Billy's just a few feet away.

"Right Sarah, thanks again for the fare. See you around." Kate pushed the gate to behind her, Sarah still harping on as Kate inched towards the front door.

"You're better off without I can guarantee. Men. All a load of arseholes!" Her shrill voice followed Kate up the path.

"Bye Sarah!" Kate shouted, opening the door, knocking as she did.

Blowing out her lips as she moved inside, Kate was thoroughly glad to be rid of her and her verbal diarrhoea. But Sarah made sure her parting words pushed their way through the tiny gap of the door, knowing they would stay with Kate as she clicked it shut.

"You were too good for Owen anyway."

'You were too good for Owen anyway' What did she mean? And how did she know his name? Kate never told her. She couldn't take much more. It was constant. One thing after another.

Lies.

Contradictions.

Deceptions.

More lies. More contradictions. More deceptions. She was so riddled with confused she wasn't sure that she could even trust herself any longer. The more she tried to make sense out of everything, the worse it got.

"Kate, you made me jump!" Trish said.

In the entrance hallway of what she once considered her sanctuary, it no longer felt like a place of safety, tarnished now by the words of a stranger.

"Sorry, I did knock. Is Uncle Billy around?"

"I'm afraid not, but he shouldn't be long. Now come on through, you look shattered." Trish led her into the kitchen, insisting she sit whilst she made them both a coffee.

She explained it all to Trish, the newspaper article, seeing his name again and the face that had murdered him. About finding out that everything she had ever believed was nothing more than a lie. Needing air. But she never got to Sarah. Or more importantly, her words as the expression Trish wore was solemn. Not what she had expected from her. She never spoke, her gaze unsteady.

Sarah could wait.

"Trish?"

Those few moments before it registered felt like an age. She could've kicked herself, how could she have been so stupid.

"You knew...didn't you? You and Uncle Billy?" A surge of disappointment forced Kate to her feet. Her hands alternated from her hips to her head to her face, surplus to requirement and she had no idea what to do with them as she began to move from foot to foot.

"Why Trish? Why didn't anyone think to tell me? How could you not tell me?" She was stood at the back of the chair, her hands gripped the cold leather, needing that physical barrier between them.

"Kate, I...I don't know what to say. I'm sorry. So, so sorry...you have no idea how much." Her turn to search Kate now, seeking forgiveness. "Billy made me promise him that no matter what, I would never tell you. I tried explaining to him that it would not end well but he wouldn't listen. Insisting that it was the best thing if you never knew."

It wasn't Trish's fault. Kate knew that. It had happened years before she and Billy had even got together. She couldn't lay the blame with her, but she was there and Billy wasn't. The only target for her anger, confusion, and sadness.

They sat in silence. The storm of emotions continuing to brew. They both heard Billy close the door behind him. Both heard him kick off his work boots. But neither looked at the other. He came in to the kitchen, unaware of what was about to hit him. He saw them sat apart, quiet. He wasn't stupid. He knew something was wrong.

"Trish? Kate?" He looked from one to the other.

Trish turned. "She knows. About Mark."

Kate remained silent, waiting for the penny to drop.

It took Billy a moment to process what lay beneath those words. It was up to him now to move this forward. "Kate, let me explain, please."

There was no desire to look at him but she needed to see his face as he gave defence and enlightened her as to why he thought she was not worthy of knowing the truth about the man she had intended to spend the rest of her life with.

It was not a decision they should have made.

Any of them.

Whatever the circumstances, she should not have been denied her right to know the truth. She wasn't even aware she had been deemed mentally unstable back then. Something else they'd failed to tell her.

The statement that the police had taken from her shortly after she had found him, together with the forensic evidence they had and the guilty plea was enough to charge and sentence him, quickly. It was feared that owing to her 'state of mind', should she be told then the consequences could be dire. The professionals and her parents discussed at length that her recovery was the most important thing back then. Kate was pretty certain that a decision like that couldn't be made nowadays without huge ramifications.

"Your parents took the secret to their graves Kate, leaving just me, and as time went on, well it just got harder to tell you. I thought you'd turned a corner, moving away, meeting Owen. Rightly or wrongly, I thought it best left where it was, in the past. Concentrate on you forging a new life for yourself, a happy one."

Even though Kate could taste the remorse that overlaid Billy's words, she couldn't find the strength to tell him she understood for she understood nothing in her fractured life.

"Kate, say something."

She could hear him, but didn't want to answer, not

then. There was something far more pressing that needed what little strength she had. The newspaper article was etched into her mind. The headline, Mark's name, the murderer's picture. She tore herself apart, forcing herself back to that time, wondering if it was someone they had known. She needed to know why he had done such a vicious, cruel thing, cross with herself for not reading the whole of the article.

"I need to see the paper. I have to read it. Do you have one?" Her response wasn't what Billy had expected.

"Kate...I don't think that's a good idea, why torture yourself even further, I have told you everything." He tried his best to dissuade her but she was standing her ground on this one.

"Not everything Billy. I need to know *how* he did it." A shred of mettle had arisen, enabling her usual soft voice to be firm, direct.

Something no one was used to.

"Kate, what..."

She cut across him, her voice raised, slicing through his words. "Just give me the paper!"

Reluctantly, Trish fetched it for her. Kate knew she was in a difficult position but whether she liked it or not, was caught up in all of this and as much a part of it as Billy.

"Thank you," Kate said, not forgetting her manners as her fingers clamped the grubby pages.

But Trish was hesitant to let go. The hesitance holding words she decided were best left unspoken as she released the paper fully.

Unfolding it, Kate set it down on the table in front of her, not wanting her fingers to touch its evil any longer than she had to. This time, she forced herself to read it, word by word, not wanting her eyes to miss anything that might help piece this jigsaw together. She made herself look at the picture, look into his eyes. Her flesh crawled, shivered, even though it was just a black and white image from well over twenty years. It was no one she knew. Or at least remembered. The article gave no details of why or how, but then why would it?

SUICIDE MURDERER EARLY RELEASE

Paul Hilkins was last week released from prison for good behaviour. Having served twenty two years of his original sentence without a single incident of bad behaviour against him, the parole board felt he had served his time and was no longer a threat to the public. He will be fitted with an electronic tag and have a strict curfew in place which will be reviewed after six months. In June 1996, the town of Paignton was shocked by its worse crime ever. Paul Hilkins pleaded guilty to the murder of Mark Blackwood who was found at home in his bedroom with his wrists slashed. Upon investigation, it was found that this was not an act of suicide but one which had been made to look that way. The cause of death was suffocation. The presiding judge took no time in deciding that the crime had been committed in cold blood, with the defendant carrying out a second act to cover his tracks and imposed a life sentence with a minimum served term of twenty years.

Kate read the article five, maybe six times, each time the word suffocation jumping out at her. Slivers of broken images floated in her head. The image of this man, this cold evil man depriving Mark of the very thing we all take for granted, forcing him to struggle and gasp until that last breath left his body.

Then the scene that had shook her world. Mark lying there, lifeless, surrounded by pills, wrists slashed apart. Covered in blood. Her mind tormented her as it showed her this man, she couldn't bring herself to speak his name, he didn't deserve one after what he'd done. Showing her this man, knife in hand as he took Mark's lifeless arms and cruelly tore into them. Standing there cackling, distorted images of what her mind was trying to construct. A cold, shallow voice repeating his name over and over, keen for her to put it with his face. Then something happened, the movie in her mind halted, the lights switched back on and she could see it clearly.

That name, Paul Hilkins. She knew it. Didn't she? How could she have not known?

Chapter 39

Owen

Knowing exactly what he needed to do, he made a call to Suzi, his PA, letting her know he would be away for a few days. He wasn't quite sure how long, explaining only that he had some business crop up that needed his full attention so he wanted no interruptions, from anybody. Suzi knew not to question him. Even when she knew he was not telling the truth. She had worked for Owen for many years and had come to learn what was expected of her, which boiled down in the end to one word.

Discretion.

Even though Owen trusted Suzi, he made the hotel reservation himself. It was best if she knew nothing. He hadn't been able to tell the reservation team how long he would be staying but they were happy to oblige when he said he would pay for a week upfront, buying into his business trip story. There was one more phone call he knew it was time to make. But it could wait just a while longer and he could play them, just like they had him.

Ensuring everything in the flat was switched off,

he unhooked his keys from the rack he could never get Kate to use and lifted his bag.

It was time to sort this mess out.

And get Kate back, where she belonged.

Chapter 40

Kate

Kate decided long ago that the mind has a funny way of showing you things in an order that never quite makes sense. Maybe it interprets what your eyes see first, not bothering to take in the whole picture. She didn't know but was sure someone somewhere would.

If she was going to make any sense out of this and get this picture complete, she had to remain impartial, there was no place for emotion. She had done it before, become immune to feeling, she could do it again.

"Please tell me Billy that this man, this Paul, is not who I think it is?"

"I wish I could tell you it's not Kate." Billy hung his head.

"Is that why H went? Not because of Aunt Pam dying but...Did you get rid of him?" Kate had so many questions but one jumped the queue, tripping off her tongue. "Oh my God, has this Paul moved here?"

Billy perched himself on the bar stool. "No. He hasn't. I believe he moved back to Paignton and has to stay in the town. Conditions of his release."

Relief washed over her, the thought of what she would have done had he moved back here incomprehensible.

Billy continued. "I had to let him go Kate. How would it have looked if I'd have kept him on? His son was a murderer and the whole sorry mess, well, it involved you too." He rubbed his forehead, the tan leathered skin pinched between thumb and index finger as he moved them back and forth.

Trish changed seats, moving to be next to Billy, her hand resting on his knee, her half smile on Kate. She was stuck between a rock and a hard place, unsure which should have her attention and Kate genuinely wished she hadn't had to go through this.

"I didn't just get rid of him Kate. We had a long discussion, and we all agreed there was no other option."

"But he relied on that job, on the money. How could you!"

This whole thing reeked of unfairness and it was one thing Kate couldn't stand, injustice.

"Kate, listen, I never just cast him aside, him or Mary, it's not how it looks. I made ..." The high-pitched ring of Billy's mobile interrupted him mid flow. He pulled it from his shirt pocket, asking them to give him "Just two minutes...sorry."

Decision made that whoever was calling was far more important than the people that were sat in front him, even after Trish's protests. His walk to the other side of the room full of purpose, moving out onto the balcony, sliding the door shut behind him.

She never took her eyes off him once as he paced up and down the balcony, quietly seething that again he had avoided facing the truth. But his expression was one of worry, his free hand made invisible patterns in the air.

Uncomfortable with the wait and the silence, Trish cleared the cups from the table, apologising as she went back to the kitchen to fill and boil the kettle again, clanking clean cups onto saucers. Sounds that Kate was fully aware of but never once looked round, continuing to observe the man she not so long ago regarded as her rock, her safe place. As much as she wanted to deny the feeling that had made itself known to her, she couldn't. There was something that he wasn't telling her, and she had to find out what.

After Uncle Billy had, mid phone call, announced that he had to go out, unavoidable, Kate had borrowed money from Trish for the ferry to get back. She needed to talk to Bernarde. And Jack. He deserved an explanation and she hoped he would listen. She needed both of them by her side.

"Kate, you're back. My God you look frozen, come and sit down sweetie." Bernarde was the first to greet her as she walked back into the apartment, furiously rubbing his hands up and down her arms. He was right, she was cold, bitterly so. A chill that had started to go much further than skin deep.

"Thanks B. Where's Jack?" Kate allowed Bernarde to escort her to the sofa.

"Right here." He sat beside her, cradling her into him, echoing Bernarde's concern about her temperature, or lack of.

"Brandy Jack. Do you have any?"

"Try the cabinet over by the bookcase, there should be some in there. And a bottle of whiskey."

Bernarde found the medicine as he preferred to call it, poured out two brandy's, one for himself and one for Kate and poured a whiskey for Jack. Assuming from the mention of there being a bottle it was his preference. Kate didn't want the brandy, the smell of it made her gag but she necked it back all the same, maybe it would do her good. Everyone always said it did.

Taking the glass from her, Jack asked if she wanted to talk, that Bernarde had told him about Mark.

As she spent the next hour recoiling everything that Uncle Billy had told her, Jack and Bernarde listened intently, both by her side. Glad there were two people in her life who were not part of this deception.

Jack's answer had been no when she asked if he knew of the Hilkins as a family. He had only moved here two years ago, taking over his father's business after he had passed away, deciding to move here for a fresh start. He'd only met Billy and Trish as their boat was moored up next to the one he'd bought.

She had wanted to get to know Jack better, but not like this. It was like they were zooming through his life on fast forward, his history being forced out, bullet pointed. But then so too had hers. And she should know you can't always have things turn out the way you want.

"I have to go and see the Hilkins," Kate concluded. "There is something Billy isn't telling me and I have to find out what it is. Will you both help me?"

Readily agreeing, the support from them meant so much to her, providing her with a new source of energy to see this thing through. But it could wait until tomorrow. Even though it was only early evening, she had done with talking for the day. What she needed more than anything was a hot bath, something to eat and sleep.

Chapter 41

Owen

The drive to Dartmouth had been unexpectedly easy and Owen was in good spirits. He'd had a long chat with himself on the journey, deciding that there was no place for regret if he was to come out of this unscathed and get Kate back where she belonged. With him, in London. She might not think that was where she should be but he figured her head would be a mess after everything and the best place for her was with him. He could keep her safe. He had always done everything in his power to keep her safe and happy, giving her everything she could ever want.

At least that was what he believed.

He was angry with her at first for leaving. Angry that she could just up and leave but she wasn't thinking straight. She couldn't have been. She was just confused, maybe even a little lost like she had been all those years when he first met her. He would forgive her for her moment of weakness, whoever this man was he had obviously taken advantage. Now he was going to make it all better.

And he wasn't going to let anyone get in his way.

Chapter 42

Kate

T he day had dragged on for what seemed an eternity and it was a mixture of relief and apprehension that Kate felt when Mrs Clifford asked her to pop the closed sign round at four pm. It hadn't gone unnoticed that her attention was scattered and she felt bound to explain – at least in part - when the old lady had queried what was troubling her for the third time.

She had watched Kate thoughtfully as she told her about Mark, the newspaper article and how her family had concealed the truth from her, sensing the disappointment she felt in Billy. Mrs Clifford asked her no questions or gave her any of the usual type of advice, just simply answered with another one of her riddles, repeating two words Kate had begun to dread hearing, dark and light.

"Allow this darkness into your life Kate, don't push it away for it is of paramount importance. Navigate it wisely, for there will be bumps along the way, and you will find the light that will illuminate your life once and for all. Fear holds us back Kate and, sometimes, it is not only our story we have to tell."

Sharing her lack of understanding, Kate begged her to put it into plain English what it was supposed to mean. But Mrs Clifford insisted that as much as she wanted to help, it wasn't her place to meddle, just to guide and she would be with her every step of the way.

Glad to be outside, to feel the cold air sting her cheeks and hear the everyday chatter of people as they went about their day brought a sense of reality to Kate.

Before leaving for work that morning, Jack had insisted on going with her to see Mr and Mrs Hilkins. At the time she was unsure, but seeing him stood there on the corner of Market Street waiting for her filled her with something indescribable.

"Ready?" he checked, hands on her shoulders as she stood before him, depositing a tender kiss on her lips.

"Ready."

"Katelyn...what a lovely surprise."

She wasn't sure if it was a welcome surprise or not as Mr Hilkins opened the lavender coloured door of his terraced cottage to them. It crossed her mind if he actually knew she had been part of this awful mess so long ago. He must have, that was why Billy had let him go.

"Is it a good time?" Kate asked, fingers crossed behind her back that he would say yes.

"Anytime is a good time to see you my dear girl, now come on in. And you young man." He welcomed them into his sitting room, a small cosy square room with an open fireplace that took up most of the back wall.

"Sit yourselves down by the fire and get warm, it's still nippy out there. I'll just go and get Mary; she'll be so thrilled to see you." Tom Hilkins shuffled off into the room beyond.

He was right, Mary was thrilled to see her, they both were and to make acquaintance with Jack. The time passed by quickly and as lovely as it was to catch up, Kate had to broach the real reason she was there.

It was hard to believe that this adorable couple who would give you their last penny had a child who was capable of such cruelty and whatever happened next, she wanted them to know her feelings towards them would never change.

Mary had offered them more tea, popping back into the kitchen to make a fresh pot, Tom followed closely behind. When they came back through, Kate would seize the moment and begin.

"Here we go my lovelies. It is nice to have company, isn't it Tom?" Mary chuckled in the kindly way Kate remembered from all those years ago. She was doing remarkably well considering she'd not long since had a heart attack, but she always did look on the positive side of life.

"Tom, Mary, I have to ask you something."

"Of course, dear, ask away."

They knew what was coming, Kate was sure they did, noticing Mary reach over for Tom's hand, lacing her fingers through his.

"Okay." She shuffled to the edge of the chair, pulling herself upright, hands clasped together on her lap. "This isn't easy for me to say this but...I know, about Paul."

"Everyone around these parts does Kate, how did you find out? Billy? Trish?" Tom was not surprised in the slightest at her disclosure.

"I saw it in the newspaper Tom but..." Something stopped her from asking if they knew who she was to Mark. Or had been. She skipped that bit, jumping forward to afterward. "When I saw it in the newspaper, it was the name I recognised. I asked Uncle Billy and he confirmed it. It made me question then why you stopped gardening for Aunt Pam. I mean it wasn't your fault."

Jack shot her a puzzled look, unsure why she was taking this approach. She wasn't exactly sure either, shooting back her own puzzled look in response.

"Your Uncle Billy was in a difficult position. Had it of come out that Paul was working for him at the time it would have ruined him. You see Billy didn't know that Paul was using violence against these... let's say clients. He was acting completely off his own back. But Paul was never one for listening to anybody. We told Billy but he thought he could get him back on the straight and narrow. Wanted to give him a chance." Tom shook his head, the strain of having to dredge up the past again taking its toll and as clear as it was how jaded they both were, she couldn't let it go.

"What do you mean working for Uncle Billy? What exactly was he doing?" Another bombshell had been dropped her way.

Mary answered, sharing the burden of voicing the past. "Billy lent money to people. It was all above board and from what I was told, the interest he charged was minimal, not like some of these companies you hear about. Anyway, Paul was getting into bother frequently and the older he got, the harder it was for us to get through to him. You see he never got over losing his parents, neither of them did. And if we hadn't of taken them in, then social services would have." Mary was back there, her eyes glassy with tears.

Tom took the baton. "Like Mary said, Paul, he began to get into bother. Mainly shoplifting and anti-social behaviour. We couldn't get through to him. Your Uncle Billy thought he needed some structure and discipline in his life and so offered him a job, as a payment collector. For a while, it appeared that he was settling down, but then he began to get moody, staying out all night and not telling anyone where he was. They both did. Anyway, the man that he killed had apparently borrowed money from Billy, not much as I understood and he wasn't behind on his repayments. But for some reason, still to this day unknown, he went to his address, off his own back and... well...you know how it ended." The rims of Tom's eyes matched Mary's now, the weft of sadness clear.

This sweet couple, full of kindness and bursting with love that touched everyone they met, hadn't deserved this, none of it.

Full of new discoveries, Kate's head was spinning, but at last things were beginning to make sense. A little anyway. So, Mary and Tom were Paul's grand-parents, not his parents explaining why she had never seen him around when she was a little girl, staying here during the holidays. And there was a sibling. That was irrelevant though. Uncle Billy had been a money lender and Paul had worked for him. Something else he hadn't told her yesterday. There were so many pieces to this puzzle she was starting to question if she would ever get to finish it. For a moment, she had forgotten Jack was in the room. What the hell must he have thought listening to all of this was anyone's guess, the reason why she had been reluctant for him to come.

"I'm beginning to understand, I think. I know this must be dreadful for you both, talking about it after all this time but there's something else I think you should know." As much as it pained her to tell them, they had a right to know, just like she had. The closet was open and the doors were not closing until every skeleton had been discovered.

The anxious look that passed between them as they waited for her to tell them had them squeeze each other's hand a little harder.

"Mark Blackwood. The man that Paul murdered. He was my boyfriend."

They hadn't known, didn't know. That was evident from the shock that bolted through them both as they let out an exasperated sigh in unison. Mary struggled to hold back the tears, her eyes growing glossier with each passing second. Tom was just still. Stock still. Even the lids of his eyes never blinked. The impact of letting out these painful memories had affected them all, even Jack. He hadn't known her for five minutes yet there he was, by her side helping her through this shitstorm. He was too good to be true and her mind was made, she was not letting him go, no matter what.

After the initial shock had passed and questions had been answered, Kate assured them both that nothing had changed, apologising for dredging up the past. They were both heartened that the great affection she had had for them both remained unchanged and of the promise of another visit, soon.

In the narrow hallway, as they took it in turns to apologise to Jack for having to meet under such circumstances, a photograph grabbed Kate's attention. A framed photograph that sat proudly on the wall above the mahogany telephone table near the front door.

A photograph with a face she would never forget.

"H, who are the people in the photograph?"

"What this one?" He nodded his head towards it, a nod of hers back to confirm.

"That's Paul. And his cousin Sarah."

Chapter 43

Owen

Owen had known that if he waited, eventually he would be led to him. She hadn't noticed him watching her throughout the day, following her in the shadows, waiting for her to make her next move. Him two paces behind. This was the last place he had expected to see her but he lay in wait, ready to catch his prey.

It wasn't long before he turned up, saw the two of them together at last, exactly what he had been patiently waiting for. He listened in to their whispered exchanges, mentally storing anything that was important to his cause, biding his time until he had everything he needed in place.

He slunk away, he had seen and heard enough.

Next on his agenda was to make that call.

Chapter 44

Kate

S he could've sworn someone had been following them. Every few minutes she checked back behind her, convinced she had seen a flash of something move, felt the icy chill of menace stroke her but there was nothing there. Nothing that she could see anyway. Nothing except her imagination casting jagged images in the fading light. She didn't tell Jack, there was something else she had to share.

"Jack, you know the picture on the wall I asked H about, well, there's something odd about it. I brushed it off at first as coincidence but now I'm not too sure. The girl, Sarah, I saw her...yesterday."

"With him?" Surprise muddled with concern sprang from Jack, slowing down his pace.

"No, on her own." Kate linked her arm firmly through Jack's, her hand gripping her wrist for added security. "When I left yesterday after the whole thing with the paper, I went out without my purse. Anyway, I had no money for the ferry to get to Billy's and she paid my fare for me."

"Nice thing to do."

"Yeah, it was, if that was all it was." She cast her

mind back to yesterday and to Sarah. A stranger who knew way too much. "I get the feeling though Jack that she had somehow been waiting for me. You see I couldn't shake her off when we got off the ferry, she insisted on walking with me. But it was what she said that made me shudder. She told me I was too good for Owen. But I hadn't told her his name or that I had come here because I had broken up from him. So how did she know?"

"Okay, that is odd. Where was she going?"

"Well that's just it, she never told me, just hinted probably my way. It was like she knew where I was going."

"Well, let's say she knew Billy too. If Paul had there's no reason why she wouldn't, right? So maybe she guessed that that was where you were going. It's a small place and word soon gets out amongst the locals about anyone new in town, then before you know it, everyone knows your business." Jack unhooked his arm from hers, wrapping it around her shoulder to pull her in closer.

"Hmmm...Maybe."

As they walked down through the streets to the river front, Kate understood what Jack was saying, it was like that everywhere no doubt but once again something didn't sit right with her. It was the way Sarah had said it. The snideness that had travelled with her words, that was what bothered her. That and the flash of happy torment in her eyes. Jack's reassurances were not enough this time, her head may have been clouded but she couldn't deny the stab of dread that filled her veins.

∞∞∞

"Hey you're back! So...how did it go?"

She retold the whole sorry story to Bernarde, from Billy's involvement to her encounter with Sarah, as the three of them sat drinking a glass of one of Jack's finest bottles of chianti. Each sip of the wine taking the edge off the growing deception and confusion that was continuously building.

"Hells bells sweetie, I'm speechless." Totally out of character for Bernarde. He always had something to say.

They sat quiet, fulfilling the temporary need to each be alone with their own thoughts. In the distance, the sky had begun to slip into its evening darkness as stars twinkled against their dramatic backdrop. This was the first time Kate had seen the stars since she had arrived and although the sky still wasn't completely clear, the heavy blanket had gone, leaving behind scatter cushions of clouds in its place.

The chime of Jack's phone made them all jump, pulling them back from their distant worlds.

"It's Billy," Jack said, checking the screen, "wanting to know if you are okay."

"Okay? Seriously? In the space of two days I have had more strange dreams than I care to remember, had a guy leave his book only to vanish, received flowers from god knows who and found out that my family kept the murder of my boyfriend from me and not only was the murderer my Aunt's gardeners' son but worked for my precious Uncle Billy. Oh tell him I'm hunky bloody dory!" Seething, sarcasm the only way she could deal with the cataclysm that had finally hit. "But then he hasn't actually told me himself that...that man...worked for him, has he?"

"Sweetie, I can't imagine how you must be feeling right now, but look, you've been through far far worse, and come through it. This will be the same but you do have to talk to Billy."

"I agree with Bernarde, talk to him, tell him how you are feeling. He is your family and I'm certain he was, is trying to protect you." Jack's words almost a plead.

She knew this wasn't fair on either of them but she couldn't help how betrayal and deceit crammed her mind. It was not the right time to talk to Billy about this latest revelation, not after alcohol, she would end up saying something she would live to regret so no, it could wait until tomorrow. After all these years one more day wouldn't hurt and maybe he might just begin to understand the pain she carried.

The gentle spring rain was welcome.
Nothing could darken this moment.
Everything so peaceful.
Full of promise.
Hope.
Just for a moment, before fear waved its hand.
Tormenting.
So cold.
A paralysing fear that wouldn't leave.

In her dream, she was somewhere else, somewhere unknown to her, at least that's what she thought. As she stepped through the scenes she found herself in, her sleep was fitful. The clothes were different, the people around her unfamiliar but she thought she knew them. Then she was out in the rain, soaked through to the skin but she was smiling, laughing. She was waiting for someone. Her heart bouncing. Then he appeared, his face lined with anger, his fists screwed tight. This wasn't who should have been here, not him. She knew it shouldn't have been him so who? Gnarled images of Mark and Paul together came, fighting for prominence in her dream. Neither of them should have had a place there. They didn't belong. As fast as they appeared, they vanished, leaving her cold. A coldness that came from the depths of somewhere unknown.

She was scared, terrified.

Paralysed with fear.

"Hey, hey, it's alright darling, you were having a bad dream."

She was sat bolt upright, eyes wide with terror. Jack held her trembling body tight against his own, his soothing whispers skimmed her ear. She didn't understand what had just happened, not yet fully awake, she couldn't even remember going to bed. Gradually her body began to loosen, allowing Jack to absorb all her weight as she relaxed into him, the recognition of her surroundings returning. Slowly and silently the tears began to fall as she tried to process the dream she had found herself in.

Jack never asked her to share with him what had happened, he knew all too well from his own nightmares how painful it could be to relive the experience once it was over. Instead he did what he instinctively knew he had to, and that was to protect her, no matter what.

Chapter 45

Frances

Frances hadn't slept well at all last night. Her usual restful sleep had been taken over with fits and starts and bad dreams. Dreams she knew were not her own.

In fact, she hadn't slept soundly since the arrival of this beautiful young woman. But that wasn't her fault, Frances held her in no way responsible.

Although physically tired from the lack of sleep, her mind was sharp, her resolve to see this through strong, to help Kate in any way that she would need.

Restful sleep would resume when all of this was over.

Of that she was sure.

Chapter 46

Owen

Owen had left early that morning, keen to make it there before she did. Her routine had been pretty consistent over the last couple of days, and he knew if he waited for the lunchtime meet up, his chance to face them would come.

He sat on the bench just outside Avenue Gardens, opposite the old station café that overlooked the river, newspaper in hand so he could, if needed, conceal himself. But she would never have expected him to find her. A smug smile tightened his lips as he reminded himself of how he had always been clever than her, than all of them. He'd learnt a lot over the years, about himself and other people. He'd learnt how to bide his time and wait for the perfect moment. Gone had the days of heavy handedness where he would have rushed straight in, he wasn't like that anymore and part of him regretted he ever had been. But it had helped him survive. And everyone had a past.

He didn't have to wait long. He saw her enter the café first, followed soon after by him. He folded the newspaper, tucking it under his arm before crossing the narrow road that stood between him and them.

They hadn't seen him open the door, too engrossed in their togetherness, holding hands across the table. They hadn't even bothered to look up as the chair he pulled out at the table nearest to them crudely scraped across the tiled floor. He ordered his expresso, wondering how long it would take her to notice him, his patience beginning to thin.

Then as the waitress set down his coffee, his moment came. A casual glance in his direction. Her brain didn't process what her eyes had seen immediately, prompting a time delayed reaction. But then her head spun back around; shock drenched her face as her eyes met his straight on.

"Owen...what the hell are you doing here?"

Chapter 47

Kate

Ignoring the pleas from both Jack and Bernarde to stay at home, Kate insisted work was the best possible distraction for her. She had no intention of letting Mrs Clifford down. And anyway, she felt drawn to be there.

"Good morning my dear, how lovely to see you."

Kate considered her statement odd seeing as it was Friday after all.

"Morning. I'll just pop my things in the back and stick the kettle on shall I?"

"No need dear, already made a pot. It should be ready by now if you would like to bring the tray back through with you when you come. We can sit and drink it in here, enjoy the bit of sunshine that has made an appearance today. And I think it's time you called me Frances."

Although her voice sounded bright enough, the growing shadows under her eyes spoke otherwise and Kate wondered if whatever had bothered her so last week, still troubled her. In spite of her concern, she smiled to herself. Frances. It would be odd calling her Frances now.

Kate offloaded, at Frances Clifford's request, all the details of the last few days. Sharing her stuff with a woman she hardly knew was at first uncomfortable. Yet once she had started, she found it remarkably easy, it was nice to have a grandmotherly figure to listen to her.

Frances was mindful of Kate's apprehension, remaining quiet to allow her the space she needed. She sat perfectly straight in the chair opposite, legs to one side with one ankle neatly tucked behind the other, hands rested on her lap. A graceful demure posture which Kate admired and attempted in her own way to emulate. It didn't come naturally to her though and she soon felt the familiar slump of her shoulders as she relaxed in the chair.

"I'm so sorry to hear that my dear, I truly am. What a painful thing for you to discover. But do not allow the past define you Kate. It can be helpful to view things in a different way..." Frances words trailed off, along with her thoughts. Thoughts of whether Kate was ready to hear what she had to say. But whether she was ready or not, she knew time was not on her side. Kate would soon be thrown head on into the past and if she wanted to ensure a different ending emerged, Frances knew she and Marcel didn't have long before their bond became visible.

Kate remained quiet, sensing there was more to come. Even though she had only known Frances, for a couple of weeks she had already picked up on her little nuances.

"As I was saying, it can be immensely helpful to view things in a different way. We are conditioned to believe that things happen to us, becoming so trapped in the situation that we carry it around with us, letting it drag us down, shaping everything after that we do. But the reality is, things happen for many reasons. Sometimes to help us. To help steer us in the direction that we should be taking, bringing us back from any diversions we take. Or, perhaps one of the hardest, to help us learn lessons, things we have agreed to but have no conscious recollection of in this lifetime." Frances paused there, gauging Kate's response. This was a lot for this young woman to take in but sometimes being thrown in at the deep end meant you learnt to swim sooner. This was no different.

"For the light...to truly come...you first have to embrace...the dark..." Kate's voice was almost a whisper as she repeated the splintered words that had up until then made no sense to her. With a nervous smile, she looked up at Frances, still unsure of the full implications of that statement. "What I don't understand though Frances is..." Her voice wavered as she shifted uncomfortably in the chair, shuffling herself to the edge, shuffling her thoughts into words. "I guess I want to know...how my family dying...It just doesn't make sense."

"Sometimes my dear, awful things happen that we mere mortals will never understand. People do all sorts in great acts of service to help another on their path. Sometimes accidents do happen that were not meant to. The mysteries of life are just that, mysteries. We are not meant to understand everything." She moved forward in her chair too, wrapping her long slender fingers around Kate's scrunched up hands, her ashen hue validating how hard this was for her but Frances had to press on. "Kate, I need you to listen carefully to me now. Have you ever heard of the term channel?"

Kate shook her head. "I don't think so. Why?"

The clumsy jangle of the shop bell rang out, interrupting them, suspending the answer.

"Be with you in moment dearie." Frances looked across to the door, calling to the young man who had entered before lowering her tone to Kate. "It'll keep till later dear. Now you go and make a fresh pot of tea and I'll see to this young gentleman."

Kate did as she was told and went out the back to the kitchen, not bothering to look who the customer was. Usually she would take them in, study them discreetly from head to toe and try to guess what kind of books they would be into, but not today, she wouldn't be able to focus. As she turned on the tap to refill the kettle, the thought that stayed with her was just how much tea could one woman drink?

"Now then young man, what can I do for you. Here to browse or is there something in particular you are looking for?" Frances questioned the young man, taking in his soft blonde curls, his face vaguely familiar.

"Hello, yes. I am looking to speak with someone

called Kate, I believe she works here?"

Frances was pensive for a moment, eyeing this confident man up and down, taking him in before asking, "May I enquire as to what you would like to see her for?"

"It's a personal matter." His reply short and to the point.

She didn't care for his curt manner. His pursed lipped smile told her that whatever he wanted with Kate wouldn't be welcome.

"May I ask your name young man?"

He was hiding something and whatever his reason for being there was, she had no intention of allowing him to see Kate.

"If she is not in today, can I leave my number for her please?" He reached inside his jacket pocket, pulling out a slip of paper that contained a mobile number, holding it out to Frances.

She never took the paper, whoever he was, he clearly didn't want her to know his name. But why?

As Kate left the kitchen, Frances's steely gaze was still cast over the scrap of paper the man was holding out for her to take. It was too late for her to do anything; he'd seen her before she had.

"Kate, is that you?"

Kate froze on the spot. A rabbit caught in headlights as her fingers gripped tighter the handles of the tea tray she was carrying, bringing it closer to her body.

"Do you know this man Kate?" Frances tried to keep her tone neutral.

"No..." The word stretched out. Kate didn't want to believe what her eyes were seeing. Wasn't this the guy she had chatted to on the train? The one from the newspaper? Why hadn't she linked the two sooner?

"I suggest..." Frances was cut short as the man interrupted.

"I need to speak to you, please. Talk to you... about..." his confidence faltered, "about that night."

In slow motion, the tray slipped from Kate's hands, her fingers unable to keep hold, her grip on reality gone too as he confirmed he fears. She wasn't ready for this, ready to confront the man who had so cruelly snatched her world away.

"Who are you young man?" Frances's tone firmed, demanding of an answer.

"Paul. Paul Hilkins." His eyes never left Kate as he answered. She wasn't what he had expected. The image he had formed about her from what he had been told was far removed from what he saw standing just six feet away from him. This beautiful woman deserved to know the truth about that night and he was the only one who was prepared to give it to her.

"Right Mr Hilkins, I suggest you leave my shop at once. Kate is clearly distressed by your presence and I will not have personal matters intrude on my employee's day."

Frances knew exactly who he was as soon as he revealed his name. Knew he had been responsible of that terrible crime that had rocked a whole community all those years ago and knew that his release had caused his poor grandmother, her old friend, to suffer a heart attack. What she didn't know was what he wanted with Kate. She had to think quickly as to the best course of action for he showed no signs of moving. Maybe they did need to talk. But not alone.

"Mr Hilkins..."

"I just want to talk to you Kate, explain. Please?"

Even though he cut across Frances again, his surety had long gone, the confidence false, it had just been for show. The paper he held had become crumpled and worn as it passed between his fingers, from one hand to the other in front of him and Frances could smell the nervousness he was heavily excreting.

"Kate?" Frances moved towards her, careful to step round the pool of tea and broken china. "Let's sit down my dear."

"Your ch...china, I'm so...sorry."

"It matters not dear; it is not important."

Frances had managed to coax Kate over to the chairs, easing her down into one of them.

The air around them had grown thick and stale and Kate was consoled that Frances was there, unsure of how much more she could take as her world closed in around her all over again.

"Mr Hilkins." The instruction to sit clear from Frances's open palm to the chair opposite Kate.

Kate knew she had to look at him, knew she had to confront him. Since she had found out, her innermost thoughts had been about what she would say to him if ever she met him. Now she had her chance. He sat straight in front of her but no words would come.

After turning the sign to closed on the half glass shop door, Frances lowered the blind, concealing them from the public and initiated the conversation.

"What is it you would like to say Mr Hilkins?"

Paul was silent for a while, in his head trying to figure out the best way to approach this. The idea seeming much easier than the reality. The reality which he was now sat in front of.

"I, I want to say I am sorry Kate. I feel you need to hear me say that before anything else." All Paul wanted to do was to tell her he hadn't done it but he couldn't, not yet. She had to know the full story. Deserved to.

Kate raised her head slowly, scared of what she would see.

Sorry.

It was fickle word.

Bandied around by people who expected it to wipe away their unacceptable behaviour. She didn't want to hear him say sorry. What she wanted was an explanation.

"That night Kate, it didn't happen like they said it did." Paul glanced over at Frances, the self-appointed mediator.

"Go on, Mr Hilkins," Frances encouraged.

"That night Kate, I had gone to see Mark because

he owed money. Drug money. But he hadn't got it. I made an arrangement with him to collect it the next week. Just as I was leaving my boss burst in and started to threaten Mark and, well, things got out of hand. There was a brawl, and Mark, he fell awkwardly. I panicked, said we needed to call for an ambulance. I was told to leave and it would be sorted out. You didn't argue with my boss, no one did, so I ran. But I swear to this day Kate that I never killed Mark. I never laid a finger on him. That I can promise." Paul dropped his head, his concentration on his fingers as he picked away at the skin, making it raw.

Kate had not taken her eyes off him as he spoke. She had to see what was this man was about. This murderer. But as his words filtered through, she didn't see a cold and calculated heartless killer. What she saw was someone who had lost just as much as she had. Someone who had lived in the shadows of his past.

He mentioned his boss.

Billy.

Her beloved Uncle Billy.

She felt sick to the pit of her stomach, unable to think of him as her own flesh and blood anymore. No wonder he hadn't wanted her to know. A violent shudder left her; she was ready to ask her questions.

"So, what happened then? I mean, you confessed."

"I don't know what happened Kate, I really don't. Yes, I confessed, but confessions aren't always what they seem. You see a witness had seen me go in to Mark's flat, and then leave, running. But no witness ever came forward to say they saw anyone else either go or leave. No one believed what I had to say. I had a motive and I was at the scene. As were my prints. In the end, they made me believe that it must have been me that had killed him, making reality appear hazy. Drugs do terrible things to you Kate but I swear to you I never killed Mark."

Kate was well aware of how drugs could tear things into shreds, stripping away everything of value, including your dignity. Part of her felt repulsed by this man but another part felt sorry for him. If what he was saying was true then how could she harbour any resentment towards him. And if it was true, that left one person responsible. The knowledge of who she now knew had killed Mark coiled in her gut, the rising bile stung her throat. She swallowed hard, sending it back down, determined not to let herself be taken over. She no longer wanted to run to escape the past, she was ready to face it head on.

Paul had pushed the screwed-up bit of paper that contained his number at Kate shortly before leaving, in case she ever wanted to talk. It seemed Kate already knew who his boss was so there would be nothing gained from dragging this on further. He had said what he had come to say and she had heard from him what she needed to hear.

After Paul had gone, Frances had closed the shop early, insisting that Kate needed to go home. Their chat would have to wait, she couldn't drop anything else on the poor girl today.

Jack had appeared not long after to escort Kate home. Frances was right to call him, he didn't want her out there on her own after what had happened. Paul could still be out there, waiting for her.

Waiting to tell her anything.

She locked the door behind them, letting the tension of the last couple of hours to leave with her breath as her fingers lingered on the bolt. This was far more complex than she could have ever imagined and she needed her strength.

She would call Marcel; they would have to speak to Kate together.

Sooner rather than later.

Kate had ignored the calls from Billy, he was the very last person she wanted to speak to. After numerous attempts he gave up. He wasn't stupid, he knew how much finding out about Mark would have hurt her. A message flashed up across the screen, it was Trish. So, he'd got her to do his dirty work now.

"Just let them know you are okay, please. I know you don't want to hear it but they will be worried," Jack urged her as they stood, backs against the cobbled wall to shield off the drizzle that had started again as they waited for the ferry to take them home.

Knowing he was right, she sent a brief message in

return, letting her know she needed time and how sickened she was by what Billy had done. None of this was Trish's fault and she couldn't, shouldn't be angry with her.

As the ferry glided across the water in the gloom of the late afternoon, the warmth from Jack as he brought her closer to him still wasn't enough to shake away the cold that nipped at her body. All she wanted to do was climb into bed and sleep and shut out the world around her.

She was backing away, from him, from this place.
She didn't understand how this had happened.
It wasn't supposed to have happened.
The cold pricked at her cheeks as it met her tears.
She turned and ran, into the crowd.
Not knowing where to but she had to go.
Her feet burnt as they rubbed hard against her new shoes but she dare not stop.
She couldn't let him see her.
Find her.
She had to get away, from here, from him.
She had to get to him.
Where was he?

Chapter 48

S cotch in hand, Owen sat back on his balcony, watching as darkness swept away the last of the evening light. Only the river sat between him and Kate now, yet she seemed a million miles away, out of reach. The love he had only recently recognised he had for her touched every inch of him. If he closed his eyes, he could see her stood there, dark soulful eyes that at times he couldn't meet, struggling with the intensity. Her smooth chocolate brown hair that would never stay where she wanted it to. Thoughts of her filled every waking moment. Small things that used to drive him insane now touched his heart, bringing a warm smile to his lips, briefly. He missed the passion she conveyed whenever she would talk about injustice and lack of resepct. He remembered fondly the way she would talk in her sleep, deep in conversation with someone, totally unaware of it the next day. It irritated the hell out of him at the time but now he missed it, immeasurably, unable to sleep knowing the only voice he would close his eyes to was the one in his own head.

But it wouldn't be long before he had her back in his life and this time, he would treat her with the love she deserved.

He drained the last of his scotch, its heat catching his throat. He had an early start tomorrow if he was to make it there and back the same day, a meeting he could've done without so resisted the temptation of another. He closed the balcony door shut as he stepped back into his room, twisting the catch to lock it and drew the curtains to shut out the night. As he climbed into bed, a sense of accomplishment comforted him.

He'd dealt with Sarah. And that meant Paul. The money of course helped but they weren't getting anymore.

Tomorrow he would deal with Billy.

Then it was time to get Kate back.

Chapter 49

Kate

Before leaving the shop yesterday, Kate had made a promise to visit Marcel. An urgent necessity Frances had called it.

On her arrival, Marcel's door had swung open almost immediately. The heat that filtered from the hallway welcome against the chill she still couldn't shake off. The weather had continued to stay dire; another day of grey skies and damp air and she was totally fed up with it now. As she handed her wet coat to Marcel, a strange sense of de ja vu struck her.

"Kate." Marcel said. "You were miles away."

"Hm? Yes sorry, just cold that's all."

Opening the door to the kitchen, she was taken aback when she saw Frances sat in one of the wicker chairs. She forced a smile, hoping it would ease the feeling that had surfaced telling her that this didn't bode well.

Sat in the double aspect lounge, they drank yet more tea and discussed the weather. That's all everyone seemed to do, talk about how long it had been since they'd seen such a spell of prolonged grey and damp. And she was sick of tea. It did nothing to quench Kate's impatience. Irritability moved her fingers, tracing the pattern on the mug, feeling the bumps from the transfer. Her heartbeat quickened, inching out of her chest as the familiar fluttering began to surface. She pushed the mug onto the table, pushing herself back into the chair, pulling the sleeves of her jumper down over her hands. She wished one of them would speak about the real reason they were all here. She couldn't bring herself to ask though, desperate to know but petrified of their reply.

Both ladies could see the immense discomfort that had worked its way through Kate. They hadn't wanted that; they had wanted her to be calm and relaxed, soon realising they should have gotten straight to the point. Prolonging it with small talk only seemed to add to her anxiety. They should have known that Kate would not offer up any conversation.

"My dear, you must be wondering why I asked you to come and see Marcel and why I too am here. We never did finish our conversation yesterday, did we? Remember I asked you if you knew of the term channel." Frances's glow had returned, not even the merest hint of a shadow on her face.

"Yes, I remember but I have no idea what it means, other than the conventional sense." Kate's eyes full of questions, moved from Frances to Marcel and back again.

"Sometimes Kate," it was Marcel who took up the task of answering, "there are people who are placed on this earth to help orchestrate change. To help bring more peace and love to the world. And there are many ways in which people do this. I myself for example, help individuals to make peace with themselves, with things that have happened in their lives in order to help them lead a more joyous life. Peace on a personal level helps facilitate change more widespread. Does that make sense up to know?"

"I guess so. But I don't understand what that's got to do with me. Is this to do with yesterday? With Paul and all that stuff?" She searched them both, needing to know. The seconds before Frances spoke stretched endlessly to Kate.

"No, my dear, not yesterday. This is about your dreams." Frances was careful not to go too fast, this was a delicate matter.

"My dreams? But I don't understand, I...I haven't told anyone."

"Both Marcel and I are on the edge of your dreams and I believe that is to help you through them. You see my dear, dreams aren't always what they seem..." Frances stopped, her eyes spoke a silent language totally foreign to Kate, but fluent to Marcel as she effortlessly picked up where Frances had left.

"Dreams can be many things. They can act as messengers to us when we need answers or simply to help the body let go of stress. And very rarely they can act as a bridge. A bridge to the past." Marcel kept her attention on Kate as she spoke, needing to see if her words were acknowledged or brushed away.

Kate was still, hands firmly shrouded in her sleeves as they rested on her knees, feet wedged on the edge of the chair. Quiet.

"We think Kate that somehow, your dreams are serving as a bridge to the past. That something, or someone is trying to tell you something. You told me you had these happenings as you called them as a little girl then they stopped, arising again not long before you came here. Only now, they have become clearer, more graphic, real."

Kate's head moved slowly, unable to process and speak at the same time.

"Most children dream of times past and see or hear things that adults don't, then as they get older, they stop, for one of several reasons. But for some, these things never stop. And can manifest in many different ways. Everything and everyone are divinely connected and some of us, in afterlife, might have agreed to return to help others in ways we as humans cannot even begin to comprehend, or remember. I understand Kate how peculiar all this might sound, and I am trying to explain to you in the easiest way possible." Marcel threw Kate a warm smile, wanting to reassure her everything was good.

But as normal as all this might be to them, it was anything but that to Kate who sat weighted in her chair, emotions sewing together to form a clumsy patchwork.

"Everything that has happened in your past Kate

has led you here today. By unravelling the truth of your own past, you have cleared the way to help uncover the truth of a buried past, not of this lifetime. It has all played a role in bringing you here. What's important is that you don't try to analyse all that we are telling you because it will complicate things further for you."

Kate wondered how things could possibly get any more complicated than they were already and as for analysing, she was struggling to take it in let alone analyse it.

Frances knew a change of approach was needed, if they were to help Kate and stop her from retreating within herself, a direct attitude was now for the best.

"We cannot tell you my dear what these dreams are trying to tell you. Only you can decipher them, that is your path. And for you to know that, you have to embrace them. And that becomes easier when you have made peace with your past. I could see yesterday you were searching for forgiveness for Paul. But you must also forgive yourself. Marcel and I are here for you, every step of the way but for us to help you, you have to be honest with us and let us in."

A chord had been struck; she wasn't sure what it was but there was a definite shift in her. The need to shield herself lessened as she lowered her feet to the floor, her thighs ached from holding them up in one position for so long. Discreetly, she unfurled her fingers, allowing them to poke free from her sleeves, to rest on her lap. She straightened her back, breathing in hard as she did, letting it out slow and steady. She was ready to talk.

"I'm not going to say I understand because I really don't. But something seems to make sense, even though I can't tell you what or why. A contradiction. Something that my life has always had in abundance." Kate had no idea why she let out a laugh.

"Ask anything you want of us my dear, anything at all. Our role is to help you understand." Frances shuffled forward in her chair, leaning over the round table to squeeze Kate's hand, a gesture full of encouragement.

"I guess there are lots of things I'd like to know. But the main one I can think about right now is why now?"

It was not directed at either, just purely thrown out for one of them to answer.

"That is something that I'm afraid we cannot answer dear." The silent language between Frances and Marcel loud once more.

"We call it divine timing," Marcel replied. "Like Frances said, we don't know why but we have to have faith that everything is working for us."

"So, all this stuff with Mark, Billy and Paul...that's the bit that I can't understand, what all that has got to do with these absences, well dreams as they have now become." Kate had slumped back into her chair, her shoulders rounded as her mind slipped back into trying to logicise everything.

"All of that will become apparent when the time is right. It might be helpful though to think of past experiences as stepping stones to the life that you are destined for. For better things to come. In some way, all our pasts are intrinsically linked."

"Really?" To Kate, it seemed cruel, heartless, to think of people and all that had happened to them as stepping stones to a better life. It was all too much to make sense of.

Even though both Marcel and Frances had told her that sometimes, because of the free will of humans, things happen that weren't part of the plan. Diversions taken because we don't always listen to the true voice that sits in our heart, fighting against the current instead of going with it. If she had to choose, the latter seemed more bearable for her, even though she knew then that she of course was responsible. The tug of war going on in her head was an uncomfortable place to be, one she feared would only get violent if she allowed herself to stay there.

"So, these dreams..." Kate asked, "why me? And when you say you're on the edge of them, what does that mean?" Her voice had become almost defensive now, a sharpness to it which made both Frances and Marcel sit up.

"That too I'm afraid, we do not have the answers for. Dream space is something that is not yet fully understood, but we do know that a dream state can be shared. I can speak only for myself when I say that when I see you, I see you watching the dream play out in front of you. A bystander if you like."

Marcel turned to Frances, keen to hear her experience, realising they had never exchanged how they saw what they witnessed.

Frances confirmed that she too saw in the same way as Marcel did. It wasn't her place to say that she saw exactly what was happening, or the messages Kate's dreams were trying to convey. Or the people that were intrinsic in all this. This was Kate's path, destiny. She could not interfere. She had seen Kate running away, seen the person who had scared her so much. Felt the blisters appear on her heels in her frantic attempt to flee. And she had seen what had followed, lingering in the dream space fractionally longer than Kate had. Always one step ahead.

The hours passed as Kate told them exactly where she was up to with the dreams. How they had moved on from the absences, the vast expanse of darkness that filled her with dread and confusion when she roused to something much more visual. Although the images came in and out of focus, she was able to recall all that had happened in them. Each one growing in clarity, lasting a little longer than the last, episodes of something she had no name for. And although scared at times, a part of her wanted to go back. Go back to where she had left to find out more.

She left Marcel's house shortly after six, a quiet ache inside of her to get back to Jack, and Bernarde. To normality. If only for a while.

Everyone comes into your life for a reason, season or

lifetime.

She hadn't noticed the hooded figure that had waited for her to leave Laburnum House, staying two steps behind as it followed her back down to Jack's. Too trapped in the cacophony of thoughts to even hear her mobile ring. Although the drizzle had stopped, the sky, bowing with dark threatening clouds, aided the fading light, bringing in darkness. Pushing her hands deeper into the pockets of her heavy coat, she picked up her pace, wanting to escape the cold.

"Kate, where have you been?"

Light poured out of the open door opened as she rounded the corner, casting shadows from the surrounding trees across the drive. Bernarde had clearly been waiting for her to return, his voice anxious.

"I've been trying to call you."

"Whatever's all this B? I've been at Marcel's, I told you. Why are you waiting for me?"

Inside the warmth of the apartment, Bernarde had still not been forthcoming with conversation. He paced the floor of the lounge, walking its length from the kitchen and back again, chewing the side of his thumb.

"Will you tell me what's wrong? And Jack, where is he?"

Kate had only ever seen Bernarde like this once before, a time both of them had never spoke about again. The worry spiralled through her now creating a wave of dizziness. She sat herself down, afraid she would fall down if she continued to stand, longing for Bernarde to tell her what the hell was going on. He joined her, unable to look at her for longer than a second to start with.

"Jack, Bernarde...where is he?" Kate demanded.

"Looking for you."

He'd been a fool, an absolute fool. Too self-absorbed to think of any consequences.

"Why? What's wrong?"

"I'm so sorry Kate, you have to believe me when I tell you it wasn't intentional. But Jack, he's looking for you because..." He broke off, swallowing hard in order to stem the shame that was rapidly creeping through him. "Because Owen is here Kate. In Dartmouth."

Chapter 50

Owen

Finding Billy's number was easy, getting him to answer had been an entirely different matter altogether. He despised old people and mobile phones, they either never heard them ring or had them switched off for most of the day. What was the point? In the end, he'd took to searching the local boat yard, assuming he would still have his boat, or at the very least be involved with people that had. Ready to approach a middle-aged woman laden with a brimming cleaning bucket and mop, he spotted him, his lucky day. Tucked away in the far corner of the yard, he made his way over.

"Well hello stranger."

"Owen, what the..." The colour drained from Billy's face as he struggled to comprehend the figure stood before him. It had been a long time and they'd had an agreement.

"We need to talk Billy."

"About what? We had an agreement. What are you doing here?" Billy spoke firm. he couldn't let him see the concern that was busy knotting inside.

"Hmm, we did Billy boy, you're right. And we still

do. But things have changed...haven't they." He gave him no time to respond. "Because Kate is here. And not with me where she should be. Now do you want to do this here or shall we go somewhere more private?" This time waiting for Billy to reply as he took another step forward.

"In here." Billy cocked his head towards the boat he'd been working on but not before checking to see if anyone was around. Although it was growing dark, he couldn't risk anyone seeing him.

"So..." Owen was growing impatient waiting for Billy to talk.

"So, what do you want me to say? Yes, Kate's here. I have no idea what's gone on between the two of you, all I know is Kate needed a break." Billy chose his words carefully, keeping the annoyance from his voice.

"So what have you told her Billy boy because I don't know what's gone on between the two of us either. I booked us a table at some crappy little restaurant to try and cheer her up after she was sacked and she never turned up. All I got was a note. After everything, all I'm worth is a god damn fucking note!" Owen turned away, just for a moment, pressing his hands down hard against the boats shiny wood interior to contain the brewing anger. "I saw the photo Billy. The five of you all looked very cosy out to dinner. Who is he?"

"What photo?"

Billy knew exactly what and who he was talking about but had no idea how Owen did.

"Good old Bernarde. Couldn't help but share his life to the world. Who is he Billy? And what have you told her for Christ's sake!" Owen banged his fist down hard, rattling whatever was kept in the drawer beneath.

In the limited space they were in, the air was suffocating, closing in.

"Owen, I think you need to take a breath and calm down mate, this isn't helping anything." Billy's suggestion more of an order than a request.

The silence between them was deafening, both as stubborn as the other but Billy was determined he was not going to ride rough shot over him. Eventually it was Owen's resolve that broke.

"I have to know Billy what she knows and who told her. She took off for no reason I can think of other than this. I take it you know he's out? I want a chance to explain. Does she know how you're involved in this?"

"Right, listen Owen. First things first. Yes, Paul is out. And yes, Kate knows, but only some of it. She arrived here out the blue, it was as much as a shock to us as it was to you. All she told us was she needed time and that, well I'm sorry, but that she didn't love you. The guy in the photo, Jack, is a friend of mine who needed someone to look after his apartment while he was away on business. If there is anything more then I'm not party to that. She turned up at ours on Tuesday, she'd seen the newspaper, about Paul. So yes, she knows Mark's death was not suicide and she knows I kept it from her. She's angry, understandably, but she has no idea that the two of us know each other and I think it's best kept that way. Don't you?"

If Billy was looking for reassurance from that last comment, he wasn't going to get it.

"Slight problem. They've been in touch. I've dealt with them for now, but I reckon it'll only be a matter of time before Paul tells her the truth."

The two men paused, suspended in time, unsure of their next move.

But it wasn't theirs to make.

Chapter 51

Kate

The wait for Jack's return had been an anxious one, neither of them able to contact him on his mobile, endless messages sent to let him know Kate was home, and safe. She vowed that she would give it another hour then she would have to swallow the pill known as pride and contact Billy. Fortunately, that moment never came.

"Thank god you're back!"

He was barely through the door when she rushed to him, wrapping her arms tight around his waist, kissing his chest, checking everything was okay.

"I might disappear more often if this is what awaits my return."

The teasing was lost on Kate. The very thought of him disappearing from her life scraped away at her, leaving her raw. Whatever bound them together had well and truly took hold now.

As the evening wore on, they talked about the one person Kate thought was finally out of her life. Bernarde had been full of apologies, over and over, for posting that photo on Instagram of them all out at dinner together. Peter had told him times it would come back and bite him on the arse, or words to that effect whenever he uploaded pictures, sharing his life with the world and he was right, because it now well and truly had come back to bite him.

He was devastated when he showed her the post Owen had tagged him in with the caption *'Guess where I am?'* Kate couldn't be cross with him though; it was just how Bernarde was. It was herself she was cross with, a fool to think that Owen wouldn't have tracked her down sooner or later anyway. If she'd had the gumption to speak to him this would never had happened. It was just a shame that Jack and Bernarde had been dragged into her pitiful mess.

There had been no sign of him, Jack had told them. He'd asked around and no one had caught sight of him lurking around. He was discreet, Jack would give him that. Exhausting all of his options, he'd had no choice but to call in on Billy and Trish, they needed to know. But he was too late. Owen had already been in touch and Billy urged Jack to not let Kate out of his sight. Despite what Kate thought of her Uncle now, she needed all the support that was available to her. Jack didn't tell her he'd been to see them, the last thing he wanted was to antagonise her any more than she already was. They would discuss it tomorrow when she'd had time to reflect.

The rain had picked up again, thrashing hard against everything that blocked its path. Kate stood by the balcony window, watching it hammer against the glass, a barrier forcing it to stop and change direction, its only way was to trickle downwards and add to the growing pools on the decking. The cold from the glass made her shiver and she pulled at her cardigan, wrapping it tighter across her body as she brought into focus Moundhill House. But it was dark and she was tired. The invisible weight she carried had grown heavier, draining her, even to stand took a great amount of effort. Her bed called, but she knew as soon as she shut her eyes, she would swap one nightmare for another. And even though she yearned for a peaceful, uneventful nights rest, she longed to know what her dream was all about.

Through the patchwork of gaps in the bushes,
she could see him, searching for her.

She dare not breathe.

She couldn't let him find her.

The stench of anger poured from his skin,
raging, carried to her on the breeze.

He turned, away from the bracken
where she was crouched.

He was moving, away from her.

He hadn't seen her.

The breath left her body hot and warm, exhaling
with it the fear it had held deep.

He must have followed her, but where was Clarence?

She didn't understand.

Why hadn't he come?

Chapter 52

Kate

"Hey Marcel, it's Kate. Can I come over and see you?"

"Kate, hi. Yes, you know you can, is everything okay though?" Marcel knew it wasn't, Kate wouldn't be calling otherwise, her chirpy voice a smoke-screen to her troubled mind.

"I have a few things I'd like to ask that's all. What time would suit you?"

∞∞∞

Waiting for one pm to come, Kate struggled to settle her mind to anything. She should've been at work but Frances had decided not to open up, asking her if she could work on Monday instead. It made no difference to Kate, but it did leave her questioning why Frances was not opening. Jack had gone out for a run and Bernarde had shut himself away in his room, his wounds of embarrassment still in need of licking. She couldn't go out if even she had wanted to; Jack had locked the door and she couldn't for the life her find her own keys to open it.

She moved around the large open plan living space, wandering aimlessly, finding comfort in her appreciation of the clean lines that were everywhere from the floor to the fittings to the soft furnishings. Stroking her fingers across the backs of the sofa's in turn as she walked round them, she paused at the third, the sideboard lugging at her attention. A sudden urge to open the book that Frances had insisted she take had her fingers clamping its spine, pulling it free. She wondered why she hadn't felt any urge to read the other book she'd shut away as she made her way to the sofa.

Nestling herself back into its plump cushions, a shudder broke free as she opened the book on the exact page that she had closed it on last time. She studied the picture more closely this time, her eyes drawn to the image of the straight-backed gentleman. Although the image was in sepia, the darkness that emanated from him came through clearly. Darkness that carried with it something far more sinister. Malevolence. Fear. She hadn't noticed it when she had first looked, but now she could easily see the fear etched into the face of his wife, his large fingers gripped her shoulder, pressing hard into her thin frame as she sat in front of him. The fear that was held in that tiny photograph managed to push its way from the page, filling the space around Kate, closing in on her, its grip palpable.

It was *him*.

The distorted face that haunted her.

The face that had begun to grow in clarity.

The face that she had seen in her dream while hiding in the bracken. The face of the man who was filled with fury. A man who she was so scared of she was left with no choice but to hide.

But why?

She stared at the page, disbelief clouding her ability to process anything rational. Why was the man from this image in her dream? None of it made any sense.

Especially the unexplainable terror she felt as her eyes met his.

Her eyes were still locked on that page, that image when Jack arrived back, not hearing him call her at first. She wanted nothing more than to break free from the image but something unknown drew her in, keeping her there, making it difficult for her to close the book.

"What you up to?" Jack leant over the sofa, kissing the top of her head.

As the heat of his kiss began to thaw the icy fear that ran through her, she put the book to her side, turning sideways to face him.

"Good run?"

"Hard run," he laughed. It had been a while since he had ran such a distance and his calves throbbed.

"Mmm, so I can smell." Kate's laugh playful as she held her nose.

"Cheeky! For that you can make me a drink while I get in the shower and then you can tell how busy you've been this morning...reading."

He stripped off his sweaty t-shirt, revealing his lightly tanned chest, throwing it at her, laughing back as he passed. His bare skin was a sight that Kate knew she would never tire of seeing. The carnal desire burned deep, making her want him.

Appearing ten minutes later, he sat himself down on the sofa next to her, still teasing her about her busy morning.

"I'd love to tell you all about it Jack but I'm off to see Marcel shortly." The serious edge to her voice unhidden.

"You seem distracted, I was only joking with you, you know that, right?"

"Yeah, course I do silly." Kate locked her fingers through his, a gentle squeeze of affection. "I was reading this right." She twisted round for the book, a pointed finger indicating where he should look. "That guy Jack, his face. That is the face I have been seeing."

Jack could feel the colour draining from him, taste the sickly sweetness that had furred the inside of his mouth. He swallowed hard, taking the book from her, snapping it shut, dropping it on the floor.

"Where did you get that book from Kate?"

"The bookshop, why? Jack what's wrong?" She hadn't seen him like this before, but then she hadn't known him that long so why would she.

"It's just, oh I don't know Kate. That house. Gives me the creeps that's all."

He couldn't tell her what really troubled him. He hadn't known her long enough to spring on her something like that. One day he would, but not now.

"I can see why it might, it's filled with such sadness. But it's not the house I wanted you to see Jack, it was the man in the photograph. He's the face I see and I have to find out why."

He wasn't looking at Kate when she spoke to him, she doubted he'd even heard her in the world of his own he was in.

"Sorry sweetheart, miles away." He had heard her but it was easier to pretend he hadn't, knowing she wouldn't press him. He didn't understand himself so how could he expect anyone else too?

"It's fine Jack, whatever it is it can wait." Her lips skimmed his cheek. "Listen, I have to go to Marcel's now if that's okay?"

He might not have known her long but he knew that he had fallen for her hook line and sinker. She was the kindest, gentlest person he had ever met, her smile able to pour light into anyone on the receiving end of it.

No wonder Owen wanted her back.

Standing in Marcel's kitchen, the two women were surrounded by esoteric knick-knacks and a nervous atmosphere.

"I'm guessing you didn't just fancy a coffee?" Marcel raised an eyebrow, holding out the hot drink to

Kate.

"Marcel there's something I need to tell you but I'm going to sound crazy. Can we sit down?"

"Sure."

Kate followed her to the wicker chairs housed neatly under the bistro table next to the French doors that overlooked an enormous herbaceous garden waiting to burst into colour.

"I called you this morning because I wanted to speak with you about the dreams I'm having. It's just that they've become clearer and...I can see faces now. Hear voices and touch things. And feel things. But they seem to just cut off, even though I don't want them to. But, after I called you, I picked up the book that Frances had told me to take home and went back to the pages I'd already read. It was there Marcel. In black and white staring right at me. The face I saw that I thought was a figment of my imagination. The face that's in my dream that I was so terrified of is the same face in this image." Kate delved into her bag, retrieving the book and laid it out on the table, opening it up at the image for Marcel to look at it.

Marcel glanced down only briefly at the picture.

"You don't believe me, do you?" Confusion shaped her expression as she turned.

"Kate, what on earth makes you think that! Why wouldn't I believe you, hey?"

The relief that rushed through Kate brought a tear to her eye. She was home to a cocktail of emotions that gave no warning of when they were about to pour. She blinked it away, not wanting anything to get in the way of this conversation.

"I'm confused Marcel, I just don't get it." Her head shook from side to side as she waited for yet more reassurance from the woman who had somehow become her mentor.

"Remember what Frances said to you, hmm? About not trying too hard to figure things out?"

She did remember but she'd panicked. She'd become conflicted between wanting this, wanting to know what she was caught in the middle of yet not wanting to experience all the associated mess that it inevitably brought with it. Conflicted as she was, there was nowhere to run to and nowhere to hide. For the first time in her life she knew that she had no choice but to front it out because whatever it was wasn't going anywhere.

"You're stronger than you think Kate, you can do this. The best advice I can give you is to focus on staying as relaxed as you can."

She wondered how many more smiles of encouragement Marcel would show her, aware she'd probably had far more than her fair share already.

"Do you think you would like another Reiki session maybe? Help restore a bit of calm?"

Kate contemplated if there was no end to the patience and generosity that this woman, who she had barely known a couple of weeks, had shown her.

"If you've not got to rush back, I can get the space ready now?"

"Marcel thank you. I would love that. Can I just

call Jack though and let him know? I told him I wouldn't be long and I don't want him to worry." She hadn't told Marcel that Owen had turned up, hadn't thought it relevant to offload more than was necessary.

"Sure. You do what you need to do while I go and prepare. I'll be about ten minutes so help yourself to a drink and use the bathroom if you need to."

Kate did just that. Poured herself a glass of water, rang Jack who made her promise to call him when she was ready to leave and then used the bathroom. Marcel was ready and waiting for her on her return. Escorting her through to the candle lit room, the heady scent of incense met her as she climbed onto the couch. Knowing the drill, she lay down and closed her eyes, ready for whatever awaited.

It hadn't taken long for the silence to take Kate. It was already there, ready and waiting to show her more.

My heartbeat slows.

I can breathe again.

He has gone, of that I am sure.

Even if just for now.

*My body stings as I straighten up from the
twisted position I'd forced myself into.*

I have to be brave and move from here to find Clarence.

*I walk back towards the train station clutching
a desperate hope that he will be there.*

*My steps are light and considered,
my senses on high alert.*

Just in case.

*The quietness around me is eerie, tugging
my spine straight, a rod of cold steel.*

I'm back on the platform, devoid of passengers.

The next train not due for hours now.

*In the distance, I catch sight of the station
master sat outside his office.*

He throws me a wave and my shoulders relax a little.

A welcome sight, a temporary safeness.

I hope.

But I don't know what to do next.

I know I can't go home, not now.

*The anger and violence that will be waiting
is too...too much to contemplate.*

I might deserve it but I know it is not my fate.

*I sit myself down on the bench nearest
to the station master's office.*

I have to wait for Clarence.

Kate's eyes flickered open momentarily. The outline of hands hovering ever so slightly somewhere over her lower body vague to her blurred vision. But the pull back to the living dream was strong and soon she was back there. Ready to experience more

I watch the hands of the station clock carry
out their rhythmic task but have no idea
of how long I have been sat here.

The station master is in front of me, asking if I'm alright.

I smile, nervously, unsure of what to say.

He asks my name but I am too afraid
to tell him in case it is a trap.

I lie and tell him my name is Mary-Ann.

He smiles back and tells me it's a shame
as he has a message in his office.

A message for a Rosalie.

I lie again and tell him that is who I am waiting for.

I'm not certain if he believes me or not.

I decide not.

My heart has turned to stone, heavy,
cold and dead in my chest.

But then I realise Victor would never
allow his business to be known.

By anyone. He never had.

He was always careful to conceal any damage
he had caused.

"Listen Miss…"

The voice was firm, bringing me from my musings.

I look up at him, I think he sees the fear that ills me.

He flips me a wink and tells me that should
Rosalie make an appearance, to tell her there
is a Mr Clarence waiting in his office.

My heart skips.

He is here.

He has been here all along.

I'm warmed by the rush of hope
and joy that finally come.

"Wait!" I shout after him, asking him to take me to him.

Though I allowed doubt to earlier consume me,
my heart knew he would not let me down.

It had been a difficult decision to make,
one that had taken time.

To leave behind my life of privilege, wealth and security.

But it wasn't difficult to know I longed
for a life that knew love.

My body ached to feel something more than
the pain it had long become accustomed to.

And Clarence gave me that something more.

He may be just one person but he is my new world.

He appears at the door and I immediately
feel invincible.

My saviour.

My protector.

He pulls me close, restoring me to life.

Every cell in me magnetised with a new
sense of freedom and hope.

For from the darkness there is now a bright, shining light.

The station master tells us to go safely, ensuring
Clarence of his confidentiality.

The notes that passed between them clearly a factor.

He takes my hand and leads me
away from the platform.

Each step a step closer to my new life.

But for tonight, we have to rest.

Clarence tells me he has booked us into
a hotel a few miles away.

Away from anyone who might recognise us.
I am tired.
I let my eyes close and allow sleep to take me …

Kate was undecided as to whether the end of her session coincided with the end of her dream or vice versa. Either way, she wished neither had finished.

So, Rosalie was running away with Clarence in search of a better life. And her hunch about the man in the picture who she knew now to be Victor was right. Although she had not witnessed the beatings Rosalie had been subjected to, she had felt the rawness of her skin where her dress had rubbed up against it. Had flashes of the pain where the buckle had ripped into the flesh so cruelly and felt the swelling in her abdomen when she had crouched to hide. There was no disputing he was a cruel, vicious man and she was pleased Rosalie had found a way to break free from him.

Marcel and Kate discussed at length what she had experienced. It was strange to be a part of something that was in the distant past yet was happening right now. She had stepped inside a film set, complete with costume dress of another era. But it was more than voyeurism. She had not only slipped into another's story but had now, somehow, become the main character. Marcel listened earnestly as she brought to life the train station and its kindly master. The very station that sat here in Kingswear that tourists could only imagine what their paid glimpse to the past was really like. She could still feel the chiffon fabric of the drop waist dress brush against her skin, its soft pastel blue a colour she would never wear today. And Clarence. The depth of those sea blue eyes. The tiny scar above the right eyebrow that creased ever so slightly when he smiled, she would never forget. How could she? She saw it every day.

Marcel, as usual, did not seem perplexed at all as she heard detail after detail relayed in glorious technicolour. A knowing smile told Kate she need not be surprised that Jack wore the same scar as Clarence. But still she didn't know why.

"Have you considered that they are the same person Kate?" The question thrown out as more of a comment.

"Up until now, no. And I don't understand how they could be because I once saw Victor's face in Jack, staring back at me. But none of this has any reasoned logic to it. And you know what Marcel, I don't need to understand how all this stuff works. During that session, everything that happened... this time it was real. I could touch and taste things, just like I can now. It was happening to me. I was Rosalie."

Marcel clasped her palms together, holding them in front of her chest while a huge grin replaced the earlier smile.

"Yes! Oh Kate, I can't tell you how happy I am to hear you confirm what we believed to be happening."

"You knew?"

Marcel's nod provided her answer.

"Wow. Right. So, now we're all singing from the

same hymn sheet as they say, what happens next?"

"You follow this through and find out why you are bringing this story to life." Marcel brought her hands forward wrapping them over the top of Kate's. "There are reasons behind everything and there is clearly something here that needs to be outed."

"Thank you. I really mean that. Do you think I should call Frances?"

"I have to call her so could let her know if you like?"

"Thank you," Kate smiled, grateful for the offer. "Tell her I'll see her tomorrow at work."

Chapter 53

Frances

Frances had been deeply engrossed in her thoughts when the telephone rang. She had known before she picked up the old-fashioned receiver who the caller was.

"Hello my dear Marcel."

"Frances, hi."

Over the years Marcel had learnt a great deal from this quietly eccentric woman so it came as no surprise to her that she knew who was on the end of the line. Others would simply assume she had a caller display feature on her phone.

"There's been a development with Kate."

Filling Frances in with the morning news, Marcel kept the topic light and straight to the point. Thanking her for calling and updating her, Frances of course already knew. She knew how scared Kate had been when she had forced her tiny frame into the bracken. Felt the heavy weight of her heart as she waited on the platform for the man who had become her saviour from the murkiness that pervaded her everyday life. She knew because as always, she had been there too, on the edge, observing every little step and detail in this tragic story, knowing what was to come next. And although she could not stop what was to happen, this time she was determined it was not to be the end.

Chapter 54

Kate

K ate had been disappointed that her sleep had been deep and unbroken for she had longed to go back. This living dream had taken her firmly in its hold and the line between then and now had started to blur, making the boundary between what was and wasn't real hard to distinguish.

Having eventually gained enough strength, the sun burnt through the hefty cloud of late and the brightness that washed over everything in its sight was a welcome change from the recent drab grey. But amongst the brightness, a trail of darkness had managed to weave a path through, following Kate's every move, determined not to let her out of sight. For it too had a mission to fulfil, and soon it would be accomplished. Especially now Owen was in town.

"Good Morning my dear." The voice rang even lighter than usual against the tinkle of the brass bell. "Beautiful morning."

"Morning, it certainly is."

In between customers, Kate had busied herself dusting the newly organised shelves, eager for lunchtime to come so she could speak to Frances without fear of interruption. The shop had been a hive of activity that morning and she guessed the sunshine had been a factor in getting people into town. Lunchtime soon approached and after turning the closed for lunch sign round, she joined Frances out in the back.

"So dearie, Marcel tells me there has been some developments."

"Hmm, I guess you could say that," Kate replied, reaching down by her side. "I wanted to ask you something though Frances, about something in this book." She placed it carefully on the table in the gap between the hand painted china plates.

"Ah," Frances took the linen napkin, dabbing at her mouth, "The History of The River Dart. The book you took home with you last week if I am correct?"

Kate nodded.

"Ask away my dear girl, I am all ears."

"So, there's a chapter in this book about Moundhill House." Kate tapped the book, letting her hand rest atop of it, keen to contain what it held. "At first, I was interested because I have always had a strange affinity with it, ever since I was a little girl. Anyway, there's a picture, taken of the owners and the staff stood outside of it. When I first saw it, I knew there was something about it but I couldn't quite place what. The sadness I felt was unbelievably overwhelming. A couple of days later, I looked at it again, properly, and that's when it came to me. The man in that photograph is the same man that haunts my dream. The man that I was running away from. Terrified of. And as I'm saying this to you now, I realise that the lady in that same photograph has to be me because in my dream I am Rosalie."

The enormity of that last sentence brought creases to Kate's forehead as she waited for Frances to apply some kind of logic to all this.

"Oh my dear girl, please don't be taken in despair. You are unlocking the codes to a forgotten past and I am here with you every step of the way." Frances had been careful in her response, keen to keep her voice neutral.

"You see the thing is Frances, when I realised the man in the photo was the face in my dreams, it was hard not to miss it. Standing behind her, in that image you could see the power he held over her, the emptiness behind her eyes. It was like as soon as I made that connection, it gave permission for what followed. My dreams became so clear and vivid, alive with colour and emotion. I still don't understand why am I seeing all this or what is expected of me but I'm okay with that. What I really can't get my head around is why Jack looks exactly like Clarence."

Frances had to tread carefully here; she couldn't

risk frightening her. She sat silent for moment, holding Kate in a smile. Then she remembered the other book, *Passages of Time,* from the man on the train.

"Kate, I want you to remember back to the train journey down here. In particular, a gentleman who left you a book."

"How could I forget! But what has that got to do with all this?" Kate bounced her index finger on the book that sat between them, the nails from her others digging in to her palm.

"The book he left you my dear holds all the answers to your questions. And when the time is right, you'll read it and it will serve you well through life for dreams are simply reflections of the unconscious mind."

"That man Frances, do you know who he was? The one on the train I mean."

"I don't my dear but why should it bother you so?"

"Because he knew my name, that's why. And then just disappeared! And I don't ever remember telling you about it." Kate was aware her words had come out slightly too harsh from the way Frances bristled.

"People come into our lives Kate for a reason, a season or a lifetime. Certain individuals have all sorts of extraordinary gifts that they share with others in the most selfless of ways, all in the name of service. We do not need to logicise everything we experience in life for if we do, life has a tendency to lose its magic."

Frances pushed her chair away from the table and stood, lifting the teapot from the middle of the untouched spread that had been laid out. Taking it over to the worktop, she looked back at Kate and said, "Fresh tea I think."

Relieved that this lady that had so kindly taken her under her wing appeared not to have taken offence at her earlier directness, Kate wondered if the distraction of tea making was intentional. Time for her to process the words Frances had imparted. The niggle in the back of her mind told her she had to stop analysing things. A trait she had unfortunately, over the years, developed into a fine art. Maybe it was time to try a different way. Wasn't that what Frances had more or less said? In such a short space of time, this dream had taken over every part of her life. It was all she thought about, mostly. Brief interludes crammed with snapshots of Mark's death, Paul and Uncle Billy. The fire. Her parents. But all of those had happened and she couldn't go back and change anything. Marcel had finally got her to see that. The dark voids that had plagued her had now turned into dreams of glorious technicolour; insistent she should not miss a thing, even if they did fill her with a mix of raw emotion. And that was where her attention had to be if she was to ever solve this riddle.

"I take it you haven't spoken to Jack about all of this dearie?" Frances questioned, setting the teapot back in the centre of the table. "You know dear, speak to him, you might just be surprised."

Kate's mind slipped a memory of yesterday, when she had shown him the book, told him about the man in the photo. She remembered his reluctance saying the house just gave him the creeps before she asked, "Any ideas on how to broach it?"

"From the heart my dear, from the heart. Now, let's eat before this tea goes cold...again!"

The afternoon was as equally busy as the morning had been. The shop thrived on having customers enjoy its offerings, it brought the fabric of the building alive. The last lady left just before five, armed with the purchase of several books about gardens and plants. New to the area she had acquired a large overgrown garden with the house she had bought and didn't know the first thing about gardening. Beaming from the help she had been given, she promised she would be back should she require anything else. When Kate closed the door behind her, a sense of fulfilment warmed her as she slid the closed sign round. Frances was right, she had to talk to Jack.

As she left the shop behind, so too did the trail of darkness that had been patiently waiting, descending once more behind her. The eyes that watched her every move would soon show themselves to her, the time to give them a voice had nearly arrived.

Chapter 55

Kate

Kate had purposely kept the conversation light over dinner and the wine flowing. If she was going to talk to Jack, she needed them both to be relaxed, and wine definitely helped on that front. Bernarde had been only too obliging when she had called earlier asking if he could make himself scarce so they could have the evening to themselves. He figured it was the least he could do considering how gracious Kate had been over his stupid faux pas. So, after they had eaten and the two of them sat snuggled on the sofa, Kate seized the moment.

"Jack…I have to talk to you."

"I could think of better things to do." Jack teased her, tenderly nuzzling her neck, taking in the warm floral scent of her skin.

"Please Jack, it's important." The tone of urgency in her voice took his eyes up to meet hers.

"What's wrong sweetheart, you've gone all serious on me."

"I have to talk to you about something Jack and it's…well it's not easy for me. Remember yesterday when I showed you that old photograph in the book and told you I recognised the man as it was the face I had been seeing?"

"I remember, what about it though?"

"Right, I know this is going to sound crazy but just hear me out. Please?" Positioning herself sideways on the sofa, she sat crossed legged, waiting for the green light.

"Okay," Jack said, no idea of where this was going.

"So, remember we spoke about that face pareidolia thing, well I don't think that's what's happening to me. You see I've started to have these dreams Jack. Dreams of a different time, another life. And well that photo I showed you has got something to do with it, what, I'm not quite sure of yet." She looked up at Jack, unaware until then she had been staring at her knees. There was something there, in his eyes. Unspoken words that encouraged her to continue. Hope. "It's like little bits of the jigsaw are starting to slot into place, allowing more of the story to unfold each time I close my eyes. But here's the strange thing Jack, you're there too. Only you're not Jack, you're a man called Clarence. A man who I am running away with in search of a better life. A safer life." She continued to search him, hoping he would give something away but instead he turned away, the sudden discomfort too much.

The few minutes of silence that passed seemed to stretch far beyond their true time. But Kate was patient, knowing that if she gave Jack enough space he would talk. After all, he hadn't walked away which she took as being a positive sign. He pushed himself to the edge of the sofa, resting his elbows on his knees, cradling his head in his soft skinned hands. Seconds later, he sat back against the sofa, rolling his head to face Kate, a smile that melted all her immediate worries.

"My turn I guess?" A faint chuckle followed his question. "Yesterday when you showed me that photo and I said that house gave me the creeps, well I guess I owe you an explanation why. You see Kate, that house, the one in the picture, the one that still sits all lonely and sad on the hill today, well...it belongs to me."

Kate's back straightened, her hand flew over her mouth to stifle the gasp. Jack owned Moundhill House. How was that even possible? And how come no one knew? No matter how hard she tried to formulate her words; they just wouldn't leave her mouth. She couldn't remember a time when she had been so stunned, speechless. Her mind, at that moment, was overcrowded with questions, answers proving to be elusive as she struggled to push just one cohesive word from her mouth. "How?"

"It's been in the family for a long time. I inherited it when my Dad passed away a few years back."

"So, you grew up there? No, you couldn't have done because the book says no one has lived there since 1934. How come you said it gives you the creeps if you own it? And why is it always shut up?" Her thoughts immediately manifested in fired questions, full of unintended accusation.

"It's not that straight forward. Firstly, you're right

about it being uninhabited since 1934. The house originally belonged to someone called Rosalie. She came from a family of great wealth, status and privilege. The house, amongst others, had been in her family for generations and she inherited it on her twenty first birthday. Her mother by all accounts had always been incredibly astute when it came to finances and status and was determined her daughters would not have their worth pinned onto the value of whom they should marry. Rosalie did marry, two years after moving into Moundhill but she died in a freak accident. Apparently, the grief became too much for him to bear so he committed suicide. Found hung one morning by his last remaining servant. I found all this out from the local history sources shortly after inheriting the house. My great-grandad bought the house back in 1951 but as far as I know, he only lived there for a short while before shutting it up and moving on. I asked my parents times why they just didn't sell it but everyone seemed reluctant to talk about it." Jack shook his head as he looked towards Kate to take the reins.

"Jack I...I'm sorry. I had no idea." In the instant those words had left her lips she realised how stupid she must've sounded. How the hell could she have known.

"It took me some time to get my head around it when I inherited it and found out what had gone on there, but I guess a part of me has always been intrigued by it all."

The look in his eyes struck her deep as the image of Clarence faded in and out of his face. She had to focus.

"Have you never been inside of it?"

"No. I've wanted to but something has always stopped me. I go up once a year to check round the outside but that's all. It has a peculiar pull does that house."

"What I don't understand is why don't you just sell it?"

A wide smile replaced his seriousness, "If only it was that simple. There's a clause in the deeds that dictates it can't be sold while there's a living relative."

Kate's face wrinkled as she looked over her shoulder, that last sentence acutely familiar.

Jack scooped her cheek into his hand, turning her face back to his. "Sweetheart, you okay?"

"Sorry...just taking it all in."

She let her fingers touch his, wrapping around them as she lowered his hand, squeezing it on her lap.

"Listen, you know when you read the history of the house, was Rosalie's husband called Victor?"

"Yes, Victor Llewellyn. But how do you know that? I'm sure all the public documents only list him as Vice Admiral Llewellyn."

"Because he is the man in the photograph Jack. The man that I see in my dreams. My dreams as Rosalie. And you Jack, you are there too in those dreams. As Clarence."

Jack couldn't speak. As absurd as all this sounded, he contemplated why he was so at ease with it all. He stood and walked to the window, the cream outline of Moundhill house bright against the dusky evening. He flattened his palms against the expanse of glass, stretching out his body, his head hung.

"Jack, talk to me, please."

One thing Kate had always hated was her inability to read another's body language. What was she thinking blurting it out like that? Had she crossed the boundary and gone too far? What did she expect? Not what came next, that was for sure.

"I know Kate, right. I know." He lifted his head and allowed his hands to drop away from the window, turning so that his back now pressed against it. " Jesus Kate, you sure have turned my world upside down I'll give you that."

Kate couldn't fathom out if his smile was genuine or forced.

"Years ago, perhaps twenty or more, I had a period of let's say strange dreams. None of them made any sense because they were so blurred, but then I started seeing faces. Not many but I would see them often, and only for a split second. Anyway, a friend recommended I see someone who after a while diagnosed me as having this face pareidolia syndrome which I told you about. I was prescribed sleeping tablets for a while to help me break the cycle of the rubbish sleep pattern I'd adopted and after a few weeks, it had all stopped and things started to go back to normal. I put it to the back of my mind and got on with my life without anything significant happening." He walked back to the sofa, crouching in front of Kate, taking her hands in his. "And then you came into my life and changed all that." He pulled her hands to meet his lips, a gentle kiss on each. "I knew all those years ago Kate that there was something more to those dreams and faces…and that bloody house. But it was far easier to believe a diagnosis, credible science than a feeling. That first day I met you, well I can't explain it but something happened, call it an internal shift if you like and I just knew we were meant to be together. That you, somehow, connected me to Moundhill."

To hear Jack admit that he too had experienced something in essence similar to what she had overwhelmed her. Pressure built behind her eyes as tears formed, but she didn't care, the rush that swept through her as they began to fall was immense. And needed. She allowed her body to crumple into the strength of his arms, a place of safety where her worries and concerns could at last be set free. In that moment, nearly everything she had ever experienced flashed before her, all worthwhile, to know that they were once again together, after all these decades she was reunited with her Clarence.

Jack, as always held her close, gently assuring her everything would be just fine. But the rolling fear that now crowded in around him told him that the worst was yet to come.

Chapter 56

Owen

Seven missed calls. The screen flashed again, not wanting him to forget. But he didn't care, they could wait. He sipped from the fake crystal tumbler, tapping his finger on the side before placing it down on the cheap mahogany desk come dressing table.

He'd hardly recognised her. There was something different about her, a radiance that had screamed happiness. Genuine happiness. Something he hadn't ever seen in her. But he couldn't let her go. It was his job to keep her safe and make her happy. She just didn't realise it. He picked up the bottle of scotch, allowing the amber liquid to glug into his empty glass. *"Last one,"* he told himself, settling the half empty bottle back on the table, screwing the cap on tight. The screen flashed again, he cursed, snatching up the phone that sat next to his glass.

Tick Tock Tick Tock...Time is...UP!

Like hell it is he thought as he laughed at the message on the screen. He tossed the phone onto the bed, a smirk smeared across his face as he tutted, big bad Paul was still hiding behind a woman. Clearly the time in prison had done nothing to make him into a real man.

But as he gulped down his scotch, his amusement at that message began to swell into a burning ball. Anger. Again. Just who the hell did they think they were! They didn't get to decide anything and they certainly didn't get to play games in his life. They'd had his money; it was time to deal with them properly. He couldn't contact Paul and there was only one language she understood.

"It's me."

The voice on the other end of the line didn't get chance to answer.

"Just listen, get your pert arse over here, now. I want you. I knew when I saw you I wanted you. I've realised since I've been here it's not her I want, it's you. We had something good Sarah and we can again. But I need you, tonight."

Owen guessed it would be easy but he hadn't realised just how easy she would come crawling. It was a dangerous game but one he was willing to play if it meant he won the star prize, Kate. He rang down to room service and ordered a bottle of champagne, if this was going to work, he would have to make it look convincing. He swiped open the voice record app on his phone in preparation, placing it face down on the bedside table. He was ready.

Just minutes later, the gentle knock on his hotel room door told him it was show time.

Chapter 57

*A soft tender touch stroked my cheek, waking
me from slumber.*

How long had I been sleeping?

*For a moment, a strike of panic coursed
my veins and then I saw him.*

My Clarence.

We had arrived at the hotel, I was safe.

*We checked in as Mr and Mrs Clarence,
the receptionist none the wiser.*

*Soon we would be together, alone and a quiet
excitement tingled through my body.*

*We mount the stairs to our room, one two
five, locking the door behind us.*

*Clarence pours us a glass of champagne, adding
a dash of angostora bitters to mine.*

*He must have remembered when I once
asked why couldn't it be pink.*

*He strokes back my hair, the heat from
his lips press into my forehead.*

His darling, always.

*We had waited for what seemed an eternity
for this moment to come.*

And it didn't disappoint.

He gently undresses me, his touch is tender, thoughtful.

Soft, ghost like touches send tingles down my spine.

*I'm stood naked before him as his fingers
trace my scarred flesh.*

*I hear him whisper he is sorry as I notice
a tear swell in his eye.*

*He promises me that he won't let him hurt me
again, that I will now live free from pain.*

*And then his full lips kiss my belly, moving upwards
until they meet my own trembling mouth.*

And gently he takes me.

There is no force or violence.

*Not the slightest hint of a being the
usual means to an end.*

*I am not accustomed to such gentleness,
such consideration, such respect.*

He is the perfect lover.

And now I know what real love should feel like.

Chapter 58

Kate

Kate wondered whether the warmth she felt that morning when she woke was that of her own or Rosalie's. Either way, the calmness that accompanied it was welcome. She watched Jack as he continued to sleep, did he too dream of a forgotten time? She still hadn't fully assimilated everything that was happening and considered if she ever would. It all seemed so surreal.

Her mind flashed back to last night, to the conversation that had carried through into the small hours. Bernarde joining when he returned from his impromptu night out. And to the promise Jack had freely made. To take her to the house. Today. Filled with a heady mix of excitement and trepidation, she slipped out of bed to shower.

The swathe of trees that lined either side of the winding one-way road bore every shade of green imaginable. Having been near on a year since Jack last attempted the road, he nearly missed the left turn they needed, concealed by wild overgrown shrubs. He swung around the corner and brought the car to a stop.

"Right...last chance. Are you sure you are ready to do this?" His question directed at Kate.

"Are you?" She was sure she could smell his nerves.

Bernarde sprang forward between the two front seats, his childlike nature easing the tense atmosphere. "Come on you two, sitting here is not going to solve anything and Bernarde is dying to see what this old place is like!"

"He's right Jack," Kate agreed. "We can do it, have to do it...together."

Jack pressed the ignition button, bringing the car to life, his hands clamped the wheel, arms locked straight. "Here goes."

Driving up along the narrowing lane, Kates stomach had adopted an ebb and flow cycle of nerves and excitement, gaining momentum as they reached the house. All that stood between them now was a pair of rusting old wrought iron gates. Jack unclipped his seatbelt, opened his door and climbed out, walking over to the keypad that sat nestled behind the soft red flowers of the camelia bush. He jabbed the numbers of the keypad, a slight tremble to his finger, pausing momentarily over the last, knowing that when those gates opened there was no going back. As they slowly started to creak open, he climbed back into the car, releasing the brake to drive them back to the past. Turning off the ignition, the three of them sat quiet and still, overcome by the grandeur of what they now looked at.

Kate's mobile rang, startling them all. It was Billy.

"Aren't you going to answer it?"

Kate stared down at the screen, annoyed at the intrusion.

"He'll keep trying you know. Maybe best to get it over and done with now he's back, hm?"

She knew Jack was right. He'd told her last night that he'd been to see him when he heard that Owen was in town and how concerned Billy had been. But that didn't change how sickened she felt when she thought back to what Paul had told her, but she would have to speak to him, sometime.

The phone rang again. Billy.

She answered and kept the conversation brief, agreeing to call round later and talk, on her terms. Right now, there was something far more interesting jostling for her attention.

"Right, come on you two," she said, "we can't look from out here."

She climbed out of the car, quietly shutting the door behind her, not wanting to disturb anything or awake the house before she was inside.

Jack and Bernarde followed suit.

Their footsteps crunched the gravel they walked on, the noise sending a nearby blackbird darting up into the sky. They climbed the three, half-moon steps up to the door, waiting as Jack took the key from his jacket pocket. A quick glance at Kate, he pushed it into the lock, turning it anti-clockwise.

He pushed the heavy panelled door ajar, stopped from going further by a twinge that pinched his hand, feeling like a trespasser even though he owned the place. He looked at Kate, hoping to find strength in her eyes. She took the lead and pushed the door fully open, walking through to find herself in a grand, polished marble entrance hall. Turning back to Jack and Bernarde, she was surprised to see they hadn't followed her in.

After some coaxing, she managed to get them both inside and closed the door behind them.

Full of awe, Bernarde asked if he could wander round alone.

"Of course, just be respectful Bernarde, please." The uneasiness had subsided just a little in Jack when he agreed.

Kate waited as Bernarde wandered off down the hallway, disappearing into a room on the right at the bottom.

"Shall we?" She too was ready to explore.

Jack hooked his fingers through the hand she had held out to him. He was happy to be led by her for she radiated a peace which he had yet to find in the place, a museum to the past, a house where time had literally stood still.

Adorned only with alabaster wall lights, the smooth continuous curves that joined the high walls of the corridor to the ceiling screamed class and simplicity. The equally spaced out recessed alcoves that each held a solitary bronze figurine struck an odd familiarity with Kate as they strolled along the white marble floor.

She had been here before.

Of course she had.

This was the house that Rosalie had been given on her twenty first birthday. A growing excitement brewed as she asked Jack to trust her to guide him through the house.

Her once upon a time home.

Her ability to know what room they were approaching before they did left him speechless, the specific detail she gave before entering each was so precise. From the positioning of the limed oak furniture to the black Axminster carpet in the bedroom to the Siena marble chimney surround, Indian Gurjan wood furniture and black velvet sofa in the saloon. Her delight clear as she soaked up the atmosphere of each room, letting out squeals and gasps of joy when she discovered items what she'd predicted to be there. But there was one room she refused to enter, the plug pulled on all her enthusiasm and pleasure as they neared it.

"His study," she told Jack through gritted teeth.

She closed her eyes against the brutal memories that were forced into her vision, her hands tightened into balls by her side tensing her neck and shoulders. She moved her arms, wrapping them tight around her shoulders, her fingers straightening out to grip the tops as she began to sway, sinking down onto her knees. Her crouched, foetal posture flinched at Jack's attempts to comfort her, terror and pain emanating from every pore. Whatever was happening, he couldn't get to her. She was out of reach, trapped inside some memory that would end only when it was ready.

His fingers clawed through his hair, powerless as he watched her cry in pain. He screamed out for Bernarde; he wasn't sure why. Seconds later he too stood by, watching helplessly as his best friend now lay curled in a ball on the floor, clutching her knees to her chest, a fist pressed hard into her mouth stifling out the sobs that racked her body.

"Shit Jack, what the hell's happening?" Tears streamed down Bernarde's cheeks. "We have to do something!"

"I don't know what's happening and I don't know what to do!" Jack knelt down next to Kate again, his attempts to bring her round failed. "She must be caught in some memory, the only thing we can do is wait. It's too dangerous to wake someone from a nightmare!"

Both men looked on, inept to deal with what they observed as they sat together, backs up against the cold, lifeless wall.

After a long twenty minutes, she began to stir.

Her fist unfurled its fingers as it felt for the ground next to where she lay. She would be safe now; he would be long gone. Over time, she'd learnt if she counted slowly to a thousand, that gave him enough time to be gone. She never knew where and she didn't care, just as long as he was away from her. She eased herself up, her breathing laboured from the pain of the blows she'd suffered but at least this time it was just his boot. There would be no blood, she hoped. As she managed to get into an upright sitting position, she looked down at her clothes. Confusion clouded behind her eyes, then she caught a glimpse of Clarence. But it wasn't Clarence it was Jack. And Bernarde. As she turned her head around slowly, they were there, on their knees, before her. She moved her hands to her stomach, expecting to wince at tender, sore skin, but there was nothing.

"Kate, sweetheart. I'm here. You're safe. Whatever happened?" The crackle to Jack's voice as he swept her in his arms confirmed what she had just experienced was not imaginary.

"Jack, it was...so...real. Victor. He was here, thrashing, the...pain." Streams of tears caught her cheeks, whatever had happened became too much, the emotional pain profound.

"Right, come on. We have to get out of here. Back home." Jack was already on his feet, Kate still held in his arms, Bernarde at their side.

Neither objected to him taking control. Although Kate knew this was her rightful home, she didn't have the strength to argue, not now. But the brewing tsunami in her told her she would soon be back. And maybe it would be for good.

Chapter 59

Kate

N ot one of them spoke about what had happened up at the house, each having their own reasons to avoid addressing the elephant in the room. After a sleep and a bite to eat, Kate and Jack were ready to leave for Billy's, something she could have done without. Bernarde grateful of an evening of mindless escapism in front of the tv.

∞∞∞

"Kate, Jack, hi!" Trish guided them both through the door, her forced sunny disposition didn't go unmissed. "Let me take your coats."

Billy was pacing the floor as they followed Trish through into the large kitchen diner, the spiky atmosphere making it feel much smaller than usual.

Jack tried to lighten the mood with unnecessary small talk while Trish fixed them all a drink, but it never worked. The atmosphere needing more than a knife to cut through it.

"Kate, I owe you an explanation. But first I need

you to know I am sorry. For everything." Billy sat himself down at the oval glass dining table, keeping the distance between himself and Kate. A gesture he knew she would appreciate.

"Sorry." Kate scoffed. "Sorry. What does it even mean? Sorry for what you did or sorry that I've found out about your sickening past."

"My sickening past? I have no idea what you are talking about."

Snarled lines lay across Billy's face but she wasn't taken in by his puzzled look. He'd lied all these years so he'd had plenty of practice.

"I know, right. About Paul. About the drugs. About your visit to Mark. It was bad enough lying to me about it being suicide but cruelly letting an innocent man take the blame for it. Well that's low, by anybody's standard." Kate was in full swing now. She'd found an inner strength that had been buried deep for far too long and she was sick to the back teeth of being played with.

"Kate, look. Yes, I lied to you about Mark's death being suicide because your parents begged me never to tell you. They decided at the time that given your...instability, well they feared it would push you over the edge. We only ever wanted what was best for you, you know. But..."

"By killing my boyfriend! How was that what was best for me!" Kate screamed across him, hating the rage that was pumping in her veins as she turned her back on him.

"Killed him? I never killed him Kate. And I seriously have no idea what you mean about drugs. I'd never seen Mark."

"Paul, he came to see me." She turned back to him, folding her arms across her chest. "He told me what had happened, how he'd been set up. Told me how he'd been to collect money from Mark that he'd owed for drugs. He didn't have it so he arranged to come back the following week but his boss had turned up. There'd been some sort of struggle, Paul was told to go and leave him to it. I saw Mr and Mrs Hilkins; they'd told me how Paul had worked for you."

"Yes Kate, Paul did work for me, collecting money from people who had borrowed it. But it was all legit and above board. It was nothing to do with drugs, of that I can assure you. I was helping him out, trying to give him a bit of stability, get him on the straight and narrow. Ask anyone around here and they'll tell you how fair my money lending was. So just why Paul is trying to pin this on me I have no idea. And Mark never ever borrowed money from me."

"Well if you didn't kill him, who the hell did?" Kate gripped her arms tighter, digging her nails into the flesh, the pain nothing to what she felt inside.

"I don't know Kate. I wish I did." Billy stood, turning his back on them as he paced the floor again, none of this made any sense. "Something's not right about all of this and I'm determined to get to the bottom of it."

He slid open the patio window, taking his phone

from his jean pocket, closing it after him as he stepped out into the night. He dialled Paul's number, straight to voicemail. His message was short. "Paul, it's Billy. Call me as soon as you pick this message up, it's urgent." He stuffed the phone back into his pocket, returning inside along with a rush of cold air.

"Right Kate, listen to me. No shouting, no screaming, just listen, yes?" Billy positioned himself in front of Kate, adopting a fatherly stance as he spoke. A sternness about him Kate had never before seen.

"Right, everything I have told you is true. But there are a couple of things that you need to know and you need to hear them from me. After all this terrible business with Mark and then your parents and Pam, you were in a bad place and determined to go it alone. I begged you not to go to London but you insisted so I pulled a favour with an old friend of mine and got you the job at Greene's. But I was worried for you Kate and I'd promised your parents that I would always be there for you, godfather and uncle duties combined. Anyway, I knew this guy. I'm not proud of what I did but at the time it felt like the right thing to do. I asked him to get to know you, look out for you, keep you safe. He'd borrowed some money from me to set up a business and we agreed that if he did as I asked, I would write off his debt. Gratitude if you like. It was worth it to know you were safe. And it was agreed you were not to find out."

Of all the craziness Kate had experienced, this was

by far the hardest to wrap her head round. Then the penny dropped.

"Oh my god Billy, no. It was Owen, wasn't it?" Her disbelief was shared by Trish and Jack, all three sporting the same open-mouthed gape.

"Billy, no..." Trish shook her head in slow motion. "Please tell me you didn't."

"I know alright. I said I'm not proud but put yourself in myself shoes. I was the last relative Kate had and I was determined to protect her as best I could but how could I do that living here when she was in London?" Billy, guilty as charged stood in front of the three of them and their disapproving glares.

It was all starting to make sense to Kate now, the spotlight shining bright on all the little coincidences, showing them for what they were. The job and all the help they had paid for that she never questioned, she figured it must have been Billy. How she had bumped into Owen that night and how quickly it had snowballed into her moving in with him. Not an act of love but one of duty. The lack of real affection. How could she have been so stupid. She just prayed that Bernarde was not in on all of this.

"Jack. Take me home...please."

Jack was only too happy to leave, not sure how much more he could take in in one day either. But the fierce silence was ripped into by the shrill ring of Billy's mobile.

"Paul, thanks for ringing me back." He turned his back to the others, walking to the far side of the kitchen. He kept his voice low, but Kate managed to pick out one or two words. A few moments later, he returned. His leathered skin from years spent working outside now sullied by an ashen film, his expression frozen. Whatever he had just learnt had come even larger than a surprise.

"Billy, sit down. What is it?" Trish had taken Billy's arm, steered him to the chair and managed to get him seated. "Here drink this." She placed the brandy glass between his fingers.

He knocked it back in one, looking between them, nodding at Trish for another. She brought over the decanter and re-filled his glass and for the second time he knocked the contents straight back. Kate had sat herself down, she was worried. It took a lot to knock the wind out of her Uncle Billy and whatever she thought of him, she had no desire to see him like this. Jack too had sat, conscious of the hard stare that Billy directed his way, uncomfortable with the suspense that hung low in the air around them.

"Billy, what did Paul have to say? Please tell us."

He turned his attention from Jack, eyes full of anguish now on Kate and her question.

"It was him Kate. It was him that killed Mark."

"Who?" Kate begged.

No one spoke. Or moved.

The pause button pressed freezing time for them all. It was Jack who released it, bringing that murky moment to life again.

"Billy, tell me who called you?"

"Paul. He...he..." the words stammered as Billy fought with this new development.

"Take your time Billy, what did he say?"

"Owen. Paul worked for Owen. Owen killed Mark." Billy poured himself another large measure, closing his eyes as the liquid provided some relief.

"Take us through what Paul said Billy, so we can all understand." Calmness floated from Trish, cocooning them all.

After another drink had been poured and drank, Billy began.

"Paul worked for me, as I've already told you, but it appears he wasn't quite ready to give up on his old life completely. Anyway, he'd took some drugs after quite a spell of being clean, got in too deep and ended up owing the dealer. Eventually the top bloke wanted to see him, told him he could settle his debts if he did a bit of work for him. The rest I think you know." Billy looked up from the glass that he held; regret seeped out from behind his eyes as they sought forgiveness. "I am so sorry Kate; you have no idea how much. But I knew none of this, you have to believe me."

Kate remembered back to the day Paul, stood in front of her at Edmunds Book Emporium. The way he told his story and how genuine he came across. He had nothing to gain by making any of this up. And neither did Billy. Little by little things were starting to make sense, but with that sense came an emptiness.

She was in shock, they all were.

And not one of them knew what to do.

∞∞∞∞

As Kate climbed in to bed that night, despite the evening's revelations, an endless sense of gratitude lay with her. For finally knowing the truth and real- ising Billy wasn't quite the bad guy she had painted in her mind. For the organic friendship she shared with Bernarde, not at all doubting him through this.

And for Jack.

Rolling onto her side, she nestled into the crook of his arm, allowing the steady beat of his heart to lull her into sleep.

Chapter 60

Kate

"Morning gorgeous, sleep well?"

Kate rubbed at her half-asleep eyes, just able to make out Jack's blurry outline and the delicate wisps of steam that floated from the mug of tea he was holding out to her.

"I could kiss you!" she said, readying herself to relieve him of the hot drink her mouth craved.

"I have no objections but you might when you see the time."

Kate shot a look at the clock. "Why didn't you wake me?"

"Because after yesterday you needed your sleep, especially if we're going try and make some sense out of all of this." Jack lowered the mug onto the bedside table, sitting down next her, fixing a kiss on her lips. "Now drink your tea before it goes cold." He slid off the bed, blowing another kiss her way as he backed out of the bedroom door like a loyal servant.

She had, if only for a few brief minutes, forgotten all about yesterday and the deluge of debris it had brought with it. She lay back, blowing a sigh out through pursed lips, wondering when there'd be an end to all this and she could for once, as an adult enjoy a normal life.

∞∞∞∞

Most of the morning had gone by the time she had showered and dressed and Jack had been right, she had needed that lie in after yesterday. For that peaceful sleep had ignited a long-lost spark which fired her determination to see this thing through.

Bernarde and Jack both lay on the recliners as Kate appeared, balcony doors pulled wide open allowing in the warm spring air. It was such a beautiful landscape to look out over, the greens of the banks merged with the changing blues of the water, dotted with pin pricks of colour from the various boats embraced you in their peaceful tranquillity. The sun glinted off the river, creating twinkling diamonds that scattered out across the water, taking your eyes and mind with them.

"Ready to eat?" Bernarde's question made Kate jump.

Seated at the table, they were all ready for the brunch Bernarde had prepared earlier having eaten very little the day before. As they tucked in, he announced he ought to get back, afraid he had already outstayed his welcome. Kate would hear none of it, insisting he must stay, now more than ever, Jack in full agreement with her. Finally, he gave in and said he'd stay until the weekend, he'd be home for Peter then.

Stuffed from the delicious brunch, it was Kate who started the conversation about yesterday at the house, unable to contain all she had been holding on to any longer. She told them everything. Most of which Jack already knew, Bernarde just bits, but it was easier for her to start at the beginning. She reeled off the timeline of events, each bullet point rolled off her tongue in a direct, matter of fact way, her pauses purposely short so neither could interject.

So, there they had it.

The circle of the forgotten dreams of her early childhood to the fear riddled voids that had burst open into vivid dreams once more. And everything in between, the faces, the old couple in the café, the guy on the train, his book and the mystery flowers. Each day grew in clarity with more pieces of the puzzle given to her. She had no explanation for what had happened yesterday, no matter how hard she tried to find one. But every single kick to the stomach that boot had shot she had felt. There was no control over whatever this dream or nightmare was trying to show her, it would play out only at its own speed and knew no limit.

She did however have control over what she would say to Owen when she saw him. She prayed to god he would give up and leave her alone, return to the bright lights of the city. But who was she kidding? What Owen wanted; Owen got. But not this time.

"What are you going to do about Owen sweetie?" The knack of being on the same wavelength had developed over the years and Peter had teased them both about their creepy skill of knowing what the other was thinking when they were together.

"Nothing B. Until of course he finds me and then he shall get a large piece of my mind before he crawls back to his scummy rock. To think he built his business on the back of other people's misery disgusts me."

"Well, be careful sweetie and don't let him sweet talk you."

Kate assured him that there was no way Owen stood any chance of being able to do that, told him not to worry and to enjoy his day mooching around Cockington village and its quaint thatched roof shops. In return he gave her the biggest hug.

Shortly after he left, Kate pressed Jack to go back to the house. There'd had been a great deal of discussion from him about why they shouldn't and from her about why they should. Realising he could no longer resist the gentle pleading behind those deep puppy dog eyes, he gave in and agreed they could go after he'd made a couple of work calls. The restaurant he'd been in the process of buying overseas had fallen through just as he'd arrived, bringing him back to Kingswear sooner than expected but there was still things to sort out.

Kate sent a quick text to Bernarde, telling him where they would be if they weren't home when he got back and cheekily asked him to make a start on supper. She sent another one to Billy asking him if he'd heard anything from Owen, thankful his reply stated he hadn't. As she pushed the phone into her bag, Jack popped his head round from the study door and flashed his fingers out twice, he'd be another ten minutes.

Waiting, she hated waiting. There was always an underlying niggle present that something would happen to scupper her plans. Patience had never been one of her strengths. But she understood the issues surrounding the new restaurant, or lack of now. To ease the wait, she took the phone back out from her bag and pulled up Marcel's number, as luck would have it, she was at home.

"Hi, it's Kate. Do you have a few minutes?"

The change in Kate's voice as she spoke was remarkable, the tentative voice of only a few days ago replaced with confidence and enthusiasm. It warmed Marcel's heart as she replied, "Always, for you."

"There have been more developments. I haven't got long but, in a nutshell, Jack has experienced similar things. And he owns Moundhill House! But yesterday when we were up there, something peculiar happened, like I was transported back to a memory which I had to relive. Anyway, we're going back up to the house now as I need to explore more, see if I can find anymore pieces of this puzzle. Listen, are you free tonight? I thought maybe you and Frances could come round for supper and we can discuss it more? About eight? Oh, and one more thing, Owen is back in town but that's another story. I'll fill you in later.;"

"We'll look forward to it, thank you. And Kate, be careful please." As delighted as Marcel was at Kate's new found enthusiasm, she couldn't ignore the gnawing that chewed away at her. Things had certainly escalated, much faster than she had anticipated. And threatening to overflow the mix was Owen.

Happy that Marcel and Frances would join them this evening, Kate scribbled a note for Bernarde to let him know they would have company for dinner. With perfect timing, Jack appeared behind her, wrapping his arms around her as she folded the note over.

"Ready?"

Chapter 61

Frances

When she had woken that morning, Frances knew the end was near, that today was the day. The day she had waited years to come. The day she knew must happen to resolve this thing once and for all.

She had been expecting the telephone call, but from Kate, not Marcel. She didn't mind, small details such as that did not concern her, as long as the bigger picture took shape. Marcel had relayed Kate's earlier call and it was agreed Frances would meet Marcel at seven, then they could arrive at Kate's together.

As she placed the receiver back, she knew the time had come to tell Marcel the truth about the secret she had been keeping from her for all these years. When tonight came, several pieces of the puzzle would fit together with one single placement.

And she hoped and prayed more than anything it would finally be the end.

Chapter 62

Owen

He'd been in the shower when Billy had rung, the voicemail left containing none of the excuses Owen had thought it would.

"Kate knows Owen. Everything. Games over."

So, the slimy git had told her. He was impressed though that after all this time Billy had found the bottle to tell his precious little Kate how he'd paid him to take care of her. Owen was certain that would've gone down like a lead balloon. But what Kate didn't know was how, over time, he had fallen in love with her. That until she had gone, he never realised what he had. His trump card, should it need playing. She would listen to him, give him chance to explain, she always had.

He'd waited long enough. Today was the day. His day to put the record straight, get Kate to see sense and come home.

He sat and watched the two of them climb into the pristine white Mercedes, their cosy laughter as the roof unfolded, the sun highlighting both heads of glossy dark hair. He watched how comfortable the two of them were together, like they had known each for ever, a pang of jealousy nauseated him as he pressed the ignition. She should be sat next to him, laughing in his car, not with a man she had only known five minutes. He held back for a few moments before gently accelerating, not wanting them to see him. He'd hired a car, he couldn't risk his own being spotted, even with a fake number plate it would rouse suspicion if she saw it. There weren't many black Ferrari's with red alloys around.

He trailed Jack's Mercedes through the winding lanes, keeping his distance as they turned off up into a dead end. He gave it a few minutes, hanging back out of sight, after all it was a no through road so he couldn't lose them. He lowered his windows, watching them slide open effortlessly. From his seat, he checked out his surroundings, nothing but trees in every direction with just a break for the roads and the sky. It was isolated and concealed. A smug grin accompanied his thought of what a perfect location it would be to hide anything in your life, away from prying eyes and passers-by. A new found understanding of why the country might appeal to some.

He started the car, aware of its noise shattering the silence and hoped they wouldn't have paid attention to it. Driving slowly, he followed the narrowing lane for about three quarters of a mile, finally approaching tall wrought iron gates. He could see his car on the other side, sat proud and perfect on the gravel, but there was no sign of either of them. They had to be inside the house. And what a house it was. He'd clearly underestimated this guy; it was going to be more difficult than he thought to get Kate away from him.

But he had patience, he could wait.

Because he'd learnt that anything worthwhile was worth waiting for.

And Kate was more than worthwhile.

Chapter 63

Kate

As they approached the once grand gates for the second time, an overriding sense of calm filtered through Kate, strange given what she had experienced yesterday. They had both agreed that they would stay together and any inkling of anything untoward then they would leave, immediately.

Kate hooked her fingers through Jacks, her grip firm as they moved down the corridor. To Kate, each step felt like one step closer to being home but for Jack, even though he owned the house, every step he took felt like those of an intruder. She took him to more rooms within the house that had long stood empty, the doors closed shut on the life they once held. But with intricate accuracy, she knew what lay behind each and the memories they held. A time capsule of the past. Her past

At the far end of the house, just off the dining room sat the Loggia. There was no denying what a breathtaking view you got from there. Pure joy. A thoughtful design that merged the indoors with outdoors. An extension of the house that shielded you from the elements with only the front aspect open, allowing the undeniable beauty of the rolling hills that descended into the sea to be taken in in all its glory.

They sat together on the greyed wooden bench, drinking the flask of tea Kate had brought with her. She closed her eyes against the gentle glow of the spring sunshine, letting its heat to spread through her, just as contentment had.

Jack edged his arm around her, smiling at the welcome murmur she let out as he too closed his eyes to absorb the peace of that moment.

*The perfect gentleman, Clarence opens the door
of his Austin 7 for me, I climb in, smiling.*

*With the lightest of strokes, he brushes
my cheek before closing the door to.*

*Another surge of pure unadulterated joy floods
my body, right now, I am on top of the world.*

*As Clarence climbs in next to me, I notice
his brow is frowning.*

*He tells me not to worry and squeezes my knee,
his reassuring smile back where it belongs.*

*But I do worry, I can't seem to push away the
disquiet that sits like a stole upon my shoulders.*

*We drive along in silence but this time
it is not a comfortable one.*

*I don't speak, I know how to keep quiet, I'd
learnt the hard way a long time ago.*

*I see Clarence checking his mirror more often
than I have noticed him do it before.*

We start to pick up a little more speed.

*I don't like it but I am afraid to speak, to
add to the cares Clarence already has.*

*He doesn't look at me, his eyes stay
firm between road and mirror.*

Temptation gets the better of me and I look around.

I gasp at what I see.

*My hand presses against my throat to stifle
the cry that is yearning to leave.*

*Even from here, the anger and hatred he
has for me is like a bullet to the heart.*

His prized possession out of his reach.

But how did he find us?

I look at Clarence, longing to see his reassuring smile but it is not there.

In that moment a deep-seated fear spears my hopes and dreams.

My once clear path of light now flickers and fades into darkness.

Marred with a growing sense of doom.

"Wakey wakey sleepy head. I think it's time we head back and by the looks of that cloud, a shower is looking pretty imminent."

Gathering up the flask and mugs, Kate hurried behind Jack, gathering her senses as she stood inside, waiting as he locked the rear door. He had been right about the rain for within seconds the cloud had burst, releasing its contents to hammer against the windows. Short, sharp and over in the time it had taken them to move from the rear of the house out on to the front steps, the sun once again shined upon them.

With the house secured, Jack clicked his fob to unlock the car. Neither of them had noticed the face pressed against the vertical rods of iron, the face that stared directly at them. The face that took immense pleasure in startling them both.

"You don't get away from me that easy baby."

Kate jumped round, looking at Jack, searching for help.

Jack moved away from the car, telling Kate to stay where she was.

"Well, well, if it isn't the big man himself. Kate does not want to speak to you and quite frankly after what I've learnt about you, I don't blame her."

"This has nothing to do with you now back off mate and let me speak to Kate."

"I think you'll find it's everything to do with me while you're on my land so I suggest if you don't want trespassing added to your ever-growing list of crimes then you'll get back in your car and move on and leave Kate alone."

"Fuck off! You know nothing about me and I'm not leaving until I've spoken to Kate." Owen clung to the bars, a surge of anger gripped him, fuelling his demands.

Kate knew full well he wouldn't back off till she had spoken to him. "Owen, what do you want? I have nothing to say to you."

"Kate, baby, please. I just want to talk to you. Hear me out, yeah?" His condescending tone wound round her. Did he really believe he could still manipulate her after all he had done?

"No Owen. I won't hear you out. You make me feel sick to the pit of my stomach." Her harsh determination was back. "I know Billy paid you to look out for me, well look how that turned out. Convenient for you I guess, debt paid off, ready-made girlfriend that would quite happily turn a blind eye to your disgusting ways and whore addiction. Yes I know all about Trinity Owen, did you really think I was that dumb? Money can't buy everything you want, at least not the things you really want in life, when will you ever learn that. At first, I thought it was me, my broken past that made you behave the way you did towards me, I even convinced myself that on the occasions you chose to take out your anger on me, that I deserved it." With each word that left her lips came another drop of strength. "Well let me tell you something Owen, I would never come back to you. Even if you were the last man standing.

You disgust me. Now please, go back to London and leave me alone." She turned her back him and begun walk away. She stopped, turning just her head. "And I know Owen. I know it was you who killed Mark." The release of years of pent up frustration took hold as she began to tremble, turning away once more as she walked to the car.

"Kate! No! Give me a chance...please! That's not what happened, you need to hear my side of the story!" It was no good, his pleas fell on empty ground. "Kate, please, talk to me!"

"You've had your time Owen. Now please, do us all a favour and crawl back to the cess pit of a life you call home. I'll give you five minutes to get off my property before I call the police. And no, I'm not bluffing." Jack turned his back, climbing into the car to join Kate, closing the door to the indignant protests Owen spat out.

"Okay?"

Kate nodded, glad of Jack's reassuring smile as she arched over to take his kiss.

Watching Owen rev up his car and drive off at speed down the lane, Jack too pulled out of the gates, glad to be leaving this place behind.

Chapter 64

Sarah

The cold calculating eyes that had carefully observed everything from behind the lush foliage of the camelias smiled. A cruel sinister smile capable of tuning anything to stone.

So, Owen had not managed to win back his *sweet little kitty kat* and it appeared she despised him more than anything. And believed he was the one who had killed her first love.

The sadistic joy this brought was beautiful.

Music to her ears.

But how wrong she was.

If only Kate knew it had been her, Sarah, who had finished the job off that neither men could bring themselves to do. Her scheming that had seen her cousin, Paul, charged with the despicable crime who still, to this day, was completely unaware it had been her and not Owen who was responsible, the man she had once loved.

But he hadn't loved her back, not in the way he should and she always told him he would live to regret it. They all would. Even her own grandparents thought more of *kitty kat* than they did her, Sarah, their own flesh and blood. So obvious.

Owen had been easy to play, thinking he could buy her off, even have sex with her to keep her quiet. What a fool he was only he never realised. She had always let him believe he had the upper hand.

She needn't have wasted her money on buying those flowers or her time racking her brains to remember the quote from that sad little fridge magnet. Nor spent endless hours watching Kate's every move or trying to keep Paul away from Owen

But she wasn't to know.

It had worked out in the end.

Owen had lost.

There was nothing for her to do here now and her cackle echoed in the air before disappearing into the background.

Just as she had all those years ago.

Chapter 65

Kate

The earlier shower had left a glossy sheen on the lanes they drove down, leaving the house fading behind them. Tiny droplets of water hung like delicate crystals from the branches, shimmering when the light caught them and everything looked so fresh and full of life.

Hope.

The rays of the sun bounced off the windscreen and Jack squinted, pulling down his visor. As they turned out of the lane and back onto the windy main road, the approaching car showed no sign of moving. Jack tried to manoeuvre but they were on a one-way road and the other car was coming the wrong way.

The wrong way at them.

He slammed his fist down hard on the horn.

But it was too late.

The oncoming vehicle struck the side of Jack's car forcing it to spin out of control.

They were rolling, falling.

Out of control.

The crunching sounds pulsated against her own

screams.

Kate's eyes fluctuated between seeing light and dark.

Jack, totally out of reach.

Tired and scared, finally her body gave in to the darkness.

To the darkness that had always been waiting for her to return.

All I can hear is a faint hissing sound,
I don't understand.

I try to open my eyes but I can't,
they are heavy and sticky.

I can't move either.

I am stuck, pinned down, the weight bearing
atop of me oppressive.

I hear the birdsong break through the hissing.

A beautiful sound.

A pinprick of light pierces the canopy of trees
above me and serenity takes hold.

Just for a moment.

I try hard to prise my eyelids open and although I can't
manage to open them wide, the slits I can manage show
me the beautiful still blue sky between the trees.

Then the harsh reality comes flooding back.

The car.

Victor.

The impact.

I stifle a sob as I call out his name.

Clarence?

But there is no answer.

I am racked with fear.

I try to move but the pain that shoots
through me is overwhelming.

My eyelids feel too heavy as I faintly call
out his name one last time…

Clarence?

I hear my name being called but it's not
Clarence who speaks for there is no softness.

I manage to turn my head a fraction and I see
him, next to me, awkward and lifeless.

The darkness has taken him, my world.

Who then calls my name?

It is him, Victor, but how can it be?

The twittering of the birds grows fainter.

I know it is coming for me too.

My eyes flutter open, just, and for the last time,
I look up to see the light of the afternoon sun.

I feel the warmth of it against my skin,
dissolving my pain, my fear.

It is time.

I allow my eyelids to close and surrender to the darkness.

For the time has to come.

To be with my Clarence.

Chapter 66

12 Months Later

As the last of the taxis drove off, the crunching of the gravel finally fell silent. Just a few hours earlier it had been alive with the footsteps of well-wishers, scattering scented rose petals over the happy couple as they climbed out of the cream and black convertible Austin 7. Now, amongst the soft twinkle of the stars above, peace and silence festooned the night.

In the months that had passed since the accident and Owen's funeral, Kate and Jack had learnt so much that had, inevitably, brought them even closer, binding them together as they finally placed together the last pieces of the puzzle, completing the picture together.

Frances Clifford had known all along of the invisible bond that bound their lives together, but as she had told them, it wasn't her story to tell. She had just been the linchpin holding them all together. On

Kate's return from hospital, she had organised a little soiree, just for the four of them. An opportunity for Kate to finally fill in the blanks.

Frances explained how there had been three girls, descended from a long line of strong independent women that had each been given a house and money in the hope they would marry for love and not status. A clause had long been written into the deeds that the houses must always pass to a female heir and could not be sold while there were any female descendants still alive.

Moundhill House had belonged to Lady Rosalie Edmunds, Laburnum House to Lady Violet Edmunds, the grandmother of Marcel's Aunt and York House, to Lady Francesca Edmunds, Frances Clifford's own grandmother.

After the death of her mother, Rosalie had found comfort in the arms of Victor Llewelyn. An upstanding Naval Officer, she had been completely taken in by his charming ways, marrying him soon after. But his charming ways were nothing more than a disguise for the wickedness that lay beneath. Systematically. he took everything away from her, forcing her hand to sign her wealth over to him, changing the female clause to male that had been a part of those deeds for many years, leaving her broken and battered. As her grief passed, it lifted the veil on how weak she had been but, in the end, Rosalie was her mother's daughter, and when she finally found her true love, she knew that was worth far more than anything money could ever buy. Rosalie had been prepared to give up every-thing, but on that tragic day in May 1933 when help finally arrived, Victor's wife lay dead in his arms. His car had apparently been forced off the road by a reckless fool, resulting in the death of his beloved wife and injury to himself. The driver of the other vehicle, an Austin 7, also died.

Clarence.

Both Lady Francesca and Lady Violet had known of the sadness that pervaded Moundhill House, the tragic story that the history books told but nei-ther knew of the real reason Victor had succumbed to suicide, their diaries testament to this. But they had both known about Clarence. Frances however, from being a small girl, had been shown that those walls held secrets that cried out to be told. That she at some point would play a part in unearthing the skeletons that had been so clumsily buried. She had seen flashes of possibilities and knew that until the truth be uncovered, Rosalie would never rest easy.

Marcel of course was already privy to this know-ledge. Frances had shared with her, her own flesh and blood, everything there was to know when they had sat in the relatives room of the hospital, unsure if Kate would pull through or not.

Although her body had been weak, Kate's mind had been stronger than it ever had. She hadn't been surprised by what she had learnt from Frances, for the last thing she saw before her eyes closed was Victor.

And though she could never rewrite history, she

was able to confirm to those that mattered that history's account of what happened was untrue, for it was Victor, who in a jealous rage had ran Clarence and Rosalie off the road. A frenzied attempt to stop them as they made off to their new life together. To hide the shame and shift the blame for his gross actions, he moved Rosalie and held her tight in his arms, like a caring, loving, distraught husband would, having been ran off the road.

And his story had been believed.

Until now.

∞∞∞

Kate let her head fall back, laughing as Jack scooped her up to carry her over the threshold.

"I love you Mrs Richardson. Happy?"

"I love you too Mr Richardson and yes, more than."

And as Jack carried her up the stairs, she knew she had returned home.

Back where she belonged.

To Moundhill House.

Married for love and not for status.

To live her long awaited happy ever after.

Authors Note

Firstly, I want to thank each and every one of you for reading my debut novel.

It still doesn't seem quite real that what started out many moons ago as a *can you imagine* conversation with my husband is now here, inbetween your fingers.

If you would like to keep in touch, find out more or just hello, please visit my website at sharronlmiller.com

Or you can follow me on Instagram sharron_l_miller

I look forward to connecting with you as I take my journey into the exciting world of fiction.

Acknowledgement

Special thanks must go not only to my husband and son, but to the friends who stood by me and encouraged my transition. You know who you are and I love you all!

And to my neighbour Suzanne, for everything X

About The Author

Sharron L Miller

Sharron lives in the Heart of the National Forest with her husband, teenage son and crazy Dachshund.

She spent the last twenty-two years training and working as a Master Energy Healer, Meditation Teacher, Mind and Body Calm Coach, Teacher and Mentor before deciding it was time to move on and fulfil her ambition of putting pen to paper.

With a love of nature and history, Sharron spends her free time gardening, walking or visiting National Trust properties.

For more information, visit her website at : sharronlmiller.com

Printed in Great Britain
by Amazon